FOOTSTEPS, QUICK AND MUFFLED
like murder in an alley, skittered down a parallel
tunnel: something was keeping pace with them,
stalking them out of the phosphorescent dark.

Truck threw up his pistol, sent a bolt flaring and
sizzling down the passage, shadows bickering
along behind it. He couldn't see anything, but
someone was out there. He dragged Tiny along
after him, stumbling and swearing. "If he gets
behind us—run, Tiny, run!"

They reached the junction and hauled up gasping
—just in time to see the hem of a plum-colored
cloak, violently agitated, vanishing into yet a third
branch of the maze—

THE CENTAURI DEVICE

The Centauri Device

M. John Harrison

THE CENTAURI DEVICE

A Bantam Book / published by arrangement with
Doubleday & Company, Inc.

PRINTING HISTORY
Doubleday edition published November 1974
Bantam edition / August 1980

ISBN 0-553-13920-7

Published simultaneously in the United States and Canada

PRINTED IN THE UNITED STATES OF AMERICA

0 9 8 7 6 5 4 3 2 1

For John Price

*And they, so perfect is their misery,
Not once perceive their foul disfigurement . . .*
                                   —John Milton, *Comus.*

ONE

■

Truck, Tiny, and Angina Seng

It was St. Crispin's Eve on Sad al Bari IV when Captain John Truck, impelled by something he was forced to describe to himself as "sentiment," decided to visit the Spacer's Rave, on the corner of Proton Alley and Circuit (that chilly junction where the higher class of port lady goes to find her customers).

"Don't accept any cargo," he told his bosun as he prepared to leave *My Ella Speed*, "for at least two weeks. Especially don't accept any vegetable seeds. I will never haul pumpkins again, any shape or form."

"What's a pumpkin?" asked the bosun, who was a Chromian dwarf called Fix. He was good with an ax—or so he said—but backward.

"A pumpkin is what your head is," explained John Truck smugly. "Children wear them for the same reason you have filed your teeth.

"Don't forget, no vegetable seeds."

And with a jaunty wave, he quit the ship.

He reached the Alley by way of Bread Street and East Thing, a damp wind tangling his long hair. He walked with his shoulders hunched and his head bent as if he were bored with it all (which he was, to the

extent that anybody is), his tight snakeskin combat
jacket and big leather hat straight out of the questionable past of the Galaxy.

Spaceport hustlers and buskers worked the streets all
the way from the port to the service areas, their peculiar instruments glimmering in the green street light.
They solicited him, but he ignored them. He had seen
them before, shivering with cold and with fear of the
long, incomprehensible future in the night winds of a
hundred planets, waiting out their time in the bleak
hinterlands of a thousand ports. They would go home
later to the same greasy doorways and park benches
and barren flops, or ride the *pneumatique* systems until
dawn: threadbare losers for whom he could find no
compassion because they so resembled himself. Their
aimless, eccentric hearts, their odors of loss, demanded
a response he was not yet prepared to give—because it
would be an admission of kinship.

This isn't to say they made him unhappy—or that
he lacked charity; he was just hollow, nothing had ever
filled him up.

Since his demob from the Fleet, a year after all the
hysteria of the Canes Venatici incident had come to
nothing but the same kind of worn diplomacy that had
begun it, he had worked all over the sky, traveling a
slow Archimedean spiral in three dimensions, tracking
in from Venatici through the Crow and the Heavy
Stars. He had driven half-tracks on Gloam and Parrot,
built roads on Jacqueline Kennedy Terminal; he had
sung revolutionary songs and pushed meta-ampheta-
mines to the all-night workers on Morpheus—not because he was in any way committed to the insurrection
that finally blew the planet apart, but because he was
stuck there and broke. After five years, he had ended
up on Earth, where everybody ends, guarding heavy
plant machinery for the Israeli World Government.

There he was paid handsomely for every Arab he
shot, but not enough—not enough for dirty work. He
had found himself wetting his trousers every time

somebody fired a gun (in fact, that had worn off after a time, but he still told it that way, against himself with a lot of gestures and funny voices—especially to port ladies), and tapping a streak of savagery he hadn't suspected in himself. He found no sense of purpose in that stupid half-war, either. Finally, it was too terrifying to find himself going through the psychological maneuvers necessary to continue without the accompanying commitment. He left it alone, but in his customary indecisive manner. He drifted away.

Had he not saved his bounty money and bought with it *My Ella Speed* (then called *Liberal Power*, something which caused him to scratch his head), his seven-year trip from demob day to Sad al Bari IV might easily have ended at the periphery of the port— accomplished by means of his horny thumb, a cheap musical instrument, and his hat in the gutter the wrong way up to receive bread. Instead of on his head where it belonged.

Even the purchase of the boat had, at the time, assumed the air of a fortunate accident. Unused to ethanol—still the sole legal euphoric of Earth—he had stumbled, smashed out of his head and laughing, into a breaker's yard somewhere in the temperate zones; then passed out cold when he realized what he'd spent his money on. John Truck was a loser, and losers, despite the evidence to the contrary, survive on luck. Not that he'd considered it luck then, lying on his back with the rusty, twisted towers of wrecks spinning through his brain (and thinking, Oh God, what am I going to *do* with it?).

It was his personal disaster that he never learned to resist the flow of events; he never learned to make steerage way.

Proton Alley is as cold as all the other streets; any warmth you think you might have found there always turns out to be an illusory side-product of the color of the vapor signs. All its denizens have digested their experience of life so well that nothing of it remains to them. They start fresh and naïve every day, but still regard you with empty eyes. No warmth; but John Truck basked in its familiarity, which is perhaps an acceptable substitute on any evening dedicated to a saint.

Outside the Spacer's Rave, an ancient fourth-generation Denebian with skin blackened and seamed, and eyelids perpetually lowered against the actinic glare of a star he hadn't seen for twenty years, was reciting lines from the second canto of *The Fight At Finnsburg.* His hat was at his feet. His boots were cracked, but his voice was passable, booming out over the heads of passing whores and stoned Fleet men:

> The Marty Lingham discovered a bleak
> orbit; hooked by a fuchsia dwarf,
> perihelion at the customary handful
> of millions: cometary, cemetery.

He showed his nasty old teeth to Captain Truck, recognizing another loser, however well disguised. He screwed up his dreadful face, winked.

"An intellectual, am I right, bosun—?" he began his spiel, stepping craftily into Truck's bee-line.

"If it hadn't been for that," Truck swore later, "I might have given him something."

Inside the Rave, it was a different matter: inside, Tiny Skeffern, the Galaxy's last great musician, was blowing his brains out through his instrument like the contents of a rare egg.

John Truck knew him of old. He stood five foot three and slightly built in the Rave's confusion of spots and strobes and kaleidomats, tapping his right foot. His hair was sparse, curly, and blond—at twenty-two years, he already had a bald patch. When he wasn't playing, he was spring-heeled, he was a leaper; when he was, he stayed in one place for minutes on end, giving the ladies a reserved but cheeky smile. He was an enthusiastic loser from way back, and he nodded when Truck came in.

He played a four-hundred-year-old Fender Strato-
caster with all the switchgear jammed full on, through
a stack of Luthos amps—each one with a guaranteed
output of half a kilowatt—and a battery of Hydrogen
Line thirty-inch speakers. He had a loose-limbed Denebian queen, all pink flares and slashed sleeves, on
bass; his drummer was a local man, looking seedy and
aggressive by turns like all good drummers. His sound:

His sound was long-line and hairy, slow and grinding, full of inexplicable little runs and complications.
He stalked the Denebian bass through the harmonies;
he made sounds like breaking glass and exploding qua-
sars, like dead ships and orbital confrontations and
eras of geological upheaval; he made sounds like God.

"I'm a highway child," he sang, "so don't deny my
name."

Which was all as it should be.

John Truck licked his lips and bought himself a
knickerbocker glory topped with little crystals of te-
trahydrocannabinol; he had a look at the audience.
They were mostly musicians from other bands, but
there was a sprinkling of spacers, who, like John
Truck, understood that music had died out in the year
2,000 and that the New Music was the old music. Only
the winners escape, Truck thought as the old Strat
wailed (taking fours with a wholly imaginary wind
which nevertheless sent tremors of intent down the
backs of his calves and thighs: the port wind, the compass wind). The rest of us get carried by the music.
Why not?

There was only one woman in the Spacer's Rave
that night. Her name was Angina Seng, and she was
looking for John Truck. He wasn't to know it: he
could only see her back. Her hair was long and coppery, she held herself with a certain dramatic tension.
Her bottom looked nice. So while Tiny Skeffern
screwed it out of his glossy, priceless antique for the
disconnected, the discontented and the rudderless of
the whole dirty universe, John Truck fell precipitately

in and out of love with her. It was an impartial, on-off passion, for every spaceport lady seen fleetingly in a crowd. He was prone to that sort of thing.

In a hiatus between sets, Tiny brought the Fender over.

"Hello, Truck."

He bobbed about for a moment, grinning sentimentally; sat down. Truck looked with affection at his bald spot, beaded with sweat.

"Tiny, you play worse and worse. Who's the girl?"

Tiny huffed, wiped his sleeve over the guitar's immaculate white polymer finish. He shrugged. Even when the Strat wasn't plugged in, the stubby, clubbed fingers of his left hand ran up and down the frets like small, undeveloped animals looking for a way out of the wind.

"Oh, thanks. She's not regular. Can you believe it, I've been here three bloody weeks."

He rubbed his nose.

"Three weeks. Can you imagine that?"

He helped himself to some of Truck's unfinished treat.

"I don't understand how I can have done it. Outside being arrested, which I wasn't. I've been careful since I had that finger broken on Barfield Eight. Three weeks in this dump!"

"If you want to lift out of here," offered Truck.

"You've still got *Ella Speed*. What a name. I never could get over that."

He chuckled.

"I'll be around when you finish this gig," Truck told him. "Or you could find her at the dock. I had her painted up about a year ago. Fix the bosun is aboard, I hope."

Tiny got up. He did a little energetic shuffle, nodded, and went back to his band. He and Truck hadn't met much since his teen-age prodigy days, when he'd been playing the circuits on Gloam. Between riots, that had been a lot of laughs, Truck recollected. He smiled to himself and worked some THC grit from between two of his teeth with his tongue. And he laughed out loud when Tiny leaned down from the poky Rave stage and whispered something to the girl with the coppery hair.

He didn't understand how she could be so pleased to see him. How could he? He only knew that spaceport women sometimes have metaphysical hungers hard to describe riding tandem with their more common appetites. They represent a different function of space, a significance of loneliness lost on their male counterparts. They are the true aliens. So he regarded her with a certain wariness.

"Mr. Truck, I have been searching the port for you."

"Go on," said Truck. "You say that to all the spacers. It's 'Captain.' Is there something I can do for you?"

(He knew it was a mistake, even then. Tiny was driving his band through the first four bars of "Where Was Tomorrow?" He recognized it for an omen.)

She told him her name. She was a big, bony girl, but her face was pinched a little round the eyes and mouth. It wasn't simply the mark of a port lady—although they too are tense and contained as if perpetually struggling to keep their substance from evaporating off into the void.

Her clothes glittered and dissolved irregularly as the kaleidomat light found frequencies critical to the opacity of the material.

"Captain Truck, how would you like a job?"

He shook his head.

"Come back in two weeks. I shall be stoned on Sad al Bari here for two weeks." He demonstrated by waving his hands about like airplanes. "Bombed out. Unless Tiny gets desperate."

"It isn't a haulage job, Captain. You won't need to fly."

"They're the only kind I take. I've got a Chromian

bosun to support. Really, you should find someone else. Not that I'm not grateful for the offer."

He thought for a moment.

"Besides which," he said, "*you* aren't hiring me." For a loser, that was pretty acute.

She leaned forward earnestly, put her elbows on the table. She toyed with the dregs of his knickerbocker glory, then clasped her hands.

"That's true. But my sponsor will pay better for a few weeks of your time than any comparable haulage job, and you didn't make much on that last seed run."

He had to give her credit for that. "You," he said, "have been talking to somebody. They were right. But I don't need money that badly. In two weeks, yes."

"Captain Truck," she said, drawing her chair closer to the table, "what if I told you this was a chance to do something for the Galaxy?"

He sighed.

"I'd say you have picked a loser. If it's politics, Miss Seng, double screw it." He beamed at her. "I'm not very political, you see," he explained.

She got up without another word.

"You're not a port lady at all," he called after her as she threaded her way through the audience to the door. But he wasn't really talking to her.

The evening went on, the Spacer's Rave got packed out. The management closed the doors in a suicidal move to suffocate the hands that fed it. "I'm gonna rock and roll you baby," sang Tiny Skeffern, "rock and *roll* you all night long,"—an old sentiment, and enduring but Truck had lost interest. About an hour after Angina Seng had squirmed her way out, he went off to look for somewhere quiet. She had soured it for him. He couldn't imagine who might want him for himself and not *My Ella Speed*.

As he went out the door, Tiny and his drummer were exchanging strokes, playing with psychopathic detachment and gentleness.

Outside, the same old wind. East Thing was a street without apparent function, a barrack thoroughfare for the shabby privates of the great commercial army—warehouses, and the occasional front-office. Packed by day with clerks and chandlers, it was a desert of vapor lamps by night; nobody walked it then except to get to the Spacer's Rave, and most of them were already there. Truck loved it for itself. You had to.

Coming abreast of a deep doorway in the high numbers, he noticed nothing; but a sneaky foot whipped out of it nonetheless, and tangled up his long legs. He kicked his own ankle painfully and fell on the floor.

"Fuck," he said. Somebody sniggered.

A shadowy figure issued from the doorway—loomed over him as, rubbing one elbow, he got himself into a kneeling position. A quick cold flicker of vapor light reflected from wicked steel knuckles. His neck exploded, he thought that his windpipe had collapsed, but he fell carefully, knees drawn up into his stomach.

"Up, son. I'm not carrying you. Get up."

An exploratory prod in the ribs. Truck concentrated on the pain in his neck.

"Come on—" Then, calling to the dim hole of the doorway: "Give me a hand here, he's going to puke all over my feet."

Another one? Any more and they could crowd him to death, never mind anything else.

They bent over him. He slapped both arms hard against the paving to give himself traction and, feet together, shoved the heels of his boots into the nearest mouth.

Nice. Crouching and eager to maim, he chuckled. It might have been taken for a groan. He pretended to get up, sank his fingers into the second man's thigh instead, feeling for a pressure point. "Your turn to fall down."

He was drawing back his foot, preparatory to putting it in, when something hit him in the kidneys. He grunted. He staggered forward flailing his arms and tripped over his original victim. He squirmed around trying to get a look at who was hitting him so hard, pulled his head in rapidly, and rolled onto the lee side of the knuckle man as a shoe caught him in the chest. It was a lace-up shoe with a thick sole and a weighted toecap, a fact which surprised him so much that he forgot to keep his head moving. All he could do after a little more of that was curl up into a ball and wrap his arms round his face while he thought about it.

For a while, there was nothing but the quiet shuffle of feet and a ragged sound in his head which told him John Truck must be involved in it all somewhere—but not how many people were kicking him. Or indeed, why. He was beginning to feel frightened that they wouldn't stop.

Eventually, though, two of them hauled him upright and began half walking, half dragging him toward a battered black vehicle parked across the street. From Truck's position it looked about the size of a Fleet battleship, but even with both of them working at it they had a job trying to fold him up enough to get him inside.

"I think I'm going to be sick," he told them plaintively, but they ignored him.

While they were sorting it out, a late-model Lewis Phoenix with all eight headlamps on main beam hurled out of Bread Street and drifted to a stop endwise across East Thing.

"Better get a move on, lads," said Truck. He spread his legs wide and went limp. He jabbed with his elbows, bit a hand that came too close to his eyes.

Tap, tap, tap, went some heels.

"Leave him alone," said Angina Seng, her voice bright and tight.

She was supporting an ugly Chambers reaction pistol with both hands. Did he detect a slight tremor in her big bony frame? He wasn't in a condition to detect anything. A dark cloak was thrown over her indoor clothes.

Silence.

Truck spat some blood into the road.

"Don't shoot them yet," he muttered. The inside of his mouth had swollen, he kept biting his cheek by accident. "I would just like a go with one of their knuckledusters first."

With sulky looks, they left him alone. Plucky Angina watched them rat off down the street, heading for the dock. They were dressed almost like spacers. She put her Chambers away and helped him into the Phoenix.

"Well, Captain Truck," she said. "You would think, wouldn't you, that they'd at least leave their own kind alone. Do you want the window down?"

Truck said nothing. One of his lower canines was giving him trouble; and between tentative explorations of his mouth, he was listening to the wind.

"Suit yourself then." She smiled encouragingly at him.

TWO

◼

The Long,
Uncomprehending Migration of
"Spaceport Annie" Truck

"Where have you brought me?" he asked suspiciously.
It was all the same to him. He was a heartbreaking
sight, slumped in the lift cage with his long chin on his
chest, his hair all tangled and dirty.

"Where's my hat? I can't go anywhere without that
hat."

He was shivering with reaction. He had a puffy lip,
an immense purple bruise stretching from under his left
ear down to his shoulder, and swollen glands in his
neck. Not that it was anything new. Morosely, he stuck
a finger into the great rent in his snakeskin jacket.

"There was nothing wrong with that hat. Christ, I
hate being sick."

Angina Seng smiled sympathetically at him. He
hoped it was sympathy.

"I thought you might like to speak to my sponsor after what happened," she told him. "Once you know all
the facts, you might change your mind about that job."
It was an affront.

"Facts," he chuckled. "Sponsor. Ho ho."

He glared at the wall above her head. An uncomfortable silence descended.

"How did you get this way?" she asked suddenly.

Stuff you.

"I don't know what you mean," he said.

They didn't speak again, but she wasn't downhearted. Wagging her tail and already anticipating the plaudits of the shepherd, she sheepdogged him out of the lift and into a reception area. There, she vanished behind an unmarked door, leaving him stranded in a front-office landscape of fake-antique carpets like fine soft cellar mold, power-sculptures cunningly designed to achieve optimum blandness and the castration of the art of the time, and no chairs. He didn't care if he never saw her again.

All the dispossessed and wayward have a fear of frontages. He discussed going back to the Spacer's Rave there and then, but he knew it was probably too late for that: gravitational tides had thrown him up here and, for the moment, he was marooned. He leered at a receptionist (who sat behind the keyboard of her input terminal as long-legged and unapproachable—by losers—as any ice-princess). She smiled back politely, because that year it was polite to be polite to the underprivileged. He scratched his head.

Far away, somebody shouted, "Don't come to me! I told you I couldn't answer for the cluster sampling!" A door opened and shut. Clearly: "*Run* off and lick her boots then."

"You may go in now, Captain Truck," said the receptionist.

So far, nobody had offered any options. Suddenly remembering Angina Seng's big Chambers gun, he wondered just how much of her gravitational attraction it represented. What was really keeping him here?

"I can see *you're* wearing a girdle," he said. "As a matter of interest, where am I?"

Her smile curdled: it was polite that year for the underprivileged to be polite back. "The Israeli Consulate," she said, "and I don't think you ought to go round saying things like that to people."

But he was already on his way through the unmarked door, shouting "You can just entirely forget about it, Miss Seng!" She wasn't there, of course. "Oh hell!" He went to leave, but some nosy treacherous element of his make-up had already slammed the door behind him and faced him up to the room's other occupant.

General Alice Gaw, postmenopausal but hardly decayed at all: onetime vacuum-commando, late of the Fleet Police, now prime executive of IWG's military arm, with a roving commission and *carte blanche* in any matter of hemiglobal security. Decorated and feted, she had been one of the six enigmatic "wardens" of the discontinued Environmental Prison experiment—that nodal myth of the hinterlands, its seeping ducts peopled with ghouls, its vaults packed with lost souls in Gothic decaying orbits about the solar enormity of their own innocence, administered by Fungus Men with cattle prods for arms and ECT machines for heads; and closed down eventually, so rumor had it, by the revulsion of the very elements of IWG politics that had demanded its institution. Rumor had it also that Alice Gaw was the only one of the Six ever to regret the move.

She was short and heavily built. She wore the sleeves of her Women's Army uniform perpetually rolled up to display chapped muscular forearms, and affected the coarse jocularity of a male psychiatric nurse. Truck knew her by repute: her eyepatch was a Galactic curiosity, her hands were thick and square. She radiated a fiercely ambiguous sexual energy which was more disturbing for her consciousness of it than for its actual effect.

Lineal descendant of that characteristic blossom of the twentieth century, the "National Security Manager," with a grasp of the art of *ad hoc* politics almost as breath-taking as the speed of her rise in the IWG hierarchy, she fixed Truck with an eye the color of concrete and said:

"I want to talk to you, boyo, and I can't do that until you pack it in and sit down."

She grinned at him and flopped herself ungracefully into the nearest chair as if inviting him by example—throwing one leg over the other, quite aware of the great expanses of powerful thigh thus exposed. She had varicose veins.

"Whatever it is," said Truck, "no. I had enough of this in the Fleet. I've got my discharge papers here—" Then, recklessly, because he was fighting down an emotion rather like panic, "You don't look like a member of the Chosen Race to me, General."

This, he managed to deliver with an insinuating snigger. The General, though, merely adjusted her eyepatch and sighed. Her bleached-out hair was chopped off all the way round her head at ear level; her nose had been broken during a police action on Weber II.

"I don't like you either, sonny, but I'm keeping quiet about it. This baiting stuff doesn't work on me, so forget it. I'm simply an executive of the World Government, doing a job. If you've got any sense, you won't make it difficult for me. I wouldn't have had you within a yard of this office if it hadn't been absolutely necessary."

She studied his clothing with distaste. "I can't believe we ever had you in the Fleet," she said. "God, what a shambles it must have been."

He had been rendered uncomfortable despite every resolution.

"You own half a world, General, and it isn't this one. Half of Earth you neither govern nor own; and to the rest of the Galaxy you have no right whatever. That lays you open."

"We govern the civilized world. We police the civilized colonies. Without the security we represent, scabs like you might have less freedom to speak. Would you chop logic with a UASR representative sitting in my place? There are three hundred billion people in the Galaxy and we have only one per cent of them. We're outnumbered, and we have what they want. Everything that happens out here affects us."

Truck shrugged. Events would carry him; it was only left to him to discover in which direction. Abruptly, two separate images welled up from the back of his head—

He recalled the Negev, the hot boredom broken only by brief violent engagements with infiltrators from the Union of Arab Socialist Republics, the dull report of a Chambers gun, the dreadful anger that welled up when he realized he had been shot at. And he saw the packed corpse-boats orbiting Cor Caroli in Canes Venatici, their cold spectral avenues limned with a faint milky light, the plastic packing cases filled with dead children, the ranked carcasses of the adults without box of any kind, the wounds glittering at him like eyes; he smelled them.

"Get on with it," he said. "Have you got anything good to smoke? Oh well."

"You may have to pay a little more attention than that, laddie."

She swung her leg, tapped the table. Truck locked his hands in his lap and played absently with them. It looked as if it might be a long session.

"We don't know very much," began General Gaw, "about the old inhabitants of the Centauri system: they were the first of the so-called 'civilized' races too intercept the wave-front of human expansion; they were wiped out as a coherent group two centuries ago in what we've been taught to call since the 'Centauri Genocide.' Shut up, Truck. You don't understand enough of anything for your opinion to be worth anything to me. That was what the intellectuals of the time called it. I'm in favor of intellectuals as a whole, but I have reservations.

"However, it was a traumatic business for humanity, that can hardly be denied; and by the time we'd finished running round getting off on our guilt complexes, the Centauri survivors had bolted off like rats and scattered themselves over the newly-colonized planets. They were absorbed fairly quickly—no drive, you see; they lacked cultural strength.

"They were enough like us to suggest common ancestry (it had already been discovered that two miscegenations out of three were fruitful or some such revolting thing); they weren't at all native to the Centauri system, although nobody ever discovered traces of them anywhere else; there was even some speculation that they might have originated on Earth, which really put the cat among the pigeons.

"But the rubbish died down, and at least one decent piece of thinking came out of it. Marsden's hypothesis of Niche Competition described the Galaxy as an ecological complex in which separate space-going races replace the separate species of a planetary ecosphere. The competition between species whose demands on the environment are identical is inevitable, natural, and harsh.

"Yes, I do believe it, as a matter of fact. Never mind that. Keep your grubby little fingers out of my head.

"Now.

"The peculiar thing about that war is that the Centaurans needn't have lost it. They couldn't have won, but for fifteen years they stood us off; then, quite suddenly, they stopped intercepting the MIEVs and the atmospheric intruders. Within three days, Centauri VII was rubbished. They did a good job of that sort of thing in those days.

"But listen to this, Truck: we had an on-planet intelligence network down there, living as Centaurans, poor sods—it's in the records—and they were sending reports through right up until Centauri VII chucked it in. So why did they commit suicide, laddie, when they'd just concluded R&D on a weapon they fully expected to finish the whole shooting match in their favor?

"You think about that, while we talk about you.

"You were born in the Pontisport hinterland on Parrot, in the rest room of a bakery. Your mother was a part-time port whore, one of the refugees who came down the Carling Line in refrigerators from Weber II. She was mainlining adrenochrome activators cut with the ribosomes of a local breed of bat. She asked for a cure, but the port authorities already had her scheduled for resettlement as a displaced person. No, I'm not asking you any of this, I'm telling you—because I know more about you than you know about yourself.

"Spaceport Annie Truck was shipped to the Heavy Stars when you were six months old. AdAcs penetrate the placenta, of course, and you had to be weaned off the stuff. She left you behind. Do you ever dream about bats?

"But what's more important about Annie is this: she was a full-blooded Centauran.

"As far as we can decide statistically, there's a ninety-four per cent chance that she was the last true Centauran to exist in the Galaxy. That makes you a half-breed, Truck. Finally, on this score at least: for some reason, Annie had the primogeniture. If you'd ever read a book, you might have recognized your bone-structure and general proportion as predominantly Centauran. Your father had weak genes, whoever he was.

"You won't find that so amusing in a minute, chummie.

"Let's go back to the Centauran War. Have it your own way, genocide; it honestly makes no difference to me. That weapon existed, you know. The MI reports worried us then, but we have our own reasons now.

"We found it, Truck.

"Some bloody lunatic of an archaeologist found it in a bunker cut three miles into the crust of Centauri VII, as nasty a little bolthole as ever I saw, and I've seen a lot.

"We found it, but we don't know how to work it. We can't even get very close to it. We can't get any instrument readings off it. I've seen it myself, and it seems half sentient. Can you see that, Truckie—a sentient bomb?

"We need your genes. They gave up and conceded Centauri without using the weapon all right; but they built its operating codes into the chromosomes of their unborn brats, because they wanted to be able to sneak back to it like dogs to sick, later. It won't go off without a Centauran.

"Annie died twenty years ago, and you're the only one we could find."

Truck mulled it over a little. He felt a wry sympathy for the port lady from Weber II. It was easy to see his own birth as a momentary lapse, a miscalculation. But again: had Annie Truck answered some unconscious urge on Parrot? In dividing, to produce another vector, a small image of herself? As if by that multiplication of possibilities, the long uncomprehending migration might be expedited—something lost by her might be gained by him.

This in the silence that followed General Gaw's monologue, while her good eye impaled him and wouldn't let go. All spacers are incurably sentimental. Eventually, he got out of his chair and stood looking down at her.

"How much good will your bomb do us when you drop it?" he asked. He wasn't sure on whose behalf he was asking. He fingered the tear in his jacket. "Who will you drop it on?"

When she said, "I expected that, Truck, it's predictable from the way you dress. You can leave it out, because I don't need it," he turned his back on her. She went on: "We blew two UASR agents in the team that uncovered the Centauri Device. There was a third, but we didn't discover that until he'd shoved off.

"That's what it's about, duckie; it always is."

Indistinctly, because he was thinking about something else: "Then get someone else to prime the thing, General."

He reached the door, went as far as touching the handle, then faced her again.

"I was on Morpheus," he said. "I stacked them up for the graveyard orbit at Cor Caroli. I've seen the library footage of Weber II. You understand, I don't care if you and the Arabs blow each other to junk. But I loaded people who'd never heard of you on to those boats."

She was still lounging, undisturbed and negligent, her thighs powerful and ugly, her eye bright and compelling. He was growing terrified less of what she represented than of the woman herself.

"That shanghai attempt," he said, "was it to persuade me that the Arabs want to talk to me too? That would have made it nice and easy to accept whatever deal you have in mind, wouldn't it? Don't do it again. I'll try and kill the next lot, so help me. The only people who wear lace-ups are Fleet Police. It only makes you look silly, you see. No spacer would be seen dead in lace-up shoes. At least the Arabs have the gumption to dress their men for the part."

She laughed, breezy and fierce.

"I told the stupid bitch it wouldn't work. I'm going to have to have a chat with her." She swung her legs out of the chair and leaned forward. "I can't say I didn't expect this. We need you, we were prepared to pay for you—but there won't be any offers now."

Truck opened the door.

"You've got yourself into my bad books, I don't mind telling you that. I'm giving you twenty-four hours to consider it, then I'll have you pulled in. Wherever you are. The charge will be trading in Fleet medical supplies when you were last on Earth, and I can prove it.

"I'll be here if you should decide to behave yourself. Bye-bye, laddie."

Truck closed the door quietly after him.

He went back to the Spacer's Rave, feeling as if he had suddenly gained a dependent. Why should Annie Truck and her AdAc habit be on *his* conscience? It was a strange reversal, but under the hinterland lamps, all kinds of dependency are possible. It assumed a kind of reality: Annie flickered into life for him there, and he accepted her.

Tiny Skeffern was winding up his gig in a desultory fashion: "Phencyclidine Dream," which he always used as his encore, was over; bass drums and most of the audience had packed up and gone home, but a cadaverous ectomorphic spacer was sitting smirking stupidly over the controls of the Rave's H-Line synthesizer, making attic, flutelike noises, while Tiny picked at the high notes with meditative fingers. Only the stoned and persistent remained to listen, wondering how they might find somewhere to go, something to do at four-thirty St. Crispin's Day morning on Sad al Bari IV.

By the time the last of them had lurched out onto the street, dirty brown light was filtering between the buildings and the vapor lamps were wan. An occasional chandler, bleary and reluctant with sleep, crept past the door of the Rave on his way to another day. Tiny turned it all off and gently laid the Fender in its hardshell case. He slapped the shoulder of the guy on the synthesizer, yawned, did a weary shuffle. "Oh, man."

There is a kind of cold particular to the dawn. All nightside losers know and revere it for its healing stimulant properties. Shivering and grinning at one another, Truck and Tiny hunched off toward the port and Truck's boat. The compass wind blew: it lay in wait for them at intersections, came whistling round the corners of warehouses to meet them. When that happened, Tiny would run on ahead, swinging the Fender case and kicking out at bits of rubbish in the gutter.

"Hey look," he said, "it's an Opener."

Waddling down Bread Street toward them in the morning chill was an enormous splay-footed, wobbling man wearing a plum-colored cloak. His head was bald and round, his features streamlined into his facial tissue so that they were mere suggestions of a mouth, a nose, a chin. His eyes were swaddled deep and tight in flaps and swathes of flesh. His cloak was open at the front.

He was an Opener all right—one of that curious sect whose members believe that honesty of bodily function is the sole valid praise of God (the existence of whom they freely and frequently aver), that function being analogous, if only through cortical representation, to the very motions of the psyche.

When the wind peeled back the cloak, he was naked. His body was shaved as hairless as his head, his skin was like a pink, shiny polymer. Let into his stomach, thorax, and belly were the thick plastic windows the Openers have surgically inserted to show off their internal processes. They were surrounded by thick callused lips of flesh, and nothing altogether pleasant was going on behind them.

He stared as he passed Truck and Tiny. His eyes were black and secretive. He had eaten a fairly light breakfast. He moved his small, indeterminate lips into a smile. Suddenly, a short thick arm whipped from under his cloak (as if the action were quite divorced from him, the arm belonging to some dwarf or ape hiding beneath the garments—his smile remained). His meaty hand clutched John Truck's shoulder.

"Here," said Truck. "Get off."

"Good morning, Captain," said the Opener. "I am Dr. Grishkin. The Lord is kind."

"What?"

Truck, gazing through the windows on Dr. Grishkin's raw and convoluted soul, recalled that he hadn't eaten for some time. The Opener still had hold of his arm. His stomach rumbled.

"I have just this moment come from your ship. Your bosun told me you were unavailable. I'm glad to find him wrong."

"That's right," mumbled Truck, "not available. Sorry."

Dr. Grishkin nodded slowly, once—until he was looking at Truck like a sad fat animal from the cave-mouth of his own brows. It was accomplished, it was dramatic. With his free hand, he spread his cloak wide. Truck began to feel ill.

"Captain, I open myself to you. I appeal to you. Although I can see by your outfit you are not one of my scattered brothers, I know from here"—he tapped each of his windows in turn—"that you are a man of principle, even of charity. Captain, I beg of you the help only you can give."

Truck shuddered. Dr. Grishkin's enigmatic eyes, full of the revelations of the organism, held his, unwavering. The grip on his arm was paternal, gentle; it was possessive. He experienced an overpowering sensation of *déjà vu*. Over Grishkin's rounded shoulder, he could see right along Bread Street, which was empty and indifferent. Having got him into this, it wasn't going to get him out. Screw all streets, he thought. He knew he had to break free: ulterior motive or mere charisma, Grishkin was too strong for him. He was fearful of discovering what the Opener wanted.

A port lady saved him. Trudging sexually down the street with a stoned deck hand hanging on her arm, she swept her long beautiful hair out of her eyes and winked at him boldly. He watched her swaying back until it was a wriggling iota in the deadly perspective of the street. Then he said:

"Grishkin, piss off."

And he walked away, leaving Tiny Skeffern and the Opener staring after him. Tiny was puzzled, but there was a certain satisfaction in Grishkin's unconvincing eye. Truck sensed that he had not won the encounter, only postponed it.

Tiny caught up, swinging the Fender case. "I think I am going to be sick," he chuckled. "How can he live with his own breakfast like that?"

Truck stopped and watched the Opener watching him. His neck ached, and the wind stung his tender lip. "Tiny," he said, "I'm going to Earth. There's no better place to be arrested."

"What?"

Out in space, other winds blew. While thoughtful Truck brooded round the exterior screens, gazing at the flying streamers of illusion produced by *Ella*'s improbable progress through the impossible medium of the dyne fields, Fix the bosun prepared him meals he didn't eat.

"You got to eat, boss."

Tiny Skeffern patched his Fender into the communications equipment. Broadcasting the "Dynaflow Blues" into the quaking, distorted universe outside—trailing slow ribbons of tachyon noise that might some day and in some unimaginably distant place be received and decoded as a stretched, alien music—the ship groped and crabbed and hurtled her way by turns a few light years closer to her captain's destiny.

Nobody mentioned Earth until it became necessary for landing procedures.

By that time, Truck had six of his twenty-four hours left.

THREE

◼

The Longest-running Party in the History of the Universe

Earth:

IWG and UASR, initially parasites of the political muscle-tissue, had eaten what remained of their twenti-eth-century hosts during the aftermath of the tragic and infamous "Rat Bomb" wars of 2003–15, when the satellite system, that uneasy and paternalistic com-promise between autonomy and empire, fragmented and fell apart.

A new Arabia swallowed the entire Sino-Soviet con-tinent, engulfed the more fertile areas of Africa, but lost its original nerve center in Egypt. IWG swelled to contain both Americas, the husk of the unsuccessful European Economic Community, and the Mediter-ranean shores.

Between them, they devasted Australasia and, in a quarrel over the missile pits of Antarctica, set fire to the Pacific Ocean.

Now, they faced one another along the crooked boundary lines of the Syrian Desert and the Taurus Mountains, the cratered wastes of the German Strip, the Bering Sea. Silos in the radio-glass puddle of the

Qattara Depression menaced Niger and the keelyards of Nubia. They disputed the Red Sea—warily, in gunboats—from the Israeli causeway at Sinai to the fifty-lane Arabian road bridge at Al Shaab.

Hydrofoil flotillas, spraying rainbow arcs of oil and semipolymers to calm the sea before them, patrolled the South Atlantic; above them, piloted missile interceptors hung in precarious fragmentary orbits; and off the tip of South America, Tierra del Fuego, enigma and threat under its power dome, humped out of the Magellan Strait like a huge, stranded alien fish.

There were many fronts, but few confrontations; they used the Galaxy for those.

It would have been naïve to consider the inheritors of the Earth as "Jews" and "Arabs": they had sold that birthright, and retained of it only the terminology. The millennial grievances that had motivated their wars prior to the last quarter of the nineteen hundreds had vanished; in consolidating their secondhand empires, they had merged a thousand nationalities and religions, only to lose their own.

More important, perhaps: each of them had surrendered its self-determination in favor of the politico-social and economic principles of the dead powerblocs —so that they were caught in the inevitable conflict of ideologies already worn pitifully thin four hundred years before, when Tiny Skeffern's shiny antique had given its first performance.

2367: the Mohorovicic Discontinuity was mined on both sides of the Red Sea Fault.

There were no more neutral zones.

Truck decided to visit his wife.

Cor Caroli was visible over the deserted inspection pits of Carter's Snort when, unaware of his position as an activator of entropy, he brought his boat down among them. He knew it for a murder-star, the killer in the houndpack of Venatici; but as yet he did not expect that his own star would eventually outshine it on all scales of magnitude.

He had to argue with Fix, the Chromian bosun, who stood stubbornly on the loading ramp of *My Ella Speed*, coughing in the dirty winter air of Earth and saying: "I'll bring the chopper, boss."

Truck shook his head.

"You stay here, Fix. Tiny will tell you if they've pinched me. The boat's yours until you hear from me again."

Fix grinned with embarrassment. His teeth were like a sawmill.

"You need big protection out there, boss. I'll just—" He made off toward the corner of the hold where he kept his stuff.

"Leave that bloody thing where it is, Fix. You're not coming."

"Stuff it."

"Sorry."

He was, too. He fastened his second-best jacket, a heavy brown leather thing lined with peculiar gray fur from some place he had never been. Some of his hair got stuck in the ornamental zip; zips were as fashionable in the hinterlands that year as Tiny Skeffern and for similar reasons. He shrugged at Fix. He left the ramp.

Tiny was still in the ship. Hearing Truck's receding boot heels, he stuck his head out of the forward lock and, silhouetted against the cabin lights, puffed ectoplasm into the frosty night.

"I'll be at the Boot Palace on Sauchihall if you need me," he called.

"Thanks, Tiny."

Gazing sentimentally back over his shoulder, Truck lost his footing among the clumps of couch-grass that had forced their way through the broken concrete of the landing field.

"See you."

He brushed himself down and trudged out into the empty, depressed streets of Carter's Snort.

Most northerly of the five major zones of Albion Megaport (that 60,000 square mile complex of bunker-docks, keelyards, freight terminals, and warehouses that had once been called "Great Britain"), the Snort had been the first of them to succumb to the domino recessions of the post-colonial period, and the only one never to have recovered.

Cargo was no longer handled there, and no ships were built—although a few keelyards still had tower cranes erected above them, as if to disguise their impotence. Only the breakers flourished, catering to the spares trade and melting down what they couldn't resell in great pig-furnaces that turned the midnight concrete arcades of Carter's Snort into a dull red maze.

Its original population dispersed in search of work, the zone had moved quickly through that process of cultural decay peculiar to ports, attracting the poor, the rootless, the ruthless—and finally the artistic and cheap intellectual elements not only of IWG but of the stars. The only music you heard in Carter's Snort was the New Music. Its feet were booted. It was the hinterland of all hinterlands.

Truck, who had once lived there long enough to make one of his more elementary errors, hunched his shoulders and walked east. He stopped for a moment to gaze at the broken spine of a refrigerator ship curving up out of its own corroding ribs, his face over-lighted by the savage glare of the plasma torches; their half-visors dark and numinous, the wreckers grinned at him, a race of amiable Vandals.

FREE ANYWHERE, said the graffiti on the walls of the dim derelict warehouses; SUSQUEMADELION LIVES, and IS THERE LIFE *BEFORE* DEATH? Truck laughed; he liked them; he felt at home. He pulled his collar up and ignored the few bitter flakes of snow that stung his face when he turned into the wind.

Ruth Berenici Truck lived in wrecker territory down

by the river. He stood in the street looking up at her windows and wondering not so much why he had come as what part of him had suggested it. Silent explosions of light from the yards, then the tolling of a monstrous girder as it flexed and fell.

The walls had been his manuscript when he still slept here: all the way up to her floor, they sent him messages from a youthful alien head.

GO HOME TRUCK.

He didn't remember doing that one.

Ruth Berenici stood outside her open door, presenting out of nervousness her left profile only, perfect and still. She was tall and thin, she moved very slowly. Her eyes were gray (devoid, though, of ice), her hair was streaked with it; her jaw muscles were a little too strong.

"Ruth."

"I saw you in the street."

Ruth Berenici had allowed the universe to wound her at every turn; because of this, she possessed nothing but a sad grace, a yielding internal calm. Truck reached out to touch her right cheek. She closed her eyes, and the left side of her mouth smiled.

"It's still there, John."

That hesitant turn of the head; the full face revealed; he bit the inside of his cheek in a kind of sexual shock.

"Why are you shivering?" he asked. He experienced a brief memory of her ascending the cellar steps of the Boot Palace some years before, a sectional assumption in the weak wet light of the Carter's Snort dawn. He found one of her long hands, trapped it.

"There are times when"—she disengaged her hand, spread the fingers, pressed them flat against his chest—"I *know* you." She shook her head. Profound bruised areas about her eyes, mark of the eternal victim. "No, you're not coming in—"

The hand moved away, leaving no bruises on his second-best hide, no marks of any kind.

"—unless you're staying this time."

Ruth recognized the significance of moments. It was her only defense.

"I am this time," he lied. The room had changed, but he found one of his hats in a cupboard. "You did it up nicely. I thought you might have gone somewhere else."

Later, placing one of his hands beneath her tiny breasts:

"Here."

Ruth worked in the front office of Bayley, the wrecker's on Lead Alley; at night, she brought him amusing presents ripped off from Bayley's stock. He stayed in the room all day because he knew it would hurt her to come back and find him out. He slept a lot. He scratched at the frost patterns on the inside of the window—stared, mildly surprised to discover himself still free.

They quarreled, crammed into her narrow hot bed.

"Why did you go?" Abruptly moving her leg, watching him seriously. And: "We ought to be able to talk about it now."

"I don't really know. Come on."

"No, wait a minute, we ought to be able to talk about things like that."

He grunted at the ceiling, rolled onto his stomach. "Oh well." He got out of bed, scratching listlessly at the hair under his armpits. With nothing to do all day, he had become a glutton for sleep, perpetually dozy. He felt as if a layer of sponge separated him from objects, from the floor.

"I have to move. I have to meet new people. I like people."

She followed him round the room, talking over his shoulder, picking things up and putting them down again.

"In the abstract, in the abstract. Liking everybody keeps individuals at a distance. If you can feel responsible for some smashed port loser you never met, why not me?"

"Oh, that's a bit simplif—"

"Right." She pressed herself against him, all that amazing white flesh, tinted smoky blue in its declivities. "You'll go again. I'll be hurt, but I'll still be here. This will always be here waiting for you."

She snatched his hand, forced him to touch her right cheek, her belly and thighs.

He shrugged. "I don't believe it's like that at all." He picked his jacket up and began to go through the pockets.

Back on the bed, Ruth sniffled. "I'm sorry." She faced the wall. "Stuff your bloody head with dope, then."

Four days.

Nobody came.

Nobody arrested him (except Ruth: the longer he stayed, the more frightened she became of his eventual departure—it was an ascending spiral of dependence). He was at the window constantly, watching the snow turn to sleet and then rain. Out in wrecker territory the plasma torches hissed; whole plantations of steel were pruned and lopped; the dark-visored gnomes bobbed and grinned.

Caught between Ruth's inability to feel anything but pain and the uncertainty of his own position, Truck grew nervous and mean. He didn't understand how General Gaw and her police could have missed him. He needed information. He picked moody bones with Ruth when she came home from work—finally put on his jacket and left the house.

Tiny Skeffern couldn't tell him anything.

"Something is moving down there underneath it all," he said, blowing on his fingers to warm them up. It was practice afternoon at the Boot Palace, but the rest of his band hadn't turned up. "But nobody's mentioning your name."

He was squatting on the dusty stage, up to his elbows in an amplifier. The Boot Palace was gloomy and cold, smelling of stale audience. Grimy swirls of fluorescent dye blinked dimly from its cavernous walls, echoes of the previous night's *satori*.

"The narcotics police are getting ready to close Chalice Veronica's import operation. You're not involved with that are you?"

He plugged in. Nothing happened.

"I'd like to see Veronica," said Truck. "He has paid ears."

Tiny kicked his amp. "Look here, fuck you, *work*," he said. He washed his hands of it. "Let's go and get smashed," he suggested. "We could drop in on Veronica later."

"I'd have to tell Ruth," said Truck. But it was past dark before he made it back to the wrecking grounds.

Somewhere between Three Jump House and the Spastic Quasar he stole a great pink Vulpeculan fruit as a present for Ruth. He and Tiny ran through the rain on opposite sides of the street, tossing this obscene thing between them until it began to show signs of irreversible wear. They giggled. Tiny was falling down a lot.

"Shush," whispered Truck, as they sneaked up the stairs.

GO HOME TRUCK, said the walls.

He missed a step. Ruth's present ballooned away through the darkness like a stupid ghost, pink and glowing. "Catch it, Tiny!"

He knocked on the door. "Ruth?" No answer. Tiny chuckled. "It went all the way down again." He tried to balance the fruit on one finger. "Not going to let you in, mate. Oops."

"Ruth?"

No answer.

Truck lowered himself carefully down, sat with his back to the door. Faint sounds of someone weeping filtered through it. They came from far away, and made him infinitely upset. "Oh, Ruth, I'm sorry." He brightened up. "Let us in and we'll give you something."

Tiny dropped the fruit. "Yes."

"Just go away," said Ruth from the other side of the door. "Just go away, John."

He left the fruit. He shrugged. Halfway down the stairs, he hung over the banister and vomited dismally. His eyes watered.

"Tiny," he said, "we're losers. What good is all this doing us?"

Ruth Berenici sat on her narrow bed, tall and gray and beautiful, tracing with her fingertips the scar that immobilized the right side of her head from beneath the eye down to that place where neck meets shoulder. It would be naïve to mistake John Truck's half of that ramshackle, enduring affair for pity.

It might well have been the other way round.

Chalice Veronica, the intellectual pusher-king, lived in a five-story converted warehouse, a grim and ancient monument behind the old rocket-mail pits of Renfield Street.

Beneath the pits, he plied his trade, in a chain of fuel cisterns abandoned during the domino recessions. There the myriad sensations of the Galaxy were cut, stored, packaged, and dispatched (it was rumored) by a hundred naked Denebian mainliners working out a mysterious debt to the King. For miles in every direction, the earth was honeycombed with traps and tunnels and boltholes.

Above ground, in twenty sumptuous rooms, the longest-running party in the history of the universe was still in progress. People were born, people died there; some were said to have lived entire lives there. It slowed, but it never stopped; the dope was benign, the cuts were appetizing—and, by agile bribery, the King kept even the least of his guests safe from harm and from all arrest.

It couldn't last for much longer.

Every six months, each room was redecorated in the style of the Important Moment: now, the moment was twentieth century. Captain John Truck (somewhat recovered from his recent malaise) and Tiny Skeffern entered the King's domain by a chromium plated vagina, passed into a plastic lobby where valuable *objets d'art*—the reheat pipe and aft fan assembly of a GEYj93, cut away to reveal V-gutters and low pressure turbine; original pressings of Bing Crosby and Johny Winter; a calf-bound set of Ethel M. Dell firsts, signed and numbered by the author—strewed their path.

Beyond, in a room full of drifting colored smoke, where the strobes jumped and hopped from one wavelength to another and Tiny Skeffern's sound fell in solid blocks from original quadrophonic equipment, Chalice Veronica himself lounged on a sofa wearing crocheted culottes.

"Hello," said Tiny Skeffern, bobbing around. "I brought a friend."

"That's so nice," whispered the King. He pulled himself languidly to his feet and smiled at Truck. His hand was icy; his skin had the texture and color of distemper, damp and powdery; he was old, and his voice was faint, destroyed; *arcus senilis*, the yellow band of decay, disfigured his eyes. It was common knowledge that he knew everything but the date of his own death.

"I want some information," said Truck.

The King laughed. "He's very direct, isn't he?" he said to Tiny Skeffern. "I do love a celebrity, though. So good of you both to come."

He studied Truck, and it was like being measured by Death.

"I've been hearing so much about you. But you're safe here. Nobody will bother you here." He tilted his blunt, lizardlike head to one side. "A lot of them would like to, though. What on Earth can you have done?"

Truck zipped his jacket up. "Thanks. That's all I

wanted to know. I'd better go. Tiny tells me you're expecting a raid."

Chalice Veronica held his hand up in the ancient mainliner's gesture, forearm stiff from the elbow, palm open.

"There'll be no raid," he murmured. "The party won't stop. Stay. Circulate. Some of the finest minds in the Galaxy are here, Artists, thinkers, revolutionaries. Criminals. Do stay."

Truck caught Tiny's eye. Tiny nodded dubiously.

"We'd love to," he said. "Only for a moment, though."

Chalice Veronica smiled distantly. He began to roll up his sleeve. Someone brought him a tray of sweet cakes. "For the Moment," he mused, "a fine sentiment. Yes, always the Moment."

As they walked into the next room, Tiny said: "He's showing his age this last year. He can't face facts any more. But we should be all right for a while."

"Ah, Hermann Göring! Now there was a true Romantic maligned by his own age. Always the fate of the innovator." In the long gallery on the fifth floor, Horst-Sylvia, the biological sculptress, was demonstrating her latest animal, something small and multimorphic. "Such excitement, such—" Upset by the hubbub, it skittered over a waxwork tableau depicting Nixon and Brezhnev and the other great landowners of the twentieth century, gazing down benignly on their peasants and bondsmen. It squealed. "Gaw hunting for him, I hear. Smoke?" In rapid succession, it became an albino marmoset, a spider, a golden salamander. It vanished into the folds of Sylvia's robe.

"Tiny's music is so . . . well . . . I just can't describe. Only the music can say it, you see. That's the beauty of the nonverbal." Finally, it took the form of a black mongrel dog and sneaked round peeing on everyone's shoes. "Harking back to the optimism—the Romance—of the Cold War, the promise of technology!"

Someone found a piece of leather for a collar, but the dog had died. It was a great success.

"They don't last very long, of course," said Horst-Sylvia.

John Truck, hanging about in a dim alcove beneath a blurred black-and-white photograph of an XB-70 ("so very characteristic of the imagination of the period"), picked sourly at his nose. Tiny had wandered off to be told what gave his music such an acute sense of aesthetic urgency.

"What did the old fool say about minds?" muttered Truck.

"You're in Carter's Snort, Captain"—a low, amused voice from somewhere in the alcove—"it doesn't do to expect too much."

Truck squinted into the gloom, positive that the recess had been empty when he entered it. He jumped. A shadowy figure wrapped in a black cloak had detached itself from the wall, eyes hidden by the brim of an enormous soft hat.

"At least they aren't dressed like silly buggers."

A hollow laugh. The mouth was obscured by a ridiculous stormcollar; beneath the cloak, bones seemed to stick out at peculiar angles.

"You have to play your part, Captain. Look here—"

A thin white hand slipped from beneath the cloak, palm upward; across it lay a single long-stemmed green carnation, uncrushed and delicately perfumed.

"Sinclair-Pater sent me. He wants to tell you this: he admires what you did on Morpheus; he wishes to help you now in any way he can."

The carnation vanished. A conjurer's gesture. It reappeared.

"What does he want from me? I've got nothing to sell. I'm no more an anarchist than an Arab."

Pater's messenger snapped his slim pale fingers. He was incredibly tall.

"An offer of help. No more. You may need it sooner than you think."

Chalice Veronica's warehouse shuddered. The lights went out. A long, rolling explosion rocked the gallery. Feeble emergency flares spluttered into life. The King's guests moaned and groaned in a sick gray twilight, gazing into each other's ghastly faces.

The anarchist swung his cloak tighter about him and stalked away into the crowd, his long legs carrying him off at great speed. Almost out of sight in the crush, he turned and shouted, "Narcotics, Captain. They'll have stopped all the boltholes. Try the roof."

And he vanished.

The emergencies died.

Truck fought his way out into the sweating, heaving darkness. Someone elbowed him in the groin. He kicked out. "Move, you—" It was useless. A Chambers bolt flared out in front of him. "They'll never take me alive!" A hysterical laugh.

"REMAIN WHERE YOU ARE," said a calm, gigantic voice.

Aerosol anesthetics hissed into the gallery.

Something blew up silently in the back of Truck's skull and he slid down into a profound hole. His last thought was that everybody seemed to know more about him than he knew about himself.

◼

FOUR

Too Much Gravity

General Gaw, Dr. Grishkin that peculiar priest, and Swinburne Sinclair-Pater the Interstellar Anarchist had each captured a piece of him.

General Gaw had the arms. "Come off it, sonny!" she cried, waving her awful spoon. Dr. Grishkin pulled his right leg off in an attempt to attract his attention. Sinclair-Pater, laughing madly, put his hands into Truck's head. "I know you!" he said archly, waggling his skinny fingers. "We all know you!"

There are mysterious troglodytic wreckers hobbling and hopping about in the gloom at the very base of the universe; for millennia, they have been searching for the one golden bolt that holds the whole surprising contraption together; Truck knew its whereabouts to the inch just before he woke up to all the vast sordid horror of a rubber restraining garment, in West Central Detention, Carter's Snort.

"I'll tell you!" he yelled, trying to thrash about. But they had all left by a back door in his head.

The only new construction in Carter's Snort since the depression: West Central Detention, thrown hastily up when the decline became apparent—conceived, built, doomed to be a slum, to deliver hinterland justice. Not that anyone inside it is interested in the latter (which is represented nonrepresentationally in a mural above the unwelcome gate and has, apparently, to do with globes, balances, and lightning—very inspiring, but all that can be said for sure is that it smells of disinfectant); no, they're deep down in all that concrete to earn a living. It bows their shoulders, as if they supported the whole steel-laced, flat faced pile on their necks.

If they have cells for souls, no one's to blame.

Outside, it's a reflection of the Snort it claims to serve: fans of rust where metal touches the walls; wet and dirty and down by the river.

Inside, John Truck. Well, he's been here before. Or in places very like it.

He was alone in a charge room with the echo of his own waking cry, the sole and total literacy of the hinterlands scratched and daubed on the pale green walls around him. This is where they write their only books: Picking Nick was here, busted for speed; Og, caught holding for a friend. All coppers do it with their mothers; if you get off, Angel, tell the Rat I didn't. Stuff and screw and stuff again. Novels of rage, futile exposés addressed to lawyers, relatives, and life; vomit and other things in corners; a cold steel door with rivets and only memories of paint through being kicked so often in silly resistance.

Truck was strapped on a bench, vertiginous from the anesthetic, already bleak and bored, wondering if the General had caught up with him at last. From beyond the door came a continual scrape of footsteps, a whole army of offenders filing past. Faint voices, the odd shout, some smashed loser who had or hadn't come down: the King's guests, paying their forfeits without the fun of the party. It was way past dawn.

He lay there for some time, silently fighting the crab lice in the restraining jacket and staring at the ceiling. People came to the door, changed their minds and went away again. Angel and the Rat and Fast Harry passed on their advice in disconnected misspelled prose, but he'd read it all before. When the door scraped open, he was half asleep. Imagine his surprise, to find Dr. Grishkin, the flabby priest, bending solicitously over him.

Cooped up in Ruth's apartment with time to consider that meeting on Bread Street, he had begun to feel a metaphysical uneasiness, even alarm, whenever he thought of Grishkin. He would have been hard put to explain why. Nevertheless, it was amplified unreasonably by the actual apparition or avatar of the man. Endeavoring to dispel some of it, he stared up into the round, lunar face where he could almost see himself reflected in a faint cheesy film of perspiration and muttered:

"I thought I told you to sod off?"

It was hardly a body blow (*One of these days, Truck,* he told himself sadly, *somebody is going to discover the real you under all this foulmouthed repartee—a foulmouthed Teddy bear*), and a mistake even to imply he might be continuing their previous exchange. The doctor had reversed his cloak, but not his stance. Black, with a thin gold stripe. Very fetching.

"Captain, it is a little more complex than that. If you could bring yourself—if you could co-operate—"

His little eyes gleamed extravagantly. Things, amorphous and juicy, shifted to and fro behind his windows like the slow stirrings of some core, some hub—something real, at any rate—which existed quite apart from his benign and greasy faith: inexplicable urgencies of the psyche mimicked in the motion of the gut, demands that perhaps only Grishkin could fully comprehend and Truck completely fulfill. Faced with such ambition— such enigma and compulsion—Truck's bravado slipped a little.

"Don't tell me you're a copper. I wouldn't have believed they had it in them."

Crucified by someone else's crabs (he hadn't yet accepted that they were now his although they evidently had—the eternal misunderstanding), wrapped up in sweaty rubber and flat on his back besides, he wasn't at his freshest; it was a stupid thing to say. But the good doctor merely smiled. He was no copper and both of them knew it. Truck hunched one shoulder.

"That was a stupid thing to say. Why *are* you here, then?"

Any port in a storm.

Grishkin beamed. He waddled very rapidly round the room once, touching the walls here, tapping them there.

"Captain," he said as he went, "you've been detained before. You aren't a fool. For an offense such as this, for a narcotics offense"—he spread his arms, the palms of his hands upwards; he stared up at the conjunction of wall and ceiling—"no one could reasonably expect a lawyer. But the twenty-fourth century admits—indeed, insists upon—your right to religious representation. Why else should I be here?" He nodded several times to himself, murmuring "Just so, just so," as if he were thinking of something else altogether.

"How you got in here I don't much care; get to the point, Grishkin."

The Opener thrust his face close to Truck's. He seemed to have had late nights recently; there were pouches of slack, slightly discolored skin beneath his eyes. He licked his tiny lips and then whispered earnestly: "To open certain avenues to you, to—"

"Grishkin, if you—"

"—to offer you a way out, Captain."

Truck felt absurdly disappointed. He chuckled sourly, thinking of the General.

Grishkin made a gesture of impatience and turned his back. "Captain, you are a difficult person to feel concern for!" When he turned back, some of the urgencies contained behind his windows had escaped into his facial musculature, pursing his mouth intermittently and drawing his forehead into two thick long labia of flesh.

"Captain," he said, "there are questions other than that of personal satisfaction, of ideology. I need an agent; if you like, an interpreter; possibly even more. Do you understand me? You are the last person in the Galaxy who speaks the language I am interested in. My doctorate is not in theology or medicine, but in archaeology; do you take my point?"

Breathing heavily, he leaned closer, supporting his gross bulk with a hand placed each side of Truck's head. Beneath the perspiration, his skin was grainy, matted.

"It is no laughing matter. The local penal system can be circumvented. If you agree to act for me, you will be released. If not—a narcotics offense, Captain—it speaks for itself."

He levered himself upright.

Truck? He was invincibly ignorant of his Time and Place, only beginning to recognize the nature of the tides. He sniggered. "Can you circumvent IWG Fleet, doctor?" he asked. "Can you circumvent General Alice Gaw?"

It wasn't really funny.

"Oh, *sod* these bleeding lice!"

Grishkin winced. The walls of his stomach contracted furiously behind the window of his soul. Of their own accord, his pudgy hands moved until their blunt fingertips touched Truck's neck. His cloak fell forward and obscured the light. After an effort, he controlled his fingers and stepped back; he wrapped the cloak about him and stood there, looking down almost compassionately.

"You are worth more than you imagine, Captain. If I suspected you were simply parroting things of which you had no understanding—you cannot be quite as naïve as—but no: you have seen her already. I had hoped to be in time." He shrugged. "Until there is some change in your circumstances, my offer will have to be withdrawn."

"You won't have anything to offer then, doctor."

There was a hiss and thud of automatic bolts being withdrawn; servos whined and the charge-room door swung slowly open to admit two uniformed policemen. Grishkin spread his cloak like a lunatic birdman, raised his eyes to the ceiling.

"The price will be right when the time comes, Captain." Then, "Open yourself to the Universal Principle, my son," he intoned. "You may not believe in Him, but He believes in you. That is my advice. Learn trust and honesty, pick only those blooms from the flora in the Gut of Matter. They may look drab to you now, surrounded by the garish petals of illusion. But later, later—

"Ah, the secular arm. Open yourself to them, my son."

He folded his arms and strode away, nodding at the policemen. They ignored him, and turned gray faces on Truck. One of them had a key to the restrainer. When the sound of Grishkin's boots had faded away down the passage, he held it up and grinned maliciously. When Truck returned the grin, his face closed up abruptly and he put it away again.

"Less of that for a start," he said.

They took him to a cell that opened off the passageway from the charge room and unlocked the restrainer so he could sit in front of a small metal-topped table on which the contents of his pockets had been spread. One of them left, the other stood behind him fidgeting and sighing occasionally as if he hoped Truck might try to engage him in conversation.

For half an hour nothing happened. A draft carried a strong smell of disinfectant into the cell.

Eventually two men came in: an IWG agent in plain clothes carrying a blue plastic folder, and a middle-aged sergeant of the civil (effectively, Port Authority) police with a long, jowled face and a rumpled uniform. They sat down on the other side of the table, not looking at Truck. The agent gave his file to Truck's guard. "Take that to Whillans for me, will you."

"Whillans is sick," the guard told him, "sir."

"Well, give it to Jansen, then." He examined Truck's papers. He seemed interested in the log book from *My Ella Speed*. He was young-looking and tanned, but partly bald, and there were deep lines running down from his nose to the corners of his mouth.

"We know he was on Morpheus, whatever the BCA have to say," he said to the sergeant. Suddenly, he turned to Truck and asked, "Who are you selling to these days?"

"I'm not selling," said Truck. He had to give them something, so he went on, "I admit I was at Veronica's place, but I was only consuming." He'd had precious little time to do any of that. "I'm not selling anything—"

The sergeant got up noisily and pointed his finger at Truck. He was slack in the belly and shoulders, which is where West Central weighs heaviest on its executives. He shook his finger accusingly.

"You'd better straighten yourself up. You're up to your ears in Earth heroin and morphine. We could break your leg and no one would care. In here we could break your leg."

Truck had always avoided the opium derivatives. Nobody wanted colonial heroin because *papaver somniforum* lacked "bite" when grown away from Earth, and its alkaloids were always either weak or peculiar. Rigid control of growing by both IWG and UASR had shut down the black market—there was simply raw material to be had; so the only trade in the genuine article was gray, a thin trickle of refined and packaged material stolen mainly from military medical supplies, traveling a precarious conveyer belt to the cutting factories of the giant H and M monopolies of Earth.

It was scarce, it was expensive, and it was profitable enough for the monopolies to protect their connections jealously. Truck had never wanted his head blown off.

(There was a second reason, one that seemed odd even to Truck. He called it squeamishness because he didn't think he had any right to a moral stance. In that, he was probably correct. But underneath his leather hat and funny clothes lived a puritan. He wouldn't sell anything he didn't believe in taking himself. He never ceased wondering about it. He thought of it as a fatal flaw in his character.)

"Earth heroin can get you killed," he said. "You know that as well as I do."

The IWG man rapped the table. "He's not playing fair with us, sergeant," he said distantly.

The sergeant sat down. "Why don't we make it harder for him?" he complained, looking at his blunt, hairy hands as if he loathed them.

The IWG man was staring vaguely up at the ceiling. "There's an easy way and a hard way of getting things straight," he agreed. He opened the log book again, flicked its pages over. He began to poke Truck's belongings about.

"You're not co-operating John," he said. "Look, this could have been harder for you personally; we've shown you a lot of consideration." His eyes were blue and watery, aimless; he gave his full attention to anything they happened to focus on, like an old animal. He blinked, and everything had equal weight for him. "We know you were on Morpheus, not too many years back, dealing in amphetamines. Your operation made a significant contribution to the Butter Putsch, so we can assume you have a political involvement. Now you turn up in a raid on Veronica's. Why shouldn't you have a heroin connection as well?

"You're in a bit of a mess, John."

In those callow days, drifting among the dark machine-tool factories and vast rolling mills, concerned only with making enough money to buy back his indentures and get off the planet, Truck hadn't been able to tell a political involvement from a vomiting fit. He was still having trouble.

"I don't know what you're talking about," he confessed. "I don't see what H has to do with politics. I've never had much to do with either."

The sergeant jumped to his feet again. This time his chair fell over. He made a fist and slammed it down on the table in front of John Truck's nose. His face had grown very red. Small objects rolled about the table top, dropping off the edge.

"You're working for Veronica!" he hissed. "Don't try to deny it." He sneered. "Just tell me one thing," he said: "Which are you? Anarcho Syndicalist or Situationist? Which is it?"

"Oh Christ," said Truck, amazed.

The IWG man winced. "Could you let me handle the political angle, Sergeant?" he murmured. He began to fumble through his pockets.

"It's bloody obvious," said the sergeant. He sat down, staring aggressively at Truck.

"Look," said the IWG man, "really this is a Fleet matter, Sergeant. Medical supplies are involved. There's a 'hold' order out on this man from General Gaw herself." He found a piece of paper.

The sergeant looked impressed. Truck felt as if a fish was trying to escape from his lungs. He squirmed about in his chair, trying to think of something to do. The local law had been allowed its pound of flesh, then circumvented.

"I'll tell you everything, Sergeant!" he said desperately. "I'm a small cog in a vast machine. A chemist on Sad al Bari is planning to flood the market with an augmented heroin-AdAc mixture. He has Trotskyist-Leninist backing—but I'll only tell you—"

The sergeant hissed and bent over the table. An expression of triumph crossed his thick features. "I knew it!" he whispered. Then he shook his head ruefully. "Taken out of my hands," he said. "Taken right out of my hands—" He glanced sulkily at the IWG man. "I could have made it to lieutenant."

Truck jumped to his feet and ran for the cell door. Furniture clattered behind him. He was halfway there when the IWG agent kicked him effortlessly in the base of the spine. He hit his head on the wall. These days, he always seemed to be falling down. He noticed that the lice had stopped biting him; he suspected they'd left the sinking ship.

The IWG man turned out to be called Nodes. He seemed peculiarly out of touch with his own situation. He even introduced himself formally as he walked Truck through the sterile but greasy corridors of West Central (institutional corridors have this quality—they combine against odds asepsis and grime, as if the ancient cycle of daylight fouling and midnight disinfectant has imparted a glaze, an intermediate patina, to their walls) toward the dreary Carter's Snort morning outside.

He said that there was no reason for them to have a negative relationship; he said that he was as human a being as Truck, since he had a wife and three fine children; he insisted on calling Truck "John," unaware that by attempting to change their traditional roles, he was simply implementing and reinforcing them. In short, he was a policeman. "We shouldn't be alienated," he said.

Truck tried to catch his watery, old-animal eyes.

"You're off your head. You know this charge is a frame? You know this General Gaw woman?"

Nodes smiled, staring off down the corridors.

"You know, that isn't much of a contribution, is it John? Honestly? If I offer you a more constructive relationship than that of officer and detainee, you should come some way to meet me, shouldn't you?"

"For Christ's sake stop calling me that."

Truck thought, *I should have kept moving, I could have been halfway across the Galaxy by now (steering*

for the bloody edge). It was too late for that. He felt
the world turn beneath him, obstinate, grinding, heavy.
"Too much gravity."

"What was that you said, John?"

The corridors paled, cooled; they came into a sort of
front lobby with wide glass doors. A drunken spacer
slumped on a bench, belching ruminatively; he glanced
up as Truck passed. "The fact is, bosun, I need
surety—" he began, blinking. He saw Nodes, shrugged,
closed his eyes, and retched disinterestedly. Outside, a
thin gray sleet was falling on half a dozen blunt, armored Fleet vehicles drawn up against the curb, spat-
tering across the wide, wet street on brief gusts of
wind. Fleet marksmen with oily reaction rifles and subtly polarized contact lenses covered the surrounding
area—lounging bored and professional, eyes slitted
against the wind.

General Gaw was waiting for him there—he saw her
through a scum of condensation on the glass. She had
discarded her Women's Army uniform for a black coverall which accentuated her small but well-shaped pot-
belly and brutal thighs. She was carrying a yellow riot
helmet in the crook of her arm. She grinned as Nodes
ushered Truck through the doors, said something to
one of the marksmen. A short, metallic laugh rang
down the quiet street.

"Welcome home, sonny. Cold enough to freeze your
bum, eh?" Truck hesitated on the shining pavement;
the wind whipped his hair across his eyes; he shivered,
and fumbled with the zip of his second-best jacket. The
General, though, was impervious to weather. She
scowled ferociously up at him like a one-eyed parrot,
her head turned slightly. Shook her index finger at him.

"Oh"—drawing the syllable right out and clicking
her tongue with huge enjoyment—"oh, but you've
done it now. If only you'd been a bit sensible about it
all, lad. I could have saved you all this—"

She took his arm in a steely possessive grip. The
Fleet executioners shifted unobtrusively into a pattern

of maximum security, placing themselves on likely lines of fire, their hard eyes flickering to and fro across Truck before going to sweep the misty intersection at the end of the block, the slick, damp rooftops. The sleet fell faster, soft and wet.

"You and I are going to have a quiet talk, laddie, somewhere nice and dry." She laughed. "A quiet talk!" she repeated loudly, grinning round at the marksmen.

Abruptly, one of them let out a high-pitched cry, raucous and mechanical. He fluttered his fingers rapidly in front of his eyes to adjust the polarization of his contact lenses, and began firing off his weapon. Bolts flared up into the sleet, vanished utterly. At the intersection, gray shapes shifted jerkily in the murk.

General Gaw shoved Truck powerfully away from her and screamed, "Get him back in there, Nodes, get him back!" She seated the yellow helmet like a bulbous growth on her head, spun away. "We'll talk later, Truck, when I've squashed these rats."

As she vanished into the gloom a great, groaning concussion shook the street, filling the air with bits of floating paper and plastic and dust.

FIVE

Under the Snort with
the King of the Moment

For an instant, the sleet fell as mud, bellying like a curtain in a storm wind as the wave front of the explosion pushed it down the conduit of the street. Truck staggered back toward the doors of West Central with his knees quivering and his hair wrapped round his face (the cilia of some wet friendly animal, tickling his eyes and filling his mouth). Above him, the concrete symbol of hinterland justice broke up into powder and stones and fell like a waterfall, the globes shattered, the balance dropping away, the grasping hand dissolved.

"Sodding hell!"

He stared up at it, terrified,

Lumps of it bruised his shoulders, beat him coughing to the floor. Nodes dragged him into the lobby, pushed him headlong into the cool plastic floor where he lay trying to ignore his soaking wet trousers. Something burned its way through the glass and battered itself into a glowing smear on the further wall, hissing furiously. The drunken spacer surfaced from some maudlin contemplation of his confinement, stared wildly about him. He shouted, "Christ, skipper, Number Five's dropped its load again!" blinked enormously, and rolled under his bench.

Truck twisted round to get a look at the street. Visibility was a dead loss. Engines raced as the Fleet tried to get its vehicles out from under; patched with a dermatitis of half-melted sleet, they maneuvered in blunt confusion, booming and roaring. General Gaw was invisible in the murk, but he could hear her voice raised in anger. Slow red bolides arced through the weather to a common vanishing point, and the reaction rifles coughed and choked like sick old men.

"Who the hell is that out there?" he demanded of Nodes.

The IWG man gave it consideration, his tired eyes resting on the commotion outside. "I'd say that's a politically naïve question even from you," he decided. His hands discovered a small Chambers pistol in one of his pockets. He pointed it at Truck. "I think we'd be safer away from here, don't you, John?"

As they backed cautiously out of the lobby, the spacer stirred beneath his bench. Down in the abused recesses of his skull some vestige of a martial emotion prodded his bruised brain. He raised a wavering contralto and, after a couple of false starts, assayed a passage from the *Finnsburg* fragment:

"Each man made his private piece with Reagan/And, at a signal, released/Heat seekers, side winders, desiccant, decorticant, defoliant;/They ran out their salvaged disrupter grids,/Swallowed their anti-sympathy pills,/Hoping for a sight of the enemy."

His delivery was round and *tremolando;* he drew great sobbing breaths between the lines and beat out the intervals with his horny hand. Pleased with the acoustics of West Central, he began on "Salute the Fleet!"—guttered into a gloomy silence three bars in.

"God bless you, bosun," he called after Truck. He

belched, gazed disconsolately round the flickering, vacant lobby. "You're a sterner man than I am!"

Later, Truck said, "I think we're—" But then, he owed IWG nothing. He shuffled along, feeling dismal and exposed, while Nodes pursued a steadily downward course, into the chilly and echoic deep-detention levels where nobody had bothered to plaster the walls. Every three or four minutes, a fresh explosion—perceptible here only as a sustained vibration in the soles of the feet—shook the peripheries of the building.

Condensation dripped from the expansion joints in the ceilings, growing milky nubs of mineral, and seeped across the sour untreated floors. It was a warren of right angles: clusters of small-bore pipes followed the passages, faithfully, like giant circuitry; dust furred the ventilators. Peculiar underground winds whistled aimlessly in the stairwells. Nodes avoided the elevators, "in case of power failure, John."

"Look, I think we're being followed," Truck admitted finally. The soft whisper of feet—receding feathery echoes, hesitant, spasmodic—had unnerved him.

The warren opened out into an underground motor pool, a wistful gray light leaking down its access ramp. It was empty but for a few Port Authority five-tonners, jacked up and incomplete. Old rags and bits of paper blew around the oily floor and there were little mounds of dust in the corners.

"That would be a pity, John," said Nodes absently, working his way round the walls, inspecting each vehicle in turn. He stopped, rubbed at a smear of oil on his gun hand with his other thumb (the Chambers threatened erratically: a support pier; a pile of sixty-inch wheels; and a notice which read DISCIPLINARY ACTION WILL BE TAKEN AGAINST OFFICERS CAUGHT—the rest was grimy and illegible). "None of these work, you see."

He stared up the ramp. "You may not be much use

to the General in other hands. In those circumstances, I suspect you would be a definite danger to security."

"*What* other hands? Come on, Nodes!"

"Frankly, John, I have orders to kill you if that looks likely." Nodes's eyes became interested in the stairwell that had dropped them into the pool. Truck backed off rapidly; he didn't know whether it was fear or repugnance; he felt entitled to either, but outrage looked like eclipsing them both.

"I've had it with you, Nodes! I'm sick of being 'John'! I'm sick of being *it!*" He waved his arms about. Evaporating sweat chilled his skin. "My God, you lot crawl out of your holes and turn the entire Galaxy into an asylum. Whose hands?" He wiped the hair out of his eyes. "And as for General bleeding Gaw's bleeding 'sentient bomb'—"

Nodes swung on him, alert and tense. The old-animal eyes focused properly on Truck for the first time since he had entered the interrogation cell.

"Don't go on," he said quietly. "That is information classified above my level, and I'm not prepared to hear it." He made a most human gesture with his free hand. "You can only damage us both by giving information I'm not cleared to hear. I suggest we—"

A scrape of bootsoles like the sound of bandages tearing.

A shadowy figure in the stairwell.

Nodes turned far too late.

His Chambers blew a pit in the concrete at his feet; splashback set his trouser-legs on fire. He tangoed back, trying to shake both legs at once, looking horrified. Fizzing and moaning like an angry cat—like Tiny Skeffern's Fender—a five millimeter shell took him full in the chest and began to burn its way in. He fell on his back, crying "Shoot! Oh, shoot!" trying to get a final desperate message to his fingers. The figure on the stairwell cackled softly, its feet scraping like torn cloth, like butter muslin, faint destroyed, on it came.

Nodes emptied the reaction pistol at the ceiling, at-

tempting to get Truck. Down on one knee over the
maimed ribcage, choking on the stink and smoke,
Truck took it gently away from him and tossed it
across the garage. It clattered and rang. Nodes
groaned, put his fingers in the soft wet edge of his atro-
cious wound. "I have an odd blood-group, Mary," he
said clearly. "Oh Jesus Mother Christ."

"You needn't have done that," accused Truck, getting reluctantly to his feet. "I swear you all take
pleasure from it."

The King chuckled faintly. He was wearing a white
leather jumpsuit of peculiar cut, tight round the crotch
and armpits, hanging loosely off his old frame elsewhere. His hands were quite steady, puncture marks
standing up among the hairs on their backs, sore scarlet against the gray junk grime deep in the very cells of
his wrinkled pachydermic skin.

"Ingenuousness spoils the Moment, Captain Truck,"
he whispered. "It can't be your cynical amorality they
all want you for. Are you out of your wits?"

He scuttled off like a lizard surprised on a warm
brick, over to a dark corner, where he scrabbled in the
dust on the floor. A section of the wall above him
creaked and slid away. His decaying voice rattled
across the garage to John Truck (puzzled and hurt and
never noted for his eager intellect), two sticks rubbing
in a dry wind:

"I prepared long ago for some much eventuality—I
sensed a similar Moment whispering back to me across
the years—H-lines alive with meaningless programs.
Escape all situations. Everything comes to me beneath
the rocket-mail pits, Captain—I—" He raised his
voice. "Come! Come in, now, my friends! You are
back in the domain of the King, and you can come to
no more harm!"

And he vanished inside.

From the stairwell came a timid susurrus of movement. White faces peeped into the motor pool, re-
treated, tasting the air this way and that. Giggling and

murmuring in hushed but rising tones, joking at last, their confidence growing by the second, the King's guests issued from their brief captivity in the West Central warren, their gauzy sleeves fluttering nervously at every disturbance of the air.

Truck stood like a mad stone over the fuming corpse, and they fled past him, giving him not a second glance, their lips parted, their eyes bright. The longest-running party in the history of the universe disappeared into the earth. He stared inarticulately after it. He thrust his hands in his pockets and hunched his shoulders.

Other, harsher footsteps rang in the corridors above—other voices, mechanical and raucous. He shook his head over the dead man. He ran.

The party having streamed on ahead of him, bent on the bright lights and the delicacies of the cutting-room floor (among which, presumably, might be numbered one hundred Denebian mainliners sweating out their unnamed obligation to the King), Chalice Veronica was alone behind his secret door. His reptilian, scrawny hand urged Truck through the gap; he cocked his head and listened; he threw the steel lever that fastened the bolthole.

"Run for it, Captain!" he hissed. "The invading faction has been embarrassed; they are preparing a final stand." And he made off down a low, ill-lighted tunnel. Crouching and lurching, scraping the top of his head on ancient stinking brick, his feet reluctant in two inches of evil water, Truck followed.

They had made perhaps four hundred yards from the motor pool when the floor sank a foot and the bolthole cleared its throat behind them with a vast, bellowing cough. Dust stormed about them, the lights went out, and they clung together in the dark, staggering about to keep their balance like practioners of a strange vice. Locked in that unpleasant embrace, the King's sour old junkbreath in his nostrils, Truck felt the earth creep and shift in the dark. He was deafened, there was foul grit in his eyes and in his mouth.

After millennia, or perhaps seconds, the subsidence stabilized. Truck disengaged himself from the King's arms, spat, and rubbed his eyes.

"The whole bloody Snort's come down on top of us," he suggested.

Veronica bared his yellow teeth in the gloom.

"I don't think so, Captain. But someone—inadvertently, perhaps—has made sure that West Central won't hold spacers for some time to come, and we seem to be safe for the Moment. Look!"

At the further end of the tunnel, a blue light glowed. They walked toward it, brushing ineffectively at the filth on their clothes.

"It's a pusher's Galaxy, Captain Truck," said the King complacently, eating white iced cakes and applying the traditional tourniquet to his upper arm with a stained silk necktie four centuries old.

The Party ebbed and flowed desultorily around them like a thick, landlocked sea as they sat in quaint inflatable chairs (vinyl gone yellow as a junkie's face with age, its transparency clouded) beneath the Renfield Street silos.

"Each in our own way, IWG and UASR, myself, even poor mad Grishkin and the masters of his idiotic religion, we keep people from remembering that they hurt, or that they are made puzzled and miserable by the immensity of the Galaxy, the irreversibility of their own humanity. It isn't a state that can *last* of course—" He snickered at himself, licked pale crumbs from his blue, anoxic lips. "Still, we never close, Captain. We make you feel nice."

Fat worms of cable ran the floor of the abandoned cistern—one of the four that served Veronica's trade—to power the drying plants and chemical vats; and batteries of floodlights slung fifty feet up in a network of girders poured out a devastating heat. The

King's court moved slowly and amiably, drenched with warmth, sleepy with it; the party had become introspective, like a frog in the sun.

"A pusher's market, and you're a prime commodity now. Alice Gaw needs you, so the Arabs must have you—oh, yes! Don't avoid the issue, Captain! Why else would Gadaffi ben Barka, nobody's fool and an astute commando, lead an absurd strike on an obsolete prison in a cold country? He's innovative, but not given to adventures."

Truck was appalled by the speed of the King's intelligence operation. Eighteen hours had passed since the escape from West Central, and he had slept most of them away. Now he sucked on a knickerbocker glory, sweating a little, and meditated on price—the King being the King and information being another pusher's market.

"I hope they wiped each other up," he said.

Veronica closed his eyes sleepily. "It's unlikely. Both are survivors. Whoever exploded himself down there, it wasn't Colonel ben Barka. And remember: it was Alice Gaw's aide-de-camp who got caught in the 'accidental' bombardment of Weber II; she'd been off-planet for five hours or more—" He tapped his fingers to the sluggish tune in his blood. "I wonder about Grishkin. If he was there as you say—"

"Grishkin!" Truck sneered.

"Ah." The King opened his eyes again. "Even he wants you, Captain. It was him who unearthed the—property—which makes you so valuable; among Openers, I'm told, the feeling is that this gives them prior right. Who's to gainsay them?" He sniggered slyly. "The old lunatic has already built a myth about it. They're calling it the Ark of the Covenant, Captain. How does that strike you for Romance? The One Entrail of the Living God, brought from Earth during some ancient migration.

"As to whether Grishkin was mad *before* he entered the bunker on Centauri, I have no reliable intelligence.

"But don't underestimate him. He is as fanatical as the other two, he has as much to gain (if less to lose), and the Opener net catches odd fish on half a dozen planets." His eyelids drooped, but failed to close. He watched Truck from two thin bright slits. "A demented archaeologist," he mused, "and a strange device. And you with a gift of tongues. Could you lead an Opener crusade, Captain? Can you imagine yourself interpreting the Word for Dr. Grishkin?"

His eyes snapped open suddenly.

"Oh, they all want you. Captain, but you're safe with me."

Truck couldn't bear his cunning old gaze, or think of anything to say. He interested himself in the murmuring guests instead. Silence stretched out, white skin over junk bones. "I suppose I'll have to leave soon," he said, finally. No answer. "I think that's somebody I know over there. It's been quite a party, though." But the lizard's eyes were closed once more. Opiates being opiates, the King had fallen into a light doze.

He got up and hovered around indecisively for a minute or two. Nobody had taken any notice of his exchange with Veronica. He bit his nails, regarding unwillingly the King's withered limbs and pinched, evil old mouth in case the audience wasn't over; but it was, and he wandered off, feeling safe no longer.

Oddly enough, he had seen someone that he knew: Tiny Skeffern, squatting on the floor with an instrument he had stolen somewhere, while an electrically thin port lady with eyes like a surprised squirrel smiled possessively down at him.

"West Central?" he said when Truck asked him. He shook his head. "Wait a minute, there was—no—I suppose I must have been there." A smile spread hesitantly over his face. "Eventually, you only remember the party," he told himself, confronting with wonder the ineffable. "But if you say so, Truck."

The port lady was warning Truck off with a green, implacable stare. He cringed politically at her and led

Tiny away, checking furtively over his shoulder for eavesdroppers. The lights had begun to poke consistently at one sore spot at the edge of his field of vision. His sense of discomfort and distrust grew moment by moment.

"Look, I don't think Veronica's going to let me leave. I'm not sure I know what to do. If he uses me to make a deal with the General—"

"Oh, he's a decent enough old boy," said Tiny politely, yearning back toward his lady (who threw Truck a glance that would have debilitated a planet and stalked off, even her shoulder blades spiky with malice). "Now look what you've done. Oh well."

In the event, it proved harrowing but not too difficult. Truck hung back, convinced of his vulnerability but afraid to commit himself to the attempt to leave, for an hour or more. Then Tiny Skeffern drew his attention to a peculiar phenomenon. The fuel cistern was becoming unbearably oppressive, the party turgid and still, lifeless, tideless—a Dead Sea of humanity in which blank sweating faces floated obstinately, determined not to drown. The music faded, stopped on an unresolved chord; people shifted their feet and stared at one another. Truck detected profound swelling undercurrents; hot, irritated interfaces.

"My God," whispered Tiny, "I really think it's ending this time." He studied the sluggish waves. "He's misjudged it. Down here—" He nudged Truck excitedly. "It couldn't be stopped from outside. But down here the system's closed. Look at those faces! Truck, they're *bored!*"

The breakdown was quick and cruel. Aimless patterns developed as the guests blundered about the cistern to the invisible rhythms of their ennui; the heat poured down unceasingly, settled in the hollows of their collarbones; their party clothes became adhesive, rumpled. Silence, but for the shuffle of feet. Some of them lay down, the rest carefully trod on them, eyes fixed elsewhere. In the face of the overwhelming quiet, they condensed like a spiral Galaxy, tracking in to the center of the room.

"The port exit, if you want to go," said Tiny. "Over there." And they set out to push their way through the congealing clot of flesh. Someone gripped Truck's shoulders: Horst-Sylvia, the biological sculptress, with her heaving coloratura bosom; yellow, motionless eyes stared into his own in passive, mute interrogation. Her jewels glittered. He dragged himself away.

"I . . ." said a voice near him, in the nightmare tones of the partially deaf, "I . . . eye . . . aye . . ." A dreadful, stammering pause. "I know . . . what you mean. Hermann . . . Hermann Göring . . . so . . . such a . . ."

The King's guests were desperately trying to reassure—reactivate—themselves, but it could never be the same again. They had allowed it to run down, they were separate, isolate. The damage was done.

The walls of the cistern lurched through a haze of heat. Despite his sleep, he felt exhausted. He was punched in the small of the back, but when he swung bloodthirstily around, no one met his eyes. He could hear himself breathing. He ground his knuckles into his eyes, fighting the drowsy hysteria emanating from the guests, who had begun to shove one another about silently like animals in a pen. When he took his hands away again, the floodlights stabbed him unerringly in that one sore spot on his retina.

He blinked. The exit was plain. But beside it, like a black beacon, had appeared a tall figure in a soft-brimmed hat. A pale hand beckoned. He thought he was hallucinating. It stood by his escape route like Death at the feast. He tried to laugh, made a dry, choking sound. It was Sinclair-Pater's courier, the anarchist in the black cloak.

"They all want me, Tiny," he whispered. A boot scraped down his shin, ground into the small bones of his foot. He fell over. The guests began to mumble;

faces hung above him like decaying moons. Tiny dragged him upright. They were ten paces from the bolthole when, flanked by two massive Denebians, Chalice Veronica, aware that the party was terminal, blocked their way.

His face was gray and awful, the corners of the lips stretched high and wide, yellow teeth and red gums peeled, the brutal revelation of the skull beneath. He chuckled, and saliva trickled down his chin.

"You're too much of an attraction to leave, Captain," he said. "They all want you, but I seem to have cornered the market. So why not enjoy yourself?" He raised his track-marked arms, swept the cistern with a gesture. "All life is here! Art, sophistry, crime—"

"You told me that before," said Truck weakly, "and all they talk about is this bloody Hermann Something-or-other."

The King's Denebians advanced in a quick, deadly crouch, but the man in the black cloak was quicker. From nowhere, he placed himself between them and the anxious Truck. His bright blue eyes glittered with laughter; his long white hands flickered hypnotically; and a perfect, long-stemmed green carnation lay along his palm, beads of moisture sparkling in the minute folds of its petals.

"Captain Truck wants to leave the party, Veronica," he said, and his voice was cold and lively, like air from outside. He watched the King closely. "Why be impolite?" The flower vanished; the white hand, amused, danced in the air, then plucked it from behind Veronica's ear. "You know, I think that's mine. Good Lord."

"You know who I am," said the King softly. "Don't be a fool. I rule down here. I am the King."

The anarchist shivered with laughter. It filled him, it brimmed out into his hands; every finger writhed with it—they flicked, clicked, produced a little disposable syringe. He looked down at it with amazement.

"You know, I believe that's yours." He went closer to Veronica and said in a low voice: "You know who

sent me. You know what the carnation means. Pater is
within striking distance, King, however far away he
seems. Pater is always within striking distance."

His shoulders shook as if he could no longer contain
his mirth. The syringe snapped in his fist. He cast the
shards up into the glare of the floodlights, and no one
ever saw them again. He clapped one hand to Truck's
shoulder, the other to Tiny's; he urged them gently forward. An entire pack of playing cards showered from
beneath his cloak. The King stepped back, his face collapsing into a senile mask, cunning and silly and
frightened.

As they left the cistern, two women began a listless
fight, rolling on the floor, kneading one another's flesh
with blunt fingers.

Out in the maze of unlighted streets behind the Renfield mail pits (where they had risen from the ground
in a fog of their own breath, three tiny figures darting
and ducking beneath the concave midnight, dwarfed by
rockets and the dark fret of access gantries), Tiny
Skeffern grinned jauntily and said: "Lucky for us you
came along, I expect." He rubbed his hands. "Christ,
but it's cold up here."

"There was no luck in it." The anarchist—his
friends called him Himation, possibly a reprisal since,
in the youthful belief that entertainment should have a
moral end, he stole their money and retrieved it from
the most embarrassing places—stared back the way he
had come. "But I got you out in time, it seems. I suspected some hours ago that Veronica had already
made his deal with the Cow of all the Galaxy." He spat
into the darkness. "If so, he'll have to face her without
you, and his party will be over for good."

Cor Caroli, the killing star, shone out above the
Snort through wisps of high cirrus. Down by the river,
the wrecking yards were silent.

"I feel quite sorry for the old fool."

Himation glared down at the little musician. "Don't

be naïve," he advised, and wrapped his cloak tighter round him suddenly. "You've been to Avernus, and seen those yellow-faced men in their alligator shoes, peddling the stuff in gangs under the lamplight at Egerton's Port. They look like vultures, they look like preachers, they look like corpses; but the King is worse than any dozen of them. He's Death's uncle, with a finger in filthier pies than Earth-heroin."

He shrugged at his own fervor.

"You can go back to your ship now, Captain," he said to Truck, who was regarding Cor Caroli as if it had done him some deep personal injustice, overcome with self-concern. "I'll come with you if you decide to take up Pater's offer. If not, I have other transport arranged. It would be worth your while, perhaps, to talk to him."

"I'll see him," said Truck. He was beginning to regard himself as a responsibility he wasn't fit to take on alone. "I can't think of anything else to do." He examined his feet. "I wonder what *he* wants me for."

Himation refused to be drawn.

"Good. As we may have to take your boat back from the Port Authority, we'd better hurry." He strode off, his cloak flying out behind him. For a moment, he looked so like Dr. Grishkin that Truck was forced to repress a shudder. But as they passed rapidly into an area of wan mercury lamps, the impression was dispelled. It was the second time he had placed himself willingly in someone else's hands.

Tiny, running to keep up, asked, "If Veronica is so dangerous, how come he gave us up so easily?"

Amusement filled Himation's hands. The green carnation appeared briefly and spectrally between them.

"Pater told me what to say. That old junkie terrified me, but he knows Pater could cut his supply-lines at a thousand places between here and the rim of the Galaxy. Pater is a little more flexible than Narcotics Section; and, unlike IWG and UASR, he has nothing to lose if Veronica closes down completely."

This gnomic accusation they couldn't get him to explain.

"Do that thing with the flower again," said Tiny. "You know."

□

SIX

The Interstellar Anarchist, an Aesthetic Adventure

Part One

A little of the previous day's snow had settled on the field where *My Ella Speed* lay grounded. Between the blockhouses and the gloomy oubliettes of the freighter silos, patches of it betrayed the unwary foot—a skim of brown slush, gelling steadily as the thermometer dropped. The field was almost deserted; the lights were doused; the earlier cirrus had blown away east and left behind it a fast-moving two thousand meter cloudbase that dyed the night as black as Himation's hat.

Truck, prone in the muck fifteen yards from his boat, awaited a signal. He was soaked from head to foot, clenching his jaw to keep it from tearing itself off and his teeth from betraying his position to the pair of General Gaw's policemen on sentry-go at the base of the unlighted ship. There was no sign of Fix the bosun, which worried him no less than the fact that the General hadn't even bothered to keep up the fiction of a Port Authority arrest.

The policemen beat their arms and stamped their

feet, cocked their heads as a distant siren fluted momentarily down empty arcades, morose and fading—2 A.M. dock stinks breathed over the field. It was the uncertain hour, when all kinds of rats dance beneath the sidewalks and the air is as bitter as lead in the lungs.

Truck sneaked a look to the left of him, where Himation lay in similar discomfort. The pale hand rose and fell, the cloak whirled like the wing of a cormorant.

Truck heaved himself to his feet and skulked toward his man. He'd gained three quarters of the distance—and the Fleet still quite oblivious—when Himation overtaxed his sense of balance on the tricky surface, flailed his arms, and went down like an empty black gunny sack. Immediately, Truck's intended victim raised a shout and sent a Chambers bolt fizzing into the slush alongside the anarchist's head. Himation wailed and began crabbing rapidly about on his hands and knees. Shadows pranced dangerously on the blistered hull of the *Ella Speed*.

"Whistle's gone, Tiny!" yelled Truck. He leaped into the air and landed on the astonished copper's back, locking his legs round the waist, left hand cupping the occipital bulge and pushing forward while the right forearm came across the windpipe and hauled back. The subject of the assault attempted to shoot one of Truck's feet off. Truck bent his head and bit an ear. The gun fell without going off.

Meanwhile, Tiny Skeffern had nipped in from the other side of the ship in a hasty ambush and kicked the legs from under the second policeman. He leaped around him, putting the boot in and jumping away again, yelping enthusiastically. He hadn't bargained, however, on the Fleet arsenal . . .

Truck gave a final wrench, dropped off his host like a dead tick and punched him in the kidneys twice. Suffering cruelly, the Fleet man staggered round to face his tormentor—took the hard vee between Truck's stiffened, separated thumb and forefinger directly in his larynx. His eyes rolled up. Truck hung over him, panting.

"Jesus!" bawled Tiny, looking down the muzzle of a Chambers gun.

Alice Gaw's law was on its feet; Tiny was rigid. Truck took a pace toward them, winced.

The first and only shell fired in the encounter was still boring its way mindlessly into the mud of the field; its fading glare lighted a quick, fishlike flicker of movement; and with a long knife sticking in his neck, the remaining policeman choked at Tiny, dropped his weapon. "Ooh." he said, kneeling down. He subsided slowly and was still.

Himation picked himself up carefully. "That was 'a dirty chance well taken,'" he said, brushing down his cloak and inspecting his gritty palms.

Truck swallowed, looked at him aggressively. "If you can do that sort of stuff, why the hell did we have to go through this charade at all?" he demanded. "You could have picked them both off from a mile away with that thing." He ran his tongue over his swelling lower lip. He knew he was going to think about what he'd just done and then be ill.

Himation retrieved his knife. He licked it deliberately, his blue eyes glittering at Truck over eight inches of stainless steel. "There's an art to murder," he explained. "And a spontaneity to Art, though Pater wouldn't agree." They confronted silently for a moment (Tiny was trying not to notice them, hands thrust into his pockets, studying some rivet-heads on *Ella Speed*'s hull); then, acknowledging Truck's sneer with a curt nod, he went over to the man who had tried to shoot him. He was limping slightly. "This one's just as dead. Captain. You'd better find it in your heart to approve."

"I don't understand what you're talking about," said Truck. but he did.

A light blazed out from the boat. The loading ramp descended, humming, to reveal the misshapen silhouette of Fix the bosun, stout legs set firmly apart, humping his ugly chopper. "You move into the light," he said, snapping his sawmill mouth. "Where I can see you. She's my boat since you took the Captain."

But they managed to pacify him and urged him to put the thing away, which he did with care, wrapping it in some filthy rags he had carried with him for the purpose since the day he fled the squirearchy in Chrome. Ten minutes later, the cubical geometry of Carter's Snort flared briefly green as the *Ella Speed* fired up and shook Earth from under her.

"I left my bloody guitar!" cried Tiny Skeffern, beating his forehead with the heel of his hand.

Himation the anarchist glanced anxiously at the exterior screens. "I hope you're skilled at evasion, Captain."

"We'll have to go back. We'll have to go back and fetch it!"

"Look, I'm sorry about all that on the field," apologized Truck, scratching the back of his neck.

They weren't followed (the General's imagination was focused elsewhere, and a violent old junkie occupied her only eye ; but they violated the operational envelope of a solitary missile interceptor on the way up, and it broke its long parabola through the upper reaches of the air to look them over.

Precarious and hungry, hovering on the edge of the time when its prey might come into season, like a huge fragile insect against the gloomy bulk of the Earth, it spun and darted—extruding its armament and making playful threatening passes—then looped away on a complicated rising curve, trailing anhedral detector vanes, satisfied that *Ella Speed* was creeping out of its sphere of concern.

They watched it with wistful admiration. A precise, composed hesitation roll through fifty miles of airspace, then it climbed away like a roman candle; to vanish—flip!—as if amazed by its own dexterity. "Arrogant sod," said Truck. A thin-skinned predator in a rarified region, it could have vaporized a city. "Will you just look at that, Tiny!"

"You mean there's a bloke in there?"

Himation shook his head. "A boy," he murmured absently. "Only a boy has the reflexes. I flew one of those things until I was thirteen. They give you amphetamines for your reactions; you get addicted fairly quickly. Nothing's the same when you come down." He gazed out at the failing atmosphere with a kind of angry yearning on his face. "A lot of them are lost from dexedrine euphoria—they try to take them where the air is thicker, they try to land them but the hulls burn out."

He took the controls soon after that. The ship shuddered fit to break its back and began its tortuous clawing progress through the dyne fields to his secret destination. It was a wholly ungraceful journey, but short, haunted by the beautiful burning boys of the anarchist's youth.

He was still morose and withdrawn when *My Ella Speed*'s Dynaflow drivers cut out with a thump and she spat herself back into reality like a grub from a mouthful of fruit. Her frame groaned and flexed; her exterior screens, confused by tachyon interference, hallucinated bizarre fish, sea horses plated with brass, unheard music from a questionable dimension. "We're out!" said Truck with relief: another time, she wasn't going to make it.

"Hey—!" as the screens cleared.

Hung out in the interminable void before them was a spherical asteroid perhaps two miles in diameter at its equator. A pretty, self-willed rock, speedwell blue and flecked with gold, it was orbiting no detectable primary body. The rest of the Galaxy seemed oddly remote, as if this fragment of jetsam had attained some absolute topological direction and was describing an intricate, metaphysical course from which everything else in the universe was equally distant. Hung out there alone, then, like a semiprecious moon; implausible.

"We are between the stars here, weaving along the gravity interface of Sol and Centauri," said Himation. "Pater found this place. He first named it 'Howell,' because it's a rogue—" He laughed at their bewilderment, and refused to explain the joke. "Lately though he's begun to call it 'Versailles.' "

He pointed at the forward screen, black shrouded arm, white finger. "Look! Watch the golden areas—"

Two bright flecks drifted out of the blue eye, expanded dizzily, and quite suddenly became two ships—two facing golden cruisers fully a quarter of a mile long, with lean flanks, raked and curved fins and curious dorsal bulges. White, gemlike flames burned at their sterns; turquoise enamelwork made flowing ideographs over their hulls, a language of delicious, tangled flower stems. They were like nothing Truck had ever seen. They bracketed *Ella Speed;* he shivered at the enticing curvature of their bellies; they were spires from a forgotten planet, they were awesome and perplexing.

"*Fastidious* and *La Vie de Bohême,*" announced Himation proudly. "Two among forty-nine. But never as dangerous as my own; she's the *Atalanta in Calydon,*

'The wolf that follows, the fawn that flies.'

She's over the horizon from here. But they'll do to shepherd us down."

Good humor spilled over into his hands again. They discovered a tiny live lizard behind Fix the bosun's ear. It sat in the cup of his palms, distending its scarlet throat, and blinked studiously up at him.

"I wouldn't have believed it," declared Fix, "if I hadn't seen it with my own eyes."

Later, after Himation had nudged *My Ella Speed* into a pit in the cyanic rock and grounded her gently,

Fix refused to leave the ship. "I got work to do, boss," he insisted. "She's coming out of the Dyne like a pregnant duck. I can't have that, not if we're going back to hauling cargo when all this"—he nodded pointedly at the anarchist—"is done with. I *suppose* they'll have tool shops for those fairy great ships out there." He stood stubbornly by the command panels, daring with folded arms Himation, General Gaw, UASR, politics, and prisons. "We got to have maintenance."

"Never argue with your bosun, Captain," advised Himation, and with flourishes made Fix a present of the lizard.

"I'm sure I don't know what to do with it," grumbled the Chromian, but you could see he was pleased.

The asteroid was hollow.

Himation let Truck and Tiny through an outer shell, a *primum mobile*, of workshops, where pandemonium reigned among powerful lifting rigs and ships components to which Truck could put no name; where masked relatives of the wreckers at Carter's Snort waved their plasma torches like hayforks and seemed to take altogether as much pleasure in putting things together as their cousins did in taking them apart. After this demonic leaping and cutting and commotion of shadows, they passed through a sphere of armories— deserted and still, racked with dyne-torpedoes and the barrels of reaction cannon like organ pipes in the chill of an ancient church. "Pater comes here often. Aren't they fine?" And finally a living area, where the air was heavy with an enigma of luxury: passages tapestried with hunting scenes by long dead artists from Oudry to Desportes, full of strangely clothed anarchists who nodded to Himation or halted their errands to attend to cheval glasses of crystal and adjust an item of dress.

They glimpsed through half-open doors a room whose tall, latticed windows seemed to look out over a pale lake among oaks where the great wet leaves of hemlock hung melancholic and inviting; another with a huge mantel on which ticked a clock shaped like a gilded elephant; a third empty but for one *fauteuil*—a woman wearing a white dress oddly spotted with crimson reclined there, slowly passing the rings on the fingers of her left hand to those of her right as she listened with immobile expression to the voice of a man they could not see. Himation smiled. "A hologram," he said. "The Hotel Pimodan, 1849. Maryx, who inspired the *Mignon* of Ary Scheffer. She is listening to Baudelaire. They are waiting for Gautier and the snake-woman and the rest of the *salon*." He entered the room and pressed his hand through the languorous, mask-like face. "See? Isn't it beautiful?"

"Are you a history professor or something?" asked Tiny politely. Truck sniggered, impressed against his will.

But Himation only shrugged laconically and, further on, rapped lightly twice at an elegant double door. The room he ushered them into was a spacious airy studio, lighted as if by a northlight as precious and passing as the Art it imitated. On a dais at the end of the chamber were easel and canvas; at the other sat a little sallow-faced girl with grave eyes and tiny breasts. Her clothes hung over a lacquered screen, and beside her was a basket of crochet work and a volume of poems; and, as she worked, she thoughtfully sang a song about artists and the way they loved:

> *"Ils aiment si artistement*
> *Ils sont des artistes gens."*

Her eyes rested briefly on the intruders, calm, uninvolved. Around her on the eggshell-tinted walls hung Hokusai prints of uncanny refinement, arranged with harmonious aloofness; ethereal porcelain ginger jars adorned with the flowers of prunus and hawthorn rested on their shelves in rapturously exact alignment; there were silken fans decorated with dim balletic shapes. It was a fabrication of Art in itself, exquisite, ephemeral.

But it was not the room, despite its dreamy invitation; nor was it the girl. It was the man before the easel, with his tube of white lead and hog-hair bristle.

He was small and dapper, with tidy brown hands. He wore a white linen suit, a green carnation in the buttonhole of the left lapel. His eyes were dark and sharp, yet bubbling—as if a constant rediscovery of their use were being made behind them. His hair was black and curly, with a strange white streak. His palette was a nocturne of grays and midnight blue. He addressed the canvas with deft, quick motions, but somehow contrived to suggest by them an air of eloquent idleness. He was a thief and a rebel, he was a man of discrimination, he was ageless. He was Swinburne Sinclair-Pater, aesthete extraordinary and Interstellar Anarchist; and he prowled the Galaxy like a brilliant tiger, stalked the self-respect of IWG and UASR; and —snap! Bright teeth.

"Ah, *le petit Manteau, au chapeau bizarre!*" he cried, waving at Himation. "Come in, dear boy! (Heloise, we are finished for today. Come tomorrow at the same time.) Captain Truck"—he dropped his brush and sprang down from the dais, extending his hand— "how wistful of you to come in fancy dress!" Truck looked down at himself resentfully. "Do you like my studio? The porcelain is K'ang, wonderful in its brittleness, hm? (Come, Heloise: out! Out!)" And he gestured extravagantly toward the door. The girl thinned her lips at him, shrugged, indolently put down her crochet hook and took up her clothes.

He forgot her and harried Himation instead. "An unimaginative time with the Queen of Cups, eh, *Manteau*? Still living in the Paltry Century? But you gave him my message. Look, we'll go into my living room shall we?"

By contrast, the suite of rooms adjoining the studio

was frugal and austere, with little chintz curtains, stained floorboards bordering Turkish carpets, and an atmosphere of cherished isolation. In the sitting room, which was achieved by way of a low passage and a Gothic doorway, there were a few short shelves of old books, a scrubbed deal table, and some stiff but charming high-backed chairs. For ornament, a bowl of dried rose petals stood in the precise center of the table. On the walls of this prim apartment were hung two pictures: one a head of some wine-god, unfathomable and sensually cruel; the other a rough sketch of a morose, stooping young man—thin, heavy-jawed, with deep, close-set eyes, dressed in the garments of a defunct High Church order.

Here, they sat down. Himation disappeared into the depths of the suite, returning shortly to flourish his cloak over the table top (rose petals stirred like leaves of another year, and a remote scent filled the room) and manifest a bottle of wine. He held up his hand—prolonged the moment—four glasses appeared, their stems between his fingers. A faint musical tone. Pater smiled on indulgently.

John Truck, like most spacers, was strictly contemporary. He preferred the latest things. He had no particular use for history, little knowledge of it except where it coincided with fashion, and no desire whatever to live in it. He regarded Pater's rose bowl with suspicion, feeling that he might be the butt of some rare intellectual joke, and Pater himself with a faint hostility. He couldn't understand the dualism of character suggested by the rich studio on one hand and this monkish living room on the other; he couldn't discover a reason for any of it.

So when Pater, eyeing Himation's hands with severe appreciation as they passed the glasses round the table, said. "I admired your effort on Morpheus, Captain," he didn't quite know how to respond. After a moment:

"I only did it for the money," he said curtly. He sensed an opening gambit and was determined not to be enlisted. "It was a long time ago, and on another world; I don't remember much about it; it was the last time I ever pushed dope. I didn't even realize your lot were organizing a revolution until quite late on. I probably wouldn't have done it if I had."

This last wasn't wholly true. He had enjoyed the last days on Morpheus when it became plain through the smoke and the smarting eyes that the putsch had succeeded. Living among the ruins had made no demand on him; and, like Himation, the anarchists who had used his peddling operation as a cover had been self-contained, amiable, demanding little. But he had been used, nonetheless. He scowled at himself, opened his mouth; but before he could make it plain that he wouldn't be used again, Himation had interrupted.

"Come on, Pater," he reproved. "Your studio's a proverb in porcelain; Chalice Veronica is quite without taste among plastic furniture; and Captain Truck's a hero on Morpheus"—his eyes glittered ironically at Truck from underneath his hatbrim—"whether he likes it or not. But he's also come all the way from Earth on your invitation; at least tell him why you asked him here." He winked broadly. Truck looked away.

"In these days of rapid and convenient travel," said Pater thoughtfully, "to come from Earth does not necessarily denote any great strength of character. Honesty does, however, despite its determination to undress all over my living room—do you imagine that I care in the least what the artist's motives are, Captain?" He showed his white teeth at Himation across the table. "As for *why*, you Philistine, you conjuror: out of courtesy. What else? Since we're going to steal the Captain's birthright from General Gaw the Bearded Lady, I feel we ought at least to tell him first."

Tiny Skeffern understood even less of his surroundings than Truck, and found even less to say. He groaned and drank his thin astringent wine. He was wondering where he could steal a decent guitar. "Take it easy, Truck," he said.

John Truck got to his feet and gripped the edge of the table. He stared at the head of Bacchus on the wall, then at Himation the anarchist. "You brought me here," he said bitterly. "You can take me back to my ship." His gaze passed on to Pater (but could only see filmy images of Alice Gaw's eyepatch and the eager gray face of the hermaphrodite pusher king). "I'm sick of saying it," he whispered. "You can stuff your bloody Centauri Device. You can *stuff* it!" He walked back along the narrow corridor and stood in Pater's studio, resting his forehead on a cool wall. He heard Tiny hurrying after him, determinedly gave his attention to a print that seemed to depict an old man standing under a tree by a chasm. Tiny went away.

After a while, though, Pater came in.

He mounted the dais and considered the easel. He took up a fine bristling hog-hair and dabbed it at his canvas. The result of this he considered lengthily. "Captain, I don't want the Device," he said, his voice echoing slightly in the tall room. "All I want to do, dear boy, is take it from General Gaw. You understand? If she wants it, if UASR want it, badly enough for them to fight openly in the street for the man who can make it work—if they are prepared to do that, then I don't care for either of them to have it. You see?" He sighed. "You don't."

Truck ignored him, but he had abandoned the print despite himself and was staring at the busy shoulders of the white linen suit. Painting unconcernedly, Pater went on:

"I certainly don't want *you*. I may have gathered my following from 'rag pickers, knife grinders and tinkers,' but at least they're decently dressed; you, on the other hand, look like one of Veronica's tramps. You have no aesthetics and less education. You fail even in your responsibility for this thing dug up on a dead planet by a lunatic. Ah! So far, you have saved the Galaxy immense pain solely by your own selfishness! If Gaw gets her hands on it, and if it's what she thinks it is, some vast new atrocity will eclipse Centauri itself; yet you've made no attempt to ensure it won't happen—all you've done so far is to run away from people you don't much like."

He swung round from his palette, an awful contempt distorting his face (for an instant, Truck glimpsed the brilliant carnivore beneath the skin and understood that, against all odds, it was a moral animal); caught Truck staring at him; laughed.

"What could you and I *possibly* have in common?"

He frowned.

"I sense in you something I'll never possess. A strength, a vast and implacable iconoclasm. We live in a sick charade of political polarities; of death, bad art, and wasted time—all in the cause of ideologies that were a century out of date in their heyday. I sense that you of all people have it in you to end that, and make me as obsolete as Earth (for I'll be redundant if IWG and UASR give up their corpse's grip). Ridiculous, isn't it?"

He left the easel.

"So: a deal then, Captain, after all! If I take the thing from the Bitch of All the Galaxy and give it to you instead, will you accept your responsibility for its final disposition? Take it, dear boy. You *are* the last Centauran, and I'll only lose it somewhere if you don't."

And he held out his hand.

They returned to the sitting room, where Pater poured more wine. Himation left them soon after that. He glittered at Truck from under his hat and said: "We'll be moving out soon, so I'd better go and arm the *Atalanta*. But we'll meet again, Captain, I hope. If not, good luck. Bore him, Pater, and I'll make you vanish in filthy smoke." He swept out, cloak billowing; and as his long legs carried away down the corridor, they heard him intone:

"Come with bows bent and with emptying of quivers,
  Maiden most perfect, lady of light . . ."

"He's good at that conjuring stuff," said Tiny Skeffern, belching reminiscently. "I'll give him that."

The Interstellar Anarchist smiled. "He's my son," he told Tiny quietly, "but despite that the best cruiser captain I've ever had."

"Christ," said Truck, rolling some wine round his mouth. "This ethanol's some rough old stuff."

Pater winced.

◨

SEVEN

The Interstellar Anarchist, an Aesthetic Adventure

Part Two

"She's transferring the Device to Earth, Captain—a decision taken against the advice of her staff nearly three days ago, when she thought she had you safe in Albion Megaport. She is most anxious to effect an introduction between the two of you."

It was some hours after the conversation in the studio. Truck had bathed, eaten, even slept a bit, and was now nearing the end of Pater's guided tour of Howell (which he did in fact insist on calling "Versailles").

"But it seems the Device will not abide the dyne fields for more than a second or two at a time, so a journey that should have taken hours is still in progress. They send the transporter into Dynaflow drive and—pop!—out it comes again, for no reason that can be discovered. They have gained a few light days. In it goes again—and so it goes on. A comic process with a real attraction for us."

Pater stood, ridiculously neat and dapper, beneath

79

the great ventral curve of a ship named *Driftwood of Decadence*, which had squeezed itself into one of the massive repair silos of the asteroid like a wasp in an apple. To his white suit and green carnation he had added a fantastic low-crowned hat of cream straw. Here at the rim of Howell, away from the generators at the core, the artificial gravity was a little feeble: Pater bounced in it as if perpetually embarking on an *entrechat*, thumbs stuck into his waistcoat pockets.

"To keep pace with its charge, the Fleet escort must spend a lot of time out of Dyne. If we catch the convoy there, they can be embarrassed—we are lightly armed, but these vessels are quicker in ordinary space, and more maneuverable, than anything IWG or UASR has ever been able to field against us."

Truck squinted the bright length of the *Driftwood of Decadence*. Turquoise arabesques glimmered mysteriously down her side; the smell of hot metal drifted about her like musk of a sleeping, barbaric priestess; the light of plasma torches exploded soundlessly off her hull to fill the silo with a ceremonial aurora. Pater—whom he had grown to like despite his incomprehensible humors and affectations—regarded him with a quizzical smile. He scratched his head. He was on the stony verge of some revelation.

"Who designed them for you?" he murmured. "Who built them?" He reached out to touch one of the great anhedral tail-surfaces; she was warm and vibrant. Suddenly, he was at the very edge of it all. *"Where did they come from, Pater?"* and—tumbling down the steep scarp of understanding—"Where?" This almost a sigh, because for spacers there is one ritual enigma, and he was within sight of something unbelievable.

Pater laughed and took his arm. "You could say I found them," he suggested, "or again, that they were given to me." He examined these ideas for a time; neither seemed to satisfy him. "Shall we walk back? I'll tell you something of it as we go." But he said nothing more until they had reached the sphere of armories, the sphere of stillness. There, head tilted as if to catch the ghost of ecclesiastical music, he gazed at a bank of long black torpedoes and began abruptly, "Imagine it, Captain!

"My ship was experimental. Some discontinuity, some lapse of topology—a woman nervously twisting a lilac stalk—had torn her out of the dyne fields. She was spiraling along the vacant rim of the Galaxy, her Dynaflow drivers gone. Imagine the horror with which I stared at the place they had occupied, watching a few thin-film control circuits drift about the engine room. Nothing more remained, just those few flakes of technology—as if *lunaria annua* had shed its seeds in free fall!

"I rushed to the exterior screens, despairing. But there! A clinker, a cinder, the merest of dim, dead suns! It took me two years to reach that place, Captain. I knew it was useless to me, I saw ahead only the cemetery orbit; but what else was I to do?

"I became irresolute, drifting for a month round that slagheap sun, the ship like a wounded arum lily. Can you see me? Then, a point-source on screens, a collision alarm! And there they were, seven times seven of them, slipping past like a train of comets approaching aphelion. I signaled them on all frequencies—they ignored me; I expended the last of my sub-Dyne fuel to overhaul them—they were undeviating; I boarded them—they were deserted.

"I boarded all of them—how bright their interiors were, how complicated and alien!—and all were empty but one; on the last, I discovered him.

"He came from nowhere you or I will ever see, Captain. He was heraldic. His exoskeleton glowed dark green like oiled metal, his wings were shot with bizarre gold veins, and his eye-clusters caught the light like globes of rough obsidian. Complex chrome-yellow symbols covered his carapace!

"He was dying, he had been dying out there for fifty years, adrift alone with his magnificent fleet. Ocher fluids leaked from his joints, strange burns cross-hatched his thorax.

"Imagine us! For months we strive to communicate. His weak forelimbs scrabble against the floor, creating pointless, agonized patterns! But he understood me long before I him. He came from outside, Captain; his ships had crossed the cruel gap between the Galaxies. He could not tell me where. He spoke of his race's millennia-long search for the metaphysical nature of space; of a disease or madness that had led his crews at last to blow their hatches and beat their wings deliriously against the vacuum, like the hawk moth against the attic lamp!

"I sent him to join them out there the day he died. In his ultimate throes he stung himself repeatedly, his long abdomen thrashing. He was desperate to explain the InterGalactic drive—he was desperate that someone should continue the search. But I could not grasp its principles, save perhaps to dimly comprehend this: the continuum has emotions—and the golden ships are the culmination of an Art addressed to Space itself!"

For some time, Pater brooded quietly over his dyne-torpedoes as if exhausted by his queer eloquence, even his gestures limp as they continued to sketch or imitate the feeble scratching limbs of the dead alien commander. When Truck prompted, "But you learned to fly the ships in Dyne?" he snapped his fingers impatiently and muttered, "Yes, of course. What does that matter? It was easy: their drivers are quite similar to our own; but what use are such engines when—?" He contemplated that wasted opportunity.

"None," agreed Truck, and walked on through the corridors of Howell—speechless, as spacers are when they consider that pillar of enigma at the closed gates of the Galaxy: the unattainable, the post-Galactic drive.

But five minutes later, Howell was shuddering to the clangor of alarms:

In the "Hotel Pimodan, 1849," the laser holograms of Maryx and Baudelaire faded like specters, caught between a whisper and a significant smile, as the asteroid drew power for the launch of Pater's raiders.

Out in the repair shops, grimy stunted engineers paused to scratch their horrid armpits and speculate about the target.

The crew of the *Driftwood of Decadence* stared at their ship and spat, gloomily reflecting that Pater would never allow her to lift in that condition.

And, pausing outside the doors of his apartments, the Interstellar Anarchist peeled his lips back off his feral teeth and winked at John Truck, his depression evaporating as the klaxons wailed. "Now! We have them located! Fetch your friends, if they want to join the dirty work—but quickly! Meet me on the *Green Carnation* within the half hour!"

It was easier said than done. Howell boiled with anarchists: mad dandified gunners wearing mutton-chop whiskers and outrageous sideburns; navigators favoring the leather flying helmets and Sidcot-suits of a forgotten war; barrel-chested mechanics in striped jerseys and tight knee-breeches—and all of them making book on their chances of survival or spoils as they scrambled, shedding tarotcards, poems, and poker dice, for their ships.

Himation, glimpsed on a crowded corridor; his crew bobbed behind him like gulls in the wake of a black-sailed lugger. Pale hands flickered and danced, but the madness was infectious. All he said was, "After the strike, Captain!" and he was gone.

Truck found Tiny in a small square room where faded charcoal sketches covered the brown and crumbling plaster. Over his knee was an old acoustic guitar with a warped rosewood fretboard; on the brass bed that filled the place sat Heloise the model, her tight sallow body glowing in the deteriorating northlight. She regarded Tiny sulkily and sang, *"Ils sont des artistes gens,"* in her pretty, muted voice. "Can't you tell him to play less accompaniment?" she appealed to Truck. "It's the song that counts." And she got up to stare out of the artificial window at the *ateliers* of a Paris long blown to hell by the Rat Bomb wars, her little bottom quivering petulantly.

"You don't need any electricity for this," explained Tiny. "Isn't that something?"

Truck dragged him through the bedlam of militant Howell. Their half hour was almost up, the asteroid was trembling to the pulse of warming engines, expectant. "What about Fix?" cried Tiny, hugging his new acquisition.

"No time. He'd only want to bring that sodding chopper."

They stumbled aboard the *Green Carnation*.

The klaxons died.

In the ensuing silence, Swinburne Sinclair-Pater smiled and adjusted the set of his coat, the tilt of his elegant hat. He raised his hand. "Go!" he commanded. With a raffish cheer the engineers fed power, the navigators touched their good-luck charms, and forty-seven golden raiders took to the aether like a pack of lush Byzantine hounds, racing and quivering and vying for the scent. But however they tried, none could outdo the *Green Carnation*, and she ran out ahead of them, an incitement, a triumph, and a hard gemlike flame.

Aboard the flagship, Truck and Tiny, immobile, awed.

A blue-gray waxy light drowned her pentacular command-bridge, running like tepid fire down the slippery perspectives of an extra-Galactic geometry, forming optical *verglas* on planes of alien metalwork, tracing the formal interlacing designs that covered the inner hull. Every four or five seconds, banks of stroboscopic lamps fired off, freezing and quantifying jagged areas of shadow, but defining no shape the eye could appreciate. Nothing was perpendicular or dependable.

Now white and dazzling, now hard black silhouettes, Pater's quarterdeck crew moved at ease through this disjointed medium, tending the bizarre original equipment of the ship or settling like insects among more identifiable machinery bolted roughly to the deck. They trailed loops of cable from portable computing facilities, calling off queries and co-ordinates in a rising chant. A subsonic ground bass reverberated through the body cavities; other voices chattered and decayed in the foreground like the cries of autistic children heard in a dream.

Above them, ribbons of circuitry framed a layout of enormous screens, on which were visible the rest of the fleet:

They hung in gay ambush, *Maupin, Trilby,* and *Les Fleurs du Mal;* the *Whistler,* the *Fastidious,* and the *Strange Great Sins.* In two long wings of twenty-four, they poised themselves "at the sharp apex of the present moment between two hypothetical eternities"—*Madame Bovary* and the *Imaginary Portraits: Syringa* and *White Jonquil.* Centauri was nearer here, a bare actinic jewel off the port bow of *Atalanta in Calydon,* from which Himation the conjurer led the second wing. Space enfolded them as they waited for their prey, they were embedded: a bracelet of gold in black volcanic glass—the *Forsaken Garden,* the *Let Us Go Hence,* and the *Melancholia that Transcends All Wit.*

"Here we begin to guess at the nature of space," said Pater softly to Truck. "Our palette is prepared. The Galaxy has given us our canvas, a dead dragonfly had bequeathed us the brushes we have to hand. We make Space. We define it. Look out there. IWG and UASR see at best a conduit for Earth's rubbish of politics. *We* infer reality. None of this belongs to Earth or to ideology. It is inviolate."

To prove his point, perhaps, space ignored him.

Truck, meanwhile, had been visited by peculiar, stealthy emotional stirrings. Oddly enough, he perceived something of what Pater was suggesting, and saw himself suddenly as a denizen of this metamathematical or aesthetical space, like poor Annie Truck, a losing vector—her life a movable analogy for hard vacuum, her AdAc habit a dyne field of the head, himself a last-minute fibril of hypothesis extending toward some once-glimpsed mental Galactic edge. He became uncomfortable.

"I don't know anything about that," he said, squinting along the optical maze of the command-bridge, "but this isn't any kind of flying I'm used to. It looks more like a one-night stand at the Spacer's Rave."

What else could he say? He was a lout.

"What do we do now?"

"We wait," said Pater (who wasn't misled, and appeared to be looking at him with a sort of compassionate irony), "but not for long."

In that, he was correct. A willowy young fellow wearing his blond beard tied up with tarred string leaped to his feet and waved a fist over his head. His arcane apparatus had discerned something leaving the dyne fields not a hundred thousand miles from their ambuscade. A few minutes later, it popped up on one of the forward screens, heading at a fair pace straight down the open anarchist throat: six IWG battleships like black and orange melons englobing an orbit-to-orbit medium haulage vehicle made of spidery girders, small ball bearings, and a big silver caterpillar—this last the hold section, with a capacity of several million tons.

Activity on the *Green Carnation* redoubled: the lights became fierce; bursts of ultrasound attacked the command-bridge like bats; the quarterdeck crew donned one-way visors and multiplied their efforts, jerking spastically from machine to machine in the stroboscopic glare, calling "It's green—it's brown—I have you on four—"

Himation came through scratchily on a battle-communication frequency, tidal RF interference grinding behind his voice. "We can knock the drive pods right off it, Pater," he suggested.

"Quick then, *Manteau*—before they can get it back into the Dyne. *On les aura!*"

The *Green Carnation* and *Atalanta in Calydon* detached themselves from the opposed files of the ambush; they raced toward one another, met head-on in a suicidal flare of retrofire, executed a terrifying Siamese turn through ninety degrees of arc, and hurled themselves side by side at the transporter, white heat blazing at their sterns and a trail of stripped and violated particles streaming out behind them.

IWG woke up, staggered about, broke formation. "They've sent us beginners!" cried Himation joyously. And as the *Green Carnation* ran on in through the broken globement, her rearward screens showed the rest of the fleet closing like a golden jaw. Dyne-torpedoes flipped end over end out of their tubes and began a misleading vibration—in and out of Reality they went, like shoals of pike seen through muddy water, and slipped among the battleships.

Pater himself took control of the flagship. He bore down on the haulage vessel like a madman, the command-bridge glare turning his buttonhole carnation black and his teeth the color of steel. "Torpedoes are so unselective, Captain!" he shouted in Truck's ear. "And I love those long reaction guns!" The caterpillar expanded until it filled the screens, huge registration numbers against its silver skin. And bigger yet—until Truck was digging his fingernails into his wet palms, until the *Green Carnation* howled with proximity alarms, until Pater threw her up into the vertical position and presented his ventral guns in a sweeping broadside skid—

Move for move in impeccable formation, the two

cruisers shuddered and shook, their gunners grinning in the red ectoplasmic backwash of the cannon—and, abruptly, the hauler was a dead whale, its drive compartments separating and vaporizing in a wild yellow rose of light, its hold sheared neatly away beneath the wrecker's torch. Before the rose was blown, *Atalanta in Calydon* and the *Green Carnation* were up and out, mirror-images tumbling and braking through a loop that brought them back to their wallowing prize.

And before that maneuver was complete, the rest of the fleet was hanging at rest in the vacuum, practicing fire-control on bits of wreckage. IWG hadn't fired a shot: they were split open, they had spilled their flesh all over the show. One of them was still trying to withdraw, caught by some failure of its drive as it faded into the dyne fields—a gray, ghostly rubber ball, perished, gaping with pain, neither here nor there.

Little Tiny Skeffern had suffered the entire circus with his eyes shut and his hands clamped round the neck of his guitar. "Truck, I'm not cut out for this stuff." he said. He sat down on the floor, drew up his legs, and jerked a thumb at Pater. "He's off his head, that bloke." He raised a feeble smile. "Next time I see you coming, remind me of this—even three weeks on Sad al Bari is beginning to look bearable."

The exterior screens caught fire for a moment as some thin-lipped gunner blew an IWG Dynaflow to pieces. Truck stared out at the drifting wreckage.

"We've got it now, Tiny. If Pater keeps his word, we can take the thing somewhere quiet and chuck it out of an airlock. Sigma-End's a nice place: we could go there and get smashed for a year—go back to being losers."

Tiny watched his fingers stalking up and down the fretboard. "We don't **have** to go there to do that," he observed astutely.

Pater relinquished the flagship to his pilot, who

grinned ruefully, made an aerobatical gesture with one hand, and murmured, "Nice time, Pater."

Pater bowed and laughed. "Dock it now," he suggested, "and be careful with the artwork." The command-bridge relaxed, its peculiar voices diminished. The severed hold section of the hauler crept back into view, toppling end over end on a heading for M41 in Orion, a target it was unlikely to reach in the near future.

"Prepare to board, *Manteau,*" said Pater over the ship-to-ship.

There was a long pause, full of the croaking whisper of the stars. Someone adjusted the gain of the receiver, shrugged.

"Manteau?"

Himation came on. "Pater," he reported thoughtfully, "we aren't boarding anything just at this precise moment. Have a look out there. The bloody Fleet's arrived."

"Oh Jesus," whispered Tiny Skeffern, and closed his eyes again.

IWG came out of the dyne fields in three waves, fifty at a time, each spherical dreadnought half a mile in diameter and mounting enough fire power to pulverize Jupiter. Their fire ports were already open, sowing torpedoes like showers of steel needles. *Syringa* and the *Melancholia that Transcends All Wit* vaporized in the first second of the engagement, trapped among the slagged embers of the ambushed convoy. The *New English Art Club* ran helplessly through the resulting plasma-front and came out limned with a fire of her own; looping and twisting, plowed into the last of the escort ships (which was still trying to vanish) and joined it half in and half out of dyne, ectoplasmic and doomed—

Aboard the flagship, Swinburne Sinclair-Pater rubbed his jaw and saw that it was impossible to disengage. The command-bridge howled and wept, the crew leaped and gyrated among their alien machinery like salmon in white water—

"I'm going to ram, bugger it," reported the *Liverpool Medici*, driving sideways across Pater's bows at a group of three Fleet vessels, and was never heard from again. Down in her belly, gunners threw up disgustingly and cheered the moment of impact—

"Get out of the way and let the ferret see the rabbit!" screamed *White Jonquil* to the *Gold Scab*. She took a hit on the bridge and, her turrets spouting erratically, cartwheeled twenty thousand miles in a halo of tangled struts and hull-plates. "*Now* look what you've done!"

"—and there's a core-melt on Number Five," whispered a faint, injured voice. "Can anybody help—" He died away without identifying himself, merged with the sea of interference—

It was murder.

They winked out one by one, the *Forsaken Garden, Les Fleurs du Mal*, the *Whistler*, and the *Fastidious*. Running on to the guns, *Imaginary Portraits* embedded herself in her assailant; they spun together disconsolately, drifting toward far Centauri. *Trilby* and the *Strange Great Sins* collided, embraced, tore through IWG like an impromptu scythe.

A distant bubbling moan, as the ship with the coremelt came back on, pleading. Himation's voice cut across him as *Atalanta in Calydon* cut across the top of Pater's screen, trying to outrun a covine of shimmering torpedoes. "We've been suckered, Pater. The jig's up. I count fifteen of us left, and I'm getting damage reports from my own crew."

"—if someone could just get a party aboard. We've lost steerage—"

In half an hour, it was all up with them. Fifteen had dwindled to five after an attempt to break out of the IWG englobement—then to two. Tiny Skeffern shook his head and stared glumly at Truck as Pater and

Himation skulked through the tragic debris, powered down and on communications silence to avoid detection. Corpses with frosty eyes knocked gently on the hull of the *Green Carnation*, and anarchist ships like filleted golden carp floated across her screens; while out beyond the eddy of wreckage IWG depended—a colony of fat spiders—from invisible threads.

Parties of pressure-suited commandos began combing the outer derelicts for survivors. The pilot with the core-melt let them on board, then gave up trying to keep it in check—he was gone in a twinkling, the last flicker of the candle. Off the port bow of the flagship hung a great black and orange moon, peeled to the honeycomb decks and still spilling power conduit into the void like mile-long cilia; to starboard, *Atalanta in Calydon* prowled, her hull blackened and scarred, more wolf than fawn.

The command-bridge was silent, full of white, listless faces, its illumination desperate and spectral. When he closed his eyes, Truck could still see frozen afterimages of the battle, the thin bodies of anarchists wrapped in white light, aspects of devotion. Beside him, Tiny Skeffern shifted uncomfortably. "Truck, why aren't we just sneaking off into the dyne?" He was used to the hinterland alleys, the boot, the hasty retreat.

The quarterdeck crew chuckled morosely at this, looking to Pater. He turned from the forward screens, from some reverie of destruction and lost opportunity. "We have become wreckage," he mused, as if discovering something behind the words. "There's a risk in operating any equipment at all now," he explained. "If we were to power up, they'd have us triangulated before we could compute a course." His face was haggard. "We can't do it, Mr. Skeffern. Even the screens are a risk."

He appeared to lose interest. After a while he went on, "While we remain wreckage we are safe. It seems as though they have retained the Device, Captain. I'm sorry about that."

Truck shrugged.

"I don't suppose I'd have known what to do with it anyway."

"You miss the point."

"There's something going on out there," said Tiny. In the distance, IWG was maneuvering indecisively, individual ships pulling out of the rubbish heap on pulses of green flame—while others seemed to be hastily retrieving their commando units. Wings and squadrons formed, grew, inclined toward Centauri. This obscure performance lasted for some minutes. Wreckage drifted and toppled, raising and lowering the curtain on it. Pater opened a channel on Fleet frequency, but no one on the bridge could separate the urgent babble from its concomitant of interference.

Atalanta in Calydon broke silence suddenly. "Pater!" shouted Himation. "Something's up—I can see—Christ!" And he began to laugh. "Pater, it's the Arabs! It's the Arabs! They've had it done all over them—" His ship woke up, quivered, took fire at its stern. It drove away through the graveyard, trailing mirth. "I'm going to try and get a better—"

Massive jamming overwhelmed his signal.

"Power up!" snapped Pater. Oscillating pulses of blue and violet light washed their faces, decaying echoes clattered around the bridge. "That fool!" A Fleet dreadnought careened past under full thrust, firing madly at something behind it the way a man stares unbelievingly over his shoulder at a pursuer in the dark. It erupted into curious boils and ran into the wreck of the *Forsaken Garden*.

The flagship groaned with mysterious voices (and Truck, wrenched out of his head by mounting alien energies, hallucinated briefly a Roman sundial isolated by a single watery ray of light in a sunken garden, smelling mint, glycol, horsehair) as Pater hurled her up and out. They shot into clear space—

To discover imprudent Himation running under the

guns of both IWG and UASR (Navy), with his ammunition spent and big dorsal holes.

Perhaps a hundred Arabs had arrived, cylindrical ships resembling mammoth nuts and bolts (they were, in fact, complete with threads, down which the command and power sections could be screwed at will) and carrying red and yellow insignia. Their ambush had telegraphed itself—unlike IWG's—and broken into small unformated skirmishes across fifty million cubic miles or so of space.

"Dyne out!" pleaded Pater. "Dyne out, *Manteau!*"

The *Green Carnation* lurched. Choking smoke began to pour into the bridge. Pater got her broadside on to his Arab and pounded it to junk. A cloud of dyne-torpedoes, released like breath from a terminal bubonic—the forward antimissile batteries coughed once or twice. Something ripped them off, and the sweating gunners with them. "We're losing pressure!" reported one of the quarterdeck crew. The ship lurched again, bellowing and creaking. Pater braced himself and bored in after Himation, drawing fire, yelling "Dyne out!"

"I'm trying to," said Himation coolly. "Don't think I'm not, Pater old chap."

Truck and Tiny groveled on the deck.

An enormous hand slapped the ship about.

"I can't hold her, *Manteau!*" cried Pater despairingly. "Rendezvous at Howell! Dyne out!"

The *Green Carnation* was withering away.

Sardonic jungle-noises squawked and twittered from her circuitry as it melted to slag, inflicting terrible burns on the dazed crew. Pater slapped a bank of rocker switches grafted on to the alien controls. She slid into dyne, but it spat her out again, twice. Her spine cracked and flexed. As they went under for the third time, Truck clutching Tiny Skeffern's shoulders and praying with horrified self-disgust that Himation would get it and not them, IWG broke into their communication channels—

"IT'S WAR NOW, LADDIE! CAN YOU HEAR ME, TRUCK? HOW D'YOU LIKE THAT?

"I WANT TO SEE YOU AFTER I'VE FINISHED WITH THESE SNOTTY JACKALS. YOU HEAR ME, PATER? HE'S MINE, AND YOU'RE FINISHED.

"TRUCK? IT'S WAR—"

Then they were somewhere else.

EIGHT

◼

An End to Art
and the Beginning of Artifice

The anarchists of Howell watched her final firework arc. She burst out of the dyne fields like a morbid comet, rolling belly-up and launching volleys of torpedoes at nothing they could see, her stern consuming itself in pale feverish radiance. Great rents had opened along her length, her bow was an agonized mouth; her golden fins were bent and charred, her turrets melted stubs. She plummeted down on them in a fog of blind murder, braking savagely; slowed, showed a queer blunt profile. Something tore, deep down inside. She broke in half. The entire northern quadrant blazed up soundlessly, drenching their appalled faces with corpse-light.

The *Green Carnation* had come home.

Four hours later, they recovered her quarterdeck section from the aphelion of a long elliptic orbit. It was intact, and under survival pressure. VR units leached on to it, opened it up with plasma torches, and went in with respirators, Earth-morphine, and a sort of dumb awe. They brought out thirty bodies and ten survivors, all of them blue with anoxia, some suffering from induction burns. Most of the deaths were from subsonic rupturing of the great organs.

Two or three of them were still on their feet, staring inertly round a dark filthy trap full of carbon dioxide and cooked flesh as if they had come the long and significant way round from Hell. They had. Swinburne Sinclair-Pater was there, a hole the size of two fists in the back of his white suit; but he wouldn't let the VR crew give him morphine until they had checked that disgusting oubliette for a small bald musician and a transit-class haulage pilot in funny clothes. They were glad to avoid his bright, somehow elated eyes.

He hung on for twelve hours, in his bedroom at the heart of Howell. Its walls were dim and glorious with blue and gold peacocks he had painted himself. They couldn't cut the suit off him, because of the induction burns, but they pulled five petal-shaped fragments of some alien machinery out of his lungs, where they had embedded themselves as he wrestled mysteriously in the supernal places of the Dyne to keep his ship from falling apart. He woke up only rarely. When he did, his eyes were sunken but amused.

John Truck and Tiny Skeffern stood awkwardly by his bed for the last few minutes, their burns dressed and their faces pallid. Truck remembered little of Pater's ride out of the night. For a while, he knew, the hull of the flagship had seemed to melt or withdraw; all of them, the asphyxiated and the dying, had worn colored glass masks, or swum in senselessness, fish of the impossible Medium; he had felt his interface with space diminish, felt it crawl through him in slow, luminous ecstasies. He knew what he'd felt, and it had seemed important at the time; but now all he saw was the stinking dark canister of the bridge, and all he found in his head was a strange embarrassed compassion for the withered figure beneath the printed silk coverlet.

Pater stirred painfully.

"Captain?" A terrible, disfigured whisper, but gaining strength: "War. The one-eyed bitch has her war at last." One of his ruined hands escaped the coverlet, touched his cheek—a short hissing breath. "For decades they've drained the Galaxy; now they'll rip it apart like beasts in an alley. Stop it, Captain. They mustn't find you."

He drew himself up, shaking fitfully; gazed without recognition at the gorgeous room.

"Did I—?" Irritated, he moved his hand feebly in search of a memory. "All pleasure devours—Captain!—Dyne out!" He tried to wet his lips, choked. Quieter: "I could never find it in me. There was too much I loved." Spurred, perhaps, by this lapse into sentiment, the old Pater returned briefly, full of gentle malice. "But you have a rich, vulgar iconoclasm, Captain. Let it speed you."

He sank back, watching the peacocks. Then, after a long time:

"You were there when she bled into the dyne fields, you saw the substance of her flaring out like ritual evidence of the future. I believe she was near to her proper purpose, then. That's our heritage. Take her. We don't belong in the murk that nurtures Earth. Take her and remember that when your times comes. You've seen Space."

He frowned. "Where's *Manteau?*" he asked puzzledly. Then: "I flung her out there for a while, Captain, against the dirty chance of dying." His voice tailed off.

Truck bent close over the savaged face. "She blew up, Pater. What can I do now? You can't give her to me, she blew up." Pater was asleep, but the room smelled just like death. He said nothing more until the end, when he pulled himself upright in the bed, winced, shuddered with horror at something beyond the painted walls. "More laudanum, Symons!" he shouted. He sighed, and a perilous calm iced his eyes. " 'Destroy all copies of *Lysistrata* and all bad drawings,' " he breathed. He looked straight at Truck and winked broadly. " 'By all that is holy all obscene drawings—' "

It was 2367. On Sad al Bari IV military bands played "Salute the Fleet!" while youths who had never seen Earth fortified the moons of Gloam and Parrot. The green carnation withered on its stem. Howell shrank to a rock. Its animating spirit had fled.

"Poor old sod," said Tiny Skeffern, out in the studio. He wandered round scratching nervously at his bandages, picking up Pater's Chinese pots and tapping them to hear their clear fragile voices. "Are you going to stare at that picture all day? Truck, honestly, it isn't even finished." He screwed his face up over a hawthorn blossom. "Do you know, that's the second guitar I've lost since Tuesday?"

"Shut up," Truck told him roughly. "He was a decent bloke." A familiar lassitude had come over him: he hung like a wrecked boat in his own skull, drawn slowly down the gravity-well of sentiment. He couldn't define his relationship with Pater, but he knew that he owed some emotion, some regret or responsibility. Something had vanished from the Galaxy forever. "Let's get out of here," yet he hung about, hoping to hear from the anarchists drifting listlessly in and out of Pater's suite that Himation the conjurer had made it back.

He hung about, but Himation never came.

"Come on, Tiny. There's nothing here for us any more."

Tiny folded up a small silk fan and put it in his pocket. It was an alley gesture, without decency, but of respect.

"Where will we go?"

The corridors were deserted: most of Howell was elsewhere, scanning the hard black sky for a destroyed fleet, shaking its head. Even the workshops were dazed and silent.

They boarded *Ella Speed* and found Fix the bosun feeding Himation's lizard from a lengthy if shallow incision in his own arm. "There's no need to go that far, Fix." Truck stood over the chart-computer, observing his fingers as they busied themselves independently about. He had an original idea for the first time in his life. It tasted like rust for all that.

"There was nothing in that transporter," he said bitterly. "She knew Pater would try for it. She even knew from Veronica that Pater had taken me off Earth." He punched the navigation display board gently. "And there she was, waiting for us. It's still on bloody Centauri, under the ground."

Pater.

He had fought both sides indiscriminately all his life, and gained nothing at the end. Out of what? A sense of responsibility? "He was just a loser like the rest of us, Tiny. The Device was never there at all."

Pater. Pater.

"What's this place we're going to, boss?" asked Fix the bosun. "Will the dope be good?"

Ella Speed left her pit and nosed gingerly through a belt of vaporized gold. Hull-plates yawned over her; miles of cable caressed her, arabesque. In passage through night—space was full of floating ribs.

"Shut your mouth and fly the bleeding thing, Fix. Don't I pay you enough?" Which was quite unfair. Truck spent the rest of the journey gawping out at the dyne fields, fiddling about with the screen adjustment, and wondering if he'd died out there during Pater's last flight.

"What the hell are we doing *here*?" asked Tiny incredulously.

Truck had harried himself to a standstill over the same question. But it remained that Pater had furnished him with an end (a purpose, fresh and raw, something he was so unused to that he couldn't keep his fingers out of it) and no means. It was the only place he could think of coming. People muddle through, he told himself, and that has to be sufficient.

The port hinterland at Golgotha stands on the periphery of an ash desert called Wisdom in the middle latitudes of Stomach (named for its discoverer) some way out in the poorly populated Ephesus-Ariadne sector, beyond the billowing CH30H clouds of "Meth Alley." Openers built Golgotha, before their sect became prominent. They had no history of persecution on Earth, but they came anyway, in 2143, and somehow (although it had nothing to do with any obvious exploitation, any crude process of blanket, bible, and Earthsyph) the pretty androgynes of Stomach lost their innocence, and many of them left the uplands for the port.

Its streets are wide. Elsewhere, the natives distill a perfume from the wings of insects; here, they have made themselves fetishes—objects of pleasure. The limestone hills at the far edge of Wisdom are strange, no one really knows what happens among them; here, day and night, dust and ash blow into the houses and the wet openings of the body on a sulky, changeable wind.

A double ghost breathes down the avenues of Golgotha in the wind: the thin twin spirit of religion and inhuman innocence—ash in the air. The delicate quick movements of the natives, who are only mirrors of your desire (who knows what they see in it, what it has replaced for them: their language has two hundred thousand separate and distinct words; they will speak it, if you ask them, at whatever climax you demand); and the Openers, in their cloaks of plum and scarlet, black and gold—they always seem to have their backs turned, to be striding away. Ash swirls round them all at dawn and dusk, when the wind thrusts little exploratory fingers beneath the door.

"Everyone comes here once," said Truck.

But no one ever went there twice. In a time when

decadence was all Earth's and anything else was imitation, there was something about that place: something to remind you of what you had voluntarily relinquished (and winked as you lost it) in other hinterlands to other more human beings. Port ladies took their lives on Stomach, and still do, slipping away in a langor of AdAcs, twisting a handkerchief—they have a crueler perception of vacuum.

An odd thing happened during the first few hours on Stomach. John Truck was later to regard it as symbolical (to the extent that he could regard anything in so abstract a way—it came in the end to little more than an itch down among the sordid experiential and intellectual gleanings of a spacer's skull), but at the time it filled him with a peculiar horror.

He had come to Stomach, obviously, to find the priest Grishkin; but since he had last seen that mysterious man on Earth, he had no idea of how he might be found. Tiny and Fix were surly, having hoped for dope in some familiar stamping-ground—so, with no better idea than that of wandering about the place until he met someone who could put him in touch with the Opener, he shrugged and left them to their own devices —took the high wire gate that leads from the landing field to Golgotha, Wisdom rolling away on his left hand in dove-gray dunes down a fifteen-hundred-mile front —the winds of Stomach already flour-papering his cheek.

Outside the gate, the androgynous whores of Golgotha crowded about him as he went, like subtly depraved children: all chemise and mutated orchids and their heads bobbing no higher than his waist, calling to him in soft, empty voices. Their minute hands plucked at his legs as he passed; some made offers of muted obscenity, others sang or raised their arms to be picked up, many simply clutched his hand and stared with ultimate cryptic promise. They flowed like a gray stream down the boulevards of the native quarter, sometimes leading him, sometimes following, all the while smiling seriously as though reflecting all acute desires.

It was impossible to think of her as "it."

She put her hands up to him; her voice was a rustle of unbelievable fabrics in a remote, passionate room. He lifted her gently by the armpits, feeling no weight but a special heat. She locked her legs round his hips and looked into his face. Disappointed, the others melted away, uttering sad, regretful cries.

" 'The cranes call as they cross to the reeds. Faint and helpless. Now I lie alone,' " she murmured. She wore an insect perfume, the crushed wings of the desert hawk moth prepared in the hills beyond Wisdom. When he stared back at her, uncomprehending, her tiny, heart-shaped face shifted and changed.

"Then perhaps we might consider mirrors," she teased, and secret languages surfaced in her eyes. "I can see you are from Earth." Her little legs tightened until they hurt. Her body became an icon, or a clue—a cool object, a revelation or alchemical tool.

"What?" said Truck, his mouth dry. He stopped there in the middle of the windy street.

"Oh hell," she muttered, uncurling her legs. "You fuck-fucky alonga me now bigfella starman?" She got down. "Why do I always get the uneducated ones?"

But he was already lost.

She led him for miles round the city, as if to tire him out—confusing precincts and alleys of native architecture. The wind turned cold, and he was forced further and further into her sphere of heat. When he complained, she said, "It is part of it, you must see us as part of it." And he did, looking down at her then up at the precarious limestone buildings. At twilight it began to rain, the ash fell plush and damp, the narrower streets became dark and inviting. She tugged him along more urgently as the lights came on; she was now a tightness in the muscles at the back of the neck. "Not far now," she whispered. Did she understand a word she was saying?

Her house was warm and bizarre. Censers swung, moths fluttered and burned amid the incense fumes. His bemusement was completed there, among mirrors. He never remembered anything of what took place there—except that he would never allow it to happen to him again.

He woke in the early hours in a bed too small for him. His throat was sore and dry, the roof of his mouth itched. "Where can I get some water?" he asked, trying to lubricate his tongue with saliva. She—it—wasn't there. He could hear footsteps in the alley outside. He went to the door; cold air seeped over his feet. Someone was in the alley, tall and obese, pacing to and fro. The ash from Wisdom had turned leprous, filling the alley with a wan illumination, patching the figure in its voluminous Opener cloak. "What are you doing?" he called. A hood was pulled over the face. Ash eddied about it, feathery.

"I was looking for—" The figure turned and pulled back its hood. It was Dr. Grishkin.

Truck got hold of the door post. His throat locked up solid. "You," he croaked.

"I can see that your circumstances have changed somewhat, Captain Truck," said Grishkin—his was a fine memory for unfinished conversations. He made no move to enter the house, stood there in the ash-storm, smiling his streamlined smile. "It would seem to be time for a review of prices—"

Truck shivered in the wind. That meeting begun in another wind on Sad al Bari IV had finally run its course. He had only postponed the preliminaries.

A stupid thing to do, he thought (thirty minutes after dawn, in an aircraft; somewhere in front of him, chronologically speaking at least, lay the transparent heart of Openerism—the city of Intestinal Revelation beyond the limestone hills). It was too late for that. Earth's vortex had sucked him in. Stomach turned beneath him like a rotting apple. "Too long in an attic."

"Mm?" said Grishkin, sprawled over two seats, his cloak open, his vast body smooth and perspiring where there was no plastic. He wasn't even half asleep. He was watching Truck out of the corner of one eye.

Truck shrugged. He pointed out of the window. "That. Look, Grishkin," he said, "I'm only doing this on certain conditions. There *is* a price." The muscles above Grishkin's left eye flexed briefly. "I want to disappear, hide. If Gaw or ben Barka find me now—"

"I can understand that, my son," said Grishkin ironically.

"Secondly, I want to know why you're interested in the Device. I'll have to know in the end anyway. On those terms, I'll agree to operate it for you—supposing you can get hold of it. As long as you don't use it for anything connected with this war. I'll cut my own throat first."

Grishkin smiled, shook his head gently. "Ah, Captain, Captain." He hauled himself up, faced Truck properly. "The war," he murmured. "Alice Gaw always wanted a proper war. One could hardly expect her to see things in their proper perspective. To listen to her description of—"

"Cut it out, Grishkin. Do we have a deal?"

"Oh yes, Captain, we have that. *Ad interim,* I'll consider your disappearance. Quite."

He seemed to go to sleep, and Truck had to be content with that. Down below, Stomach crawled on. After a while the cockpit door opened and out came the pilot, yawning. He grinned at Truck, grimaced rudely at the inert priest. "All well in here?"

"Who's flying the bloody aircraft while you're asking stupid questions?" said Truck. He hated atmosphere vehicles. There was so much to run into.

"What aircraft?" Suddenly, he slapped his forehead and stared wildly about. "Oh Christ, this aircraft!"

"Ha ha," said Truck. "Very comical."

Beyond the limestone hills there was only more desert—but uglier than Wisdom, with an air of acceptance and failure. He tripped leaving the aircraft, came up gazing at the gloomy sky with his hands coated in putrefying soil. "What a hole, Grishkin. Can't you do better than this?" In the distance over the hopeless rock flowed rivers of abrasive dust—thick and brown, miles wide. Elsewhere small furtive birds eyed their surroundings sadly, ruffling their feathers as they hopped among the fallen, decaying trees.

Finally, that revelatory city—a handful of ball bearings embedded in black sand—it closed on Truck like a trap.

"An early failure in climatic control," admitted Grishkin. "We were primitive if energetic when we came to Stomach, Captain." He spoke as if he'd been there in 2143, which wouldn't have surprised Truck in the least. "It will be rectified, like all things, with time."

He hurried Truck into a silent place with clean cool white walls. An odd smell of ozone and antiseptic pervaded it. There were static dust-collectors and ventilators everywhere, humming faintly. If you looked closely at the walls, you could see countersunk rivets. People who might or might not have been Openers moved down the passageways dressed in pale green gowns and plastic gloves, their footsteps echoing with queer calm urgency.

"Are you sick?" asked Truck suspiciously. Hospitals made him uneasy. He thought of running back to the aircraft, but the pilot had gone off somewhere to get his breakfast.

"This anxiety, Captain—it isn't necessary. All your problems end here."

"That's what I'm afraid of."

He bit his fingernails, swallowed accidentally, coughed. He lagged behind, but Grishkin took his arm possessively.

"What are you going to do with me?"

"Come now, Captain, before we tend to the first part of our bargain, you must see something of our work here." His diabolic or malefic avatar lurked just beneath his eyelids, peeping out but endeavoring to remain unobserved. "You'll find the Memorial Theater very interesting. But we mustn't be late." Things were fermenting, dissolving behind his windows. Every time they came to a fire door in the corridor, he glanced up at the clock above it. His grip tightened. He was actually pulling Truck along.

Suppose the Memorial Theater to commemorate a single genius of the movement (rather than, say, some murky instance or episode of its past) and he'd have to be a fable—a Minotaur of medicine and religion, some accidental connection between the brain of a mad vivisectionist and the hands of an inappropriate rector. Something any decent man would put a boot to without thought. On Stomach, no one had, and his spirit presided.

It was a huge room.

Normally, Truck sensed, it would be full of a seedy, vinegar-colored gloom strained through the thirty-foot stained glass windows (depicting what? Openerism is an eclectic, a catholic faith—there was a bit of everything, from Lazarus rising to Moses descending; but surely Lazarus hadn't died from a Caesarean incision?). Now it was lighted up starkly by thousands of watts of white light. Electrocorticogram operators and organists sat over their instruments while choirboys draped in thick plum felt paced slowly between the massive multifoil arches, their eyes fixed on the groined roof. The operating table, inviolate on the center of the flagged floor, was a limestone altar. The eerie modes of some plainsong chant echoed long and hollow and far away, as if from bare masonry.

Snip, pick, went the hands of the surgeons, slim and dextrous. "+&—, +&—, +&—," sang the electrical gear as, masked and gowned, Truck and Dr. Grishkin slipped into the inner circle of light and odor.

"This is one of the most impressive events in our history," whispered Grishkin. The patient lay under a local analgesic. A tent of surgical drape covered his body. Above him, spotlights and sheaves of cable hung from chrome bars. Thin bright laser beams crossed and danced. Grishkin bowed to the surgeons, moved nimbly forward—keeping hold of Truck's wrist—and whipped back the surgical tent. "Look—" he breathed.

At first sight, it was a flayed corpse: a mass of yellowish adipose tissue, great ropy blood-vessels, red and blue; all ligament and muscle, wet and sticky-looking and held together by a sac of cling-plastic. John Truck felt his throat fill up with something. He was back among the orbital hospitals and corpse-boats of Canes Venatici, packing them in their boxes. He tried to pull away, but Grishkin held on.

"For the first time, a Grand Master of the Movement is attaining total transparency—" It was plastic. The thing under the tent would never move again. It had a glass skin. "His reverence is fully aware. Would you like to speak to him? Ask him something?" Grishkin radiated an ebullience, a vast energy. "If you find this amazing, you should see what we're doing with the head Captain!"

Truck backed off, waving his free arm violently, dislodging a strand of hair from under his hygienic cap. Doctor Grishkin tucked it back for him, hissing with pleasure. The chant of the choir fell into the minor, over a pattern of unresolved chords from the organ: "Hallelujah!" they cried, and Grishkin said, "A crystal skull, Captain! The Brain Revealed!"

It poked through the back of the surgical tent, maggot-colored, patched with distended areas of cochineal, veined blue-black. It was covered with tiny squares of white paper, each bearing a number. It opened an eye and *looked* at him.

"Something's gone wrong!" he shouted. "Oh, kill it—can't you see!"

"We've had some trouble with the allografting, I admit," said Grishkin. "But foreign-body reaction is well below the acceptable minimum. Don't carp, Captain. Ask!"

Truck swallowed. "Why—" Mild, swimming blue eyes, like birds' eggs in that wreckage. It was trying to smile at him. "Why would *you* need a sentient bomb?" he managed. He was frantic; anything so Grishkin would be satisfied and take him away from there.

A faint chuckle. "You," whispered the Grand Master of the Openers. "You—"

Grishkin began to laugh. He threw back his head and roared. "Oh, Captain! You've been listening to poor, violent Alice Gaw. She has a mind like a howling desert. She's mad, my son—there's no bomb on Centauri. I was there first, I dug my way into the final bunker bare-handed. What she saw lies in her own head, not there. Didn't you realize that?"

His laughter died away. He wiped his mouth. "But I—what I saw was something quite different. It filled that place, it—" He shuddered. Condensation formed behind his windows. Anguish clouded his eyes. "There is a Mystery at the foot of Shaft Ten: a receptacle of the Spirit—and God spoke to me from it—" He swayed like a sick man, pawed his forehead. "He asked for you, Captain, he asked me to bring him a Centauran." His lips peeled back off his teeth, he seemed to be fighting the muscles of his own face for an instant, some actual battle—then he relaxed. His fingers left a red mark on Truck's wrist. "Now, Captain, the rest of our bargain."

"I don't think I want to go on with this."

Truck was always running for doors. This time he made it, and he was out in the corridor before something pricked him in the neck. For someone not getting any dope, he thought, I'm passing out more than I should.

He dreamed that pupation was almost over. Dr. Grishkin was forcing him to distend the sac on his forehead, to burst the brittle shell of the chrysalis. He hated it. His multi-jointed legs, however, scrabbled on of their own accord; his forehead strained against its confines, diminished, swelled again; the shell cracked, cold air flowed in. You could go anywhere like that, said General Gaw. Anywhere, sonny. He tried to withdraw. Let me be a grub again. But they wouldn't. His antennae waved feebly, already receiving messages of a new kind. That was an end to it: fighting to remain, he left the husk nevertheless, an imago full-formed. Woke up—

Terrified in case he discovered what kind of insect he was.

He waited for his head to clear. He looked down at himself. "I never asked for this, Grishkin. Some day I might kill you for this." He got carefully off the bed, rubbing his arms. His old clothes were gone. Wisps of the dream were still evaporating in his head. He got dressed in the only thing available (aware of Grishkin, arms folded, watching him curiously), avoiding the mirrors in the room when he could.

He flexed his hands in miserable defiance. "One day." Caught an accidental glimpse of himself— shivered.

"But Captain, *you* wanted to disappear. Now you're invisible. Who'll look at you and see Captain John Truck, a spacer? Mm?"

Truck walked blindly past him and out of the room, but he followed. "I've fulfilled my part of the bargain, Captain. Both your conditions have been satisfied. You're mine, now."

His numb misery gave way to panic. He was almost sobbing. He became lost in a maze of cool white corridors, where Openers nodded politely at him and his reflection lay in ambush for him at every glass door. He began to run, his breath scraping at his throat. But he couldn't lose the shadow behind him. "Admit it, my son—" Finally, he found the daylight, stumbled out with Grishkin waddling rapidly after. He fell down a flight of steps and into the ghastly spaces of the Stomach badlands.

He stayed there, on his hands and knees, gulping.

"The General has installed half the Fleet over Centauri VII, Captain. It will take time to breach her security. We can only wait a suitable opportunity. In the meantime, don't you see, you can take up a probationary ministry, like any other Novice of the order. You will be invisible. It's what you asked. I have provided not only security for you, but a means whereby you can remember our bargain."

"You didn't have to do it this way, Grishkin."

His cloak had fallen open. He looked up. In front of him stood the pilot of the atmosphere vehicle, a puzzled expression on his decent flier's face. "What are you staring at, you bastard?" But he could no longer avoid his reflection. It was in the man's eyes: the plum-colored cloak; the horrible naked scrawny body, shaven and goosefleshed in the wind; the *bald* head—

And the little plastic panel implanted in his abdominal wall. He stared at it and began to weep.

It was disgusting.

It hurt.

"Here," said the pilot, helping him up. "Take it easy."

But that wasn't the end of it, either, although he soon found that he could keep the cloak discreetly wrapped round him and ignore what lay beneath it—so that when he got back to Golgotha some of his composure, such as it was, had returned. It was precarious. He'd take Pater's injunction to heart and he could no longer guess what might become of him.

It was dark by then. *My Ella Speed* was blacked out. She seemed deserted, but up in the control room he stumbled over Tiny Skeffern, snoring on the floor, a ripped-off bottle of Pater's ethanol under his hand. He kicked the body gently. "Tiny? Fix, why aren't there any lights on?" He found the switches himself, worked them petulantly. "Fix, where are you?" There was something scrawled on a bulkhead in tremulous yellow crayon:

DERE BOS
IVE GOTTA JBO ONA FRATER OUT FRUM ERTH AN IF
WEER TAUKGNI ABOT PAY WEL I HAVENT BIN PAYD FRO
6 MNUTHS
FIXX

All Chromians are dyslexic from birth. It may be why their culture is still feudal. Truck sat down in one of the command chairs and shrugged at the inscription. "Fix, Fix." It was no more than he deserved. He felt unutterably weary.

Tiny, meanwhile, had stirred, rubbed his eyes, and sucked the empty bottle. "Fix left," he said, helping himself up with the edge of the chart computer. "Christ that stuff stinks." He staggered round the cabin looking for water, tripping repeatedly over the bottle, intent only on his own pain. "Took his chopper and everything."

"It's happened before. He'll be back. We're always falling out." It was true, but it didn't make him feel any better: it was always his fault.

Finally, Tiny got his sight back.

"Hey, Truck," he sniggered, "did you get converted?" He squinted across the control room, a big, silly grin spreading across his face as he took in Truck's new clothes. "Jesus, what—"

Truck, inspired by a dreadful rage, had leaped to his feet and was making determined grabs for Tiny's throat.

He skipped smartly back. "Truck, I—"

Truck got hold of him. Laugh, and I'll kick your head in, Skeffern," he said earnestly. "Come on then—" He wanted to hurt somebody. He was being driven further and further out on his own, away from even the minimal decencies of the hinterlands. He shoved Tiny up against the bulkhead until his thin blond hair was rubbing out Fix's illiterate plea for fair treatment. "Come on"—inviting with steely fingers— "say one word."

And then, from all the sick misery of his awakening in Grishkin's ghoulish city: "Oh sod it, *sod* it. Help me, Tiny."

Tiny gaped and snuffled.

Truck slumped back in his seat and set his eyes sorrowfully on the bosun's stupid half-erased note (Fix wasn't fit to be out on his own: he only got into fights with people bigger than himself, or pawned his chopper). "What am I doing, Tiny? I made a deal with Grishkin. It was the only way I could see to get hold of the bloody Device. Now I'm not sure he didn't suspect that all along. He expects me to try and double-cross him. He cut me open as a warning. What am I doing?"

"It was only a joke, Truck, I didn't—"

Truck shivered and stared at the bulkhead.

Bleak steel.

NINE

◼

Under the Lamplight at Avernus

2367: without Truck to operate it, the Centauri Device
(bomb or Totem, perhaps both) remained in its
bunker, quiescent but maybe reviewing in solitude
memories of an earlier war. Or even—sensing that
Truck was now gravitating toward it, spiraling in from
his own choice rather than General Gaw's or ben
Barka's or Grishkin's—stirring a little in its two-cen-
tury sleep.

2367: above, on the fringes of Centauri's rubbished atmosphere, hung evidence of the new war—blind black
battleships, slipping constantly into new patterns of defense, casting mechanically about like beasts that will
tear each other if there is no scent of quarry.

2367: the Galaxy had begun a horrible gavotte to
Earth's tune. On Sad al Bari IV, adolescent shock-
troops with doomed delinquent faces wore their IWG
uniforms through weekend leave in the hinterland, shyly testing their new boots in the alleys off Bread Street;
from the factories of Parrot issued the graveyard shift,
rubbing its hands to stir a sluggish, sleep-deprived con-
stitution and congratulating itself on overproduction of
long reaction guns for the mutual succor treaty with

UASR (the notorious "Salisbury" pact); while everywhere else young girls with clear winsome eyes were lifting their feet to Earth's popular songs and their skirts to dashing young Earth-liaison officers with the colonial squadrons.

2367: a brief hush out there among the stars, as it all hit a pinnacle of awed preparation. Then—lips parted in wonder and a calm dewy smile—the long graceful pratfall into Earth's mucky business.

2367: *Intestinal Revelation* (lately the *Ella Speed*, out of RV Tauri II—Stomach—with a cargo of nothing) lay at Egerton's Port. Avernus, that infamous planet at the edge of the Ariadne arm. Out there, the war seemed remote but plausible.

Egerton's Port went down the drain before it was ever a finished proposition. It never experienced that state of spiritual pioneering—during which the local Women's Institute will hang a spacer whose hair falls a centimeter below his collar (and even specify the type of collar)—through which ports on newly-colonized planets inevitably pass; but moved from raw incompletion to the decadence of an established hinterland while the earth-movers were still mapping it out of the ground. Thus, while its streets were cinders and its buildings sour corrugated plastic, its heart was as rotten as Earth's; and while its considerable warehouse facilities were still in process of development, so was the sore that came to be called "Junk City."

Before the civil engineers left there was a pusher for every street corner and every possible sensation, from AdAcs to Ziapaprothixene. By the time John Truck got there, there were ten (and the reputation of the place, had been going anywhere but in circles round Beta-X-ligo XVII, would have preceded it at every stop along the way). They fought one another in vicious obscurity through the confines of Junk City, and those who survived went out like rats into the port-proper; they were the red-eyed end, they were the continually-replaced rodent teeth and alligator shoes of the Galaxy—they were so eroded in the skull that they'd ask you one minute if scruples were shot or snorted and wonder the next if you could get them a kilo or two at the right price.

But it was their clients that made the place an agony.

They sat or slumped in groups with their backs against the shaking walls, caught like depraved family snapshots—the spike still hanging from the arm, the tiny trickle of blood from the nose—Denebian, Gygnian, Chromian, Earthman, They had given up all pretense of being spacers or whores or anything they had started out to be, and become ciphers with creased open palms, evil clothes, soft bleached voices. The whites of their eyes were gray and somehow crystalline; and whatever it is that the eyes are attached to had gone that way too. Every day just before dawn an irregular detail drawn from their own ranks would clear the streets of those who had died in the night. It kept them in dope.

It was there that Truck began to incubate the vision that was to influence his final deployment of the Centauri Device. Day after day he had to ignore the beseeching hands or listen to the alligator shoes (licking, licking the filthy untreated concrete floors) or pick his way between the O/D cases of the streets. He felt sympathy for someone other than himself, which was unusual—and more, he came to realize that it was Earth money that had built the shacks of Avernus and Earth speculators who owned them.

Further, he remembered Sad al Bari, where he had looked at the losers and, in effect, congratulated himself on escaping all that. But was it any more than a matter of degree? From a terminal H habit on Avernus to a streetsinger's pitch on Sad al Bari to *My Ella Speed* was an upward progress, maybe—but he'd consumed with the best of them, and he was no stranger to alligator shoes, either. Somehow, he'd never seen himself as quite so much a part of it—would he begin to regret his THC sundaes and his adventures on Morpheus?

People take what scraps of personal memory they want to believe in and erect a house of experiential straw. Pater had set light to his, and Avernus was fanning the flames.

He shared with Tiny Skeffern a one-room plastic shed and left it once a day to preserve his fictional Openerism. His window hurt at the edges, where the flesh was inflamed, and it still terrified him to look at it; but he hung on grimly, waiting for a word from Grishkin and thinking up ways to double-cross him when it came.

He made an unconvincing Opener, being embarrassed to undo his cloak in private, let alone public; as a Novice, he was not allowed, nor would he have wanted, to take confession; and so his sole cover-activity was the distribution of sect literature (brown bundles of which, printed on that crude paper which always seems to smell of excrement, filled the hold of his ship) among the bars and leprotic brothels of the port. It was a threadbare deception and when, after about two weeks of it, he met an earlier acquaintance, it was put paid to entirely.

TEN

◼

"He Doesn't Even Know
What Year It Is"

Afternoon on Avernus, and a thin sour drizzle beading
the plastic walls. Main Street, Egerton's Port was
poached and muddy. Outside the Boogie Shuffle it was
all AdAc habits, mainly onetime port ladies dreaming
of the teen-age barbie dolls they had once wanted to be
or the fine skinny corpses they would one day make—
their eyes fixed on the underside of the lowbrow clouds
and the rain falling into their open mouths. Truck went
in, past the vapor sign that said GET HER SOME
AND WATCH HER BITE YOUR FINGERS OFF,
and found a party of engine-room mechanics from
some visiting military vessel—haunted by the thought
of explosive decompression a thousand light years from
home and already three parts smashed—dancing ap-
ishly about to a hologram recording of Tiny Skeffern
doing "Eight Star Crawl" at the Palace.

He climbed onto a table.

"Open yourselves to the Universal Principle," he
whispered, hoping they wouldn't hear, "my brothers."

Vast appreciative catcalls.

"I have here—"

Openers aren't supposed to fight; so when Legiron Crab—a tube-reamer out from the Knuckle system and shortly to lose his left arm in the gallant wreck of the *Seventeeth Susan*—decided to have a look under Truck's cloak, Truck went for a pressure point in the neck so as not to make it obvious.

"Oy," said Legiron, quite unperturbed, "get your fingers out of me throat. I haven't got no nerves anyway." (Some weeks before, a bosun's mate—driven past the point of dispassionate logic by Legiron's talent for messing up anything more complicated than deck-scrubbing—had beaten him repeatedly about the skull with one of the larger wrenches used in shackling down Dynaflow Drivers, and been dragged off ten minutes later by some quarterdeck officers still screaming "Lie down, you pisshole, lie down," to no avail, leaving Legiron to scratch the back of his neck reflectively, well on his way to becoming a myth.) "I just want to see what you got."

And he grabbed Truck's wrist, his hairy great forearm distending like one ultimate Universal Muscle. Truck, fearing a fracture, kneed him in the hurdies.

"Now you went too far, matey!" cried Legiorn, massaging his offended morals. "Off you go."

Suiting actions to words, he flung Truck halfway across the bar and out on to Main Street, his Opener tracts fluttering expressively round his head. Which was how he came to find himself down among the lady losers of Avernus, a hard pelvic girdle making inroads into his kidneys, a small breast interfering with one ear, and face to face with Angina Seng, the girl spy from Sad al Bari IV.

"Captain," she said, hands on bony hips and smiling curiously down on him (as if it really was a coincidental meeting), "you must keep doing something nobody likes."

Truck rubbed some rain into his face to get the circulation moving in his brain. He thought of going back into the Boogie Shuffle and killing Legiron Crab.

"I don't know you," he said, "and I'm not a Captain"—he accepted her strong hand without grace and added cunningly—"my sister."

But it was his turn for not fooling her. "It won't wash, Captain Truck. I'd like to talk to you." She brushed his cloak down absently, wiped some mud from his cheek. Looking at his window: "My, you haven't *actually* got religion, have you?" He fussed about with his cloak, clicked his tongue. "Well, Captain?"

"Oh yes"—scathingly—"at the Israeli Embassy, I suppose. We could have some nice talks with the General."

"There's no IWG representation on Avernus," she said, now becoming interested in the vapor sign outside the Boogie Shuffle. "And I haven't worked for that cow since you and I last met." Her face was struggling with two expressions at once: the curled lip of disgust or disdain, certainly; but behind the eyes something else—that intimate understanding of vacuum only a port lady has, some remote pain he couldn't quite put a name to. She tugged her wet coppery hair back from her face, her body slumped sullenly over folded arms. "I hope she—"

A shrug. "Are you coming?" And she walked off down Main Street. He was fascinated.

She took him to a shack on the edge of the port and sat a rickety folding table strewn with twisted half-empty tubes and hard dried nubs of cosmetic while he mooched about looking for something to eat. They stalked one another in the rainy light. She brushed her hair, examined minutely her face (thin lines of an internal tension too secret to be politics or anything other than running-down clockwork of a port lady's life), looked his reversed image over covertly when he was occupied with the fridge.

"What have you got?" he asked round a mouthful of something local. "Another sponsor, eh? Jesus! What is this stuff?"

"It's off, I think. Here, let me taste it. How did you know, Captain?"

A weary little room. He stared oafishly round it at the cast-off underwear and open cupboards, the scuffed walls. How old was she? Was this all of it? Coming too close to her soul—continually in transit between such rooms and always arriving late—he shivered. He was fooling himself if he thought he knew the half of it.

"It was a joke. I don't want to hear anything about it. Last time was too painful."

"Look, Captain, you obviously don't want to give it to General Gaw. I could put it in safer hands. I could arrange a meeting."

His naïveté didn't extend that far; around that point, it degenerated into a sort of sly ferrety awareness. "You don't even know what it is," he told her. She pursed her lips (a hit, a hit!). "No, wait. I'll meet him." He paced up and down, munching. He could check one or two things at least.

"Good." She dropped the hairbrush. "I'll take you to him now." Got up, smoothed her dress over her stomach, stood too close to him, smiled right at him. He was touched—but.

"No. Here. Tonight. Fetch him here at eight. I've got things to do."

She frowned. "You wouldn't be working for General Gaw yourself, Captain?"

"You're a bit behind the times, aren't you?" Deep down, something was warning him that losers should never, never make decisions. He ignored it, and it sniggered horribly at him. "Just on my terms this time, that's all." It was blatant *hubris*. At the door he asked, "Don't you ever get tired of being used?" Thinking of poor old-animal Nodes, who also hadn't known what "it" was—or wanted to.

She stared out into the rain after him, tapping her fingers against one of the Opener broadsheets ("Some Words of Plain Good Sense in a Time of Trouble").

After he'd vanished down the dreary street, she went out in another direction.

"I want a gun," said Truck when he got in.

"Christ." Tiny had heard about the incident at the Boogie Shuffle. "Truck, how can you shoot a bloke just because he chucked you out of a bar?"

He put his underpants on, hopping about on one foot; he was entertaining. The lady in the bed, her voice muffled by the blanket, said, "Get that creep out of here. He gives me the willies." She raised herself on one elbow, glaring at Truck. "Tiny, how can he live with his breakfast like that? How can you live with him? You're an artist." She shuddered.

Pointedly, Tiny showed Truck the door. "Fix might have left something on the ship," he suggested. He winked and jerked his thumb back over his shoulder. "Eh?"

Fix hadn't. But in a locker on the bridge, Truck found a set of steel knuckles he'd bought long ago on Morpheus and never used. He put them on and went prancing around on his toes, feinting dangerously at the display panels. He got a couple of hours' sleep in his old bunk then, when it was dark, stuck the steel knuckles in his right boot (under his foot where they'd be safe from a cursory search, if uncomfortable), and left for the edge of Egerton's Port. He had howling colic from Angina Seng's Avernus pasty.

Half past seven saw him shivering in a pool of shadow twenty yards from Angina's door.

The compass wind was blowing inside and out, wiping the eyes with rain, buffeting the losers on the port streets (down galleries of one repeated image—a hand to the shaking wall, head down, retching dejectedly from the very brain out), and plastering Truck's cloak to him like wet cement. He wasn't sure why he was there: to hold, perhaps, for just this once, a small power over those who have the steerage way to set a course despite the wind; to get a look at Angina Seng's new sponsor before whoever it was got a look at him.

Given this, anyone can predict a disaster.

Twenty minutes later, the enigmatic Angina appeared head down into the weather from the direction of Junk City and let herself in, looking round circumspectly while she fumbled with her key. Off in the prehistoric darkness, Truck sniggered to himself. She was bundled up against rain or recognition, but unable to disguise the earthly slouch of the born port lady. Lights came on. Both of them settled down to wait. She had a mysterious trick of turning up at the window moving from right to left then, a minute later, reappearing from the same direction, as if some personal topology applied to the room. Fifteen of these manifestations took place while Truck shivered and squirmed the sole of his right foot and tried to ignore his griping stomach.

The figure that finally shuffled up to Angina's door might just as well have been Hermann Göring. He discovered immediately that he'd stationed himself too far away to pick out any characteristic (other than, say, a wooden leg) he wasn't already familiar with. He moved idiotically out of his hiding place to get a better look, still saw nothing but waterproof clothing and a white blur of face. Disconcerted by this unexpected anonymity, he raced back into cover—just a shade too late to do anything about the unfriendly movements that suddenly filled the darkness about him.

One of the UASR death-commandos who had been following him since he left *Ella Speed* rapped him quickly in the biceps to immobilize his arms while the other lugged out a Chambers gun the size of a mortuary and poked it at his groin in awful warning. "You put your hands on your head pretty fucking sharpish," they advised him. Their lean pockmarked faces were wreathed with smiles as they searched him, and then stood back to let him reflect on his obvious future if he insisted on playing by the rules of winners.

"Got any good postcards, boys?" he insinuated nastily, because he felt the fool he was. The hashishin exchanged an unpleasant glance, clearly reinterpreting their orders, and advanced on him.

"We thought you'd never come in, Captain," said someone from behind him, just in time. "You didn't have to skulk about there in the rain, old chap—didn't Miss Seng make that clear to you? You must be frozen stiff."

Gadaffi ben Barka: second Colonel or executive of the People's Army of Morocco—originally a chip off the old UNFP—and thus the nearest thing to General Gaw's opposite number in the UASR(N). He was tall and slimly built, with a back like a board and a neatly clipped mustache. He tapped Truck's hands with the tip of his little swagger cane. "You could put them down now, I think."

He affected the precise, slightly decayed English of original Arab stock unused to handling it since the cultural revolution of 2184 with its concomitant stress on the speaking of only Arab languages among the bureaucrats of the inner party. His name, which can be spelled some 400-odd ways in the English (from Quathafi to Khedaphey), was an illustrious one. His hair, shaved to within an inch of its life, had a tinge of gray to match his beautiful military suit. When he smiled he showed a lot of white teeth and one black one. He was a lot more engaging than the General, but that rotten enamel counted for a lot.

"You seem to have got caught up in my security operation. Sorry about that." Quite the part, walking with his hands clasped behind his back, he knew exactly what had happened. "But if you'd just come through the front entrance"—ushering Truck through that same door—"as we expected, you'd have been quite safe. No harm done. These mix-ups happen."

Angina Seng ignored him and stared out of the window. He hoped it was because she felt guilty. He limped ostentatiously past her and sat down on the

bed. In fact, his foot did hurt like hell, and his queasy
gut was generating long gray waves of nausea to break
cold and sweaty over his bald scalp. He looked accusingly at the fridge. His cloak fell open. "You've
bloody poisoned me," he told Angina's shoulders. She
shrugged.

Like the commander of some desert terrain poring over
his maps, ben Barka sat behind the camp table, scraping idly at its curious reliefs of dried cosmetic; planning, perhaps, fantastic miniature campaigns among its
arid wadies and exposed ridges—the wind like emery
on the eyeballs at sunset; the camels sore-footed and
refractory; the Maxim-gun bogged to its hubs in sand
again, or jamming just as the train arrived, never quite
fulfilling the promises of the Austro-Greek munitions
dealer (with his soft fat hands and celluloid collar)
who'd smuggled it by motorized dhow from Constan-
tinople—some grim expedition to redeem a heartland
lost for centuries under the dust, its cisterns poisoned,
its women under a punishment, ash interring its surviv-
ing sons. His eyes were full of some violent past—not
his own in any sense of the personal, but having
greater individual meaning than a mere heritage.
    The hashishin, meanwhile, had disposed themselves
by the door, where they seemed to fall into a state of
feral languor, giving Truck insolent grins and winks,
picking their noses with fanatical concentration. Ben
Barka brought his last dawn sortie to its desperate con-
clusion under the cold desert rimwall and said, "I see
you've been on Stomach lately, Captain. Intellectually,
I can hardly credit you as an Opener—it's an unsatis-
fying notion. Still, faith is a peculiar thing: in the past,
we Arabs have had creed enough for a Galaxy, and energy too; but, until now, no—"
    He stared past Truck at something on the wall,
shrugged. "I presume the girl has told you why I asked
you here?"

Truck sneered sideways at Angina Seng. "What would I know about it? I thought she'd found her level in the IWG embassy on Sad al Bari." He hardly knew what he was saying. He got a quick sight of his stomach, heaved; drew the sodden cloak about him, blushing miserably and thinking of Grishkin's victorious smile.

"I see. Make us some mint tea please, Angina. The Captain looks cold."

Off by the window, a sudden, impatient movement. "Oh, for Christ's sake Gadaffi tell him why he's here and then get out. He hasn't got a clue what he's got hold of. The old cow obviously never told him, and half the time he's so drugged that he doesn't even know where he is. Why should I have told him? He's never listened to a word I've said." She watched the rain, lacing her fingers, rubbing one thumb with the other. "I'm sick of both of you."

"Make us some mint tea, please, Angina."

"Oh, come *on*—"

"Make us some mint tea, please, Angina."

There was a greasy sink in one corner. She began to smash things about in it.

Truck swallowed. "She'll sell you out, too, ben Barka. She'll do it for practice."

The colonel smiled wanly to himself. "There's no need to feel injured, Captain. This is an informal sort of meeting, there was no coercion intended." The hashishin rubbed their tanned noses. "An exploratory meeting, really."

"I wasn't thinking of myself."

"There will be no betrayal," ben Barka insisted, rapping his stick briskly on the table and looking irritated for a moment or two.

"I told you he was a bloody moron," said Angina. "He doesn't even know what year it is."

"Our arrangement has certain safeguards built in, Captain. You, of all people, should be familiar with the kind of thing I'm thinking of. The General herself was good enough to institute them a long time ago. And, of course, Angina is hardly welcome in that sector any more. Now let's—Ah, thank you, Angina."

She had slopped two small plastic cups on the table between them, full of something green and steaming. Truck looked dismally into his. A slight glutinous scum had already formed at its rim, like algae at the high-water mark of an abandoned canal. Something was floating in there. Something was *floating*.

Truck staggered to his feet, eyes filling with tears, and headed blindly for the door, thinking solely of relief. The hashishin stepped thoughtfully forward to intercept him, beaming and swinging hands like edged slabs of sandstone. Simultaneously, ben Barka shouted something, kicked his chair out of the way, and came up aiming a Chambers gun in fashionable military style—feet well apart, arms out straight, left hand gripping right wrist. That he could prevent himself from firing after all that, was a minor miracle; but Truck didn't care.

He hardly saw any of it. Somewhere in a limpid personal twilight, he was groaning with fear and revulsion and heaving up the whole contents of the universe. After a while, he felt the Arabs bending over him. Somebody called his name a couple of times. The last thing he properly understood for a while was Angina Seng saying: "He's always doing that. Well, you can damn well clean it up before you go."

They dragged him through the drenching rain, dashing along like a night retreat from some El Bira or Ein Kerem of the mind. Sudden vicious squalls of wind groaned between the black violent buildings, flushing up the losers of Avernus (to drive them, mere bundles of rag, feeble impersonations of life, from one cold corner to another, all the long night through). Every time his foot went down, pain lighted him up like a dancing man in a neon sign.

They came to a halt, panting and staring about, some three hundred yards down the street from Angina's shack; pushed him into some sort of ground vehicle; took off into the dark on a wave of mud and transmission noise. Egerton's Port receded but not far. Ben Barka drove nervously, craning forward to peer through the water pouring down the windshield. In the back seat, the *fellaheen* wiped condensation from the windows then shoved their faces so close to the glass that it misted up again immediately.

Later, they left the road. Distant thunder smoked from the sky with a smell of cold-drawn steel wire and manganese slag; the car veered and bucked and smashed its underparts repeatedly down against the ruts and cinders of a ruined landscape; flares of white light bleached the faces of the hashishin. For a moment, hung between sky and waste by a particularly brutal spasm, Truck imagined Earth's war reaching out for Avernus like a bleeding hand. But when he looked for the telltale violet ionization trails of descending MIEV warheads, he could see nothing.

He retched comfortably a couple of times and fell into a doze alternately hag-ridden and beatific. His head lolled onto the shoulder of one of the Arabs. They looked across it at each other with distaste.

◼

ELEVEN

A Thin Time in
"Junk City"

Waking up ten minutes later, he rubbed his mouth and nose, sneezed. Odd silhouettes were forming and shifting somewhere beyond the streaming windscreen. He sat up and looked around. "What do you know?" he said, his respect for ben Barka declining rapidly as the car lurched its way deeper into the mean and soulless night of Junk City.

"Shut your mouth," suggested one of the hashishin.

Junk City, a fair-sized industrial complex that had processed the raw materials for the pit-warehouse quarter of Egerton's Port during the early stages of colonization, was falling apart ten years after the fact in the evil glare of a failing temporary power plant that had somehow never been shut down, its foundries and plastics factories links in a well-established chain of warrens which served the hinterland pushers.

It was a nerve-racking horizon of slag tips and cooling-towers, leaning chimneys and gutted workshops, cold furnaces sadly gravid with congealed ore and fluxes, all linked together by a black etched spiderwork of gantried, man-high conduits and precarious diagonal conveyors. Smoke and vapors vented from the overtaxed condensers of the power plant roiled between the rusting hoppers, drifted across the soaked ashy earth at the height of a man's waist to hang reeking over the terraces of the opencast mines.

Reactor-glare beat its way up and down the spectrum, now white and electric, now somnolent and purple—a constant unhealthy flicker of partially contained plasma struggling against the abused lines of force that restrained it, filling the wind with an awful, modulating, voracious roar like junk-tides on an abandoned planet at the very gutter-edge of Time. The denizens of this city, white eyes and thin demented bones, watched the light racing and arcing across their grim skyline, and huddled close. Why should they be any less desperate for comfort than their customers? That leaky old engine menaced them, but they depended on it.

"I was on Centauri VII, Captain. I know what I saw when Grishkin burst through into the final bunker. I had been operating the cutter not a minute before he began to scrabble his way through, barehanded. Yusef Karem saw it too, but later, and his report was garbled; Fleet agents were already close behind him— by then, they had cooked my sergeant's brains and knew we were there."

Ben Barka had a bolthole in the ganger's shed of an ore furnace: a dusty room with faded yellow duty rosters pinned to the walls and a collection of the shaky, scuffed furniture that always seems to find its way into such places—two or three hard chairs, some adjustable metal shelving, and a half-made folding bed.

From small grimy windows the top-gas extractors and blast pipes of the smelter were visible, crawling over its outer shell like vast slow worms. Its charging platforms and skip-inclines hung askew, creaking on their broken welds in the wind. Shunting lines ran round its base, detouring heaps of machine-tool rejects once destined for the fire. Nothing here had been built to last; its very bulk seemed to lend it an impermanent air.

"What I saw is probably the most powerful propaganda tool the Galaxy has ever known. Conceive of a sort of psychical radio of great range and selectivity, which, by broadcasting images direct to the cortex, will bypass the interpretive moment and eliminate the possibility of evasion—"

Ben Barka was pacing the shabby room nervously, slapping his cane against the open palm of his left hand and frequently consulting his watch. He seemed to be expecting someone else. "No more willful ignorance, Captain! The responsibility will be enormous!"

Truck massaged his foot, stretched. He felt rested and energetic, but wary. Down in the port he'd rather admired the desert fervor of ben Barka's eyes; this was less romantic.

"That's a disgusting little fantasy," he said. "I don't know anything about 'interpretive moments.' Whatever you saw in the bunker, the General seems convinced that it's a bomb. I suspect you're both as mad as Grishkin. *He* thinks it's God."

Ben Barka rubbed some grime from a window pane, examined the end of his finger edgily.

"Did you ever stop to think, Captain, that there may now remain no useful definition of the terms 'sane' and 'insane'? It's war. Anything else is an impersonation, a dream."

"Then stop it. You wouldn't have anything to eat round here, would you? I'm famished."

"Give us the Device and it will stop. I can promise you that."

"Oh sure. It's not a case of giving. I've never even seen the bloody thing—and if it was, I wouldn't. I don't see you as much of an alternative to General Gaw. If only you'd slaughter each other instead of the rest of us. Why don't you hold your war on Earth? I'll sell tickets and applaud."

The colonel looked nonplused.

"Now, if yours are the 'safer hands' Angina had in mind, you've been wasting your time. Can I go now?"

At this, the door of the hut scraped open abruptly and an Earth-European in the uniform of the UASR(N) Political Corps bustled over the threshold. His skin was gray, his hands were covered with small seedy scabs, and the cuffs of his shirt were frayed. Five centuries earlier, there would have been permanent ink stains on his fingers too, and secret meetings in his attic every second Wednesday.

He had obviously been eavesdropping. He glared aggressively at Truck, put his thumb in his mouth and ripped savagely at the nail, then said without looking at ben Barka, "I'll take over now."

Ben Barka shipped his stick and clasped his hands behind his back. He nodded coldly. Long, rolling dunes came back into his eyes, under a white moon. Trains full of overfed colonial infantrymen steamed out of the marshaling yards of Alexandria into the jaws of his ambush.

"I'd prefer you to sit in *that* chair," said the PCO. His nose was running. When it became evident that Truck didn't intend to resist, he wiped it on his sleeve and grinned triumphantly.

"By dint of ceaseless energy and intelligence," he began, in a vigoriously offensive voice, "the watchful peoples of the United Arab Republics have uncovered a projected violation of their sovereignty involving an antihumanitarian weapon built by the decadents of Centauri VII in an attempt to halt their engulfment by the equally corrupt expansionist forces of the so-called 'Israeli World Government.' "

He sniffed loudly. "Well, we all know what happened *there*," he said parenthetically.

"While we of the UASR would abhor and strongly protest the use of any such device as antibeneficial to

the interest of freedom-loving nationals of all the
planets, there seems a possibility that in the hands of a
properly-constituted Socialist democracy it would signal
the overture of a new era of Socialist co-operation: the
instant peaceful conversion of the Galaxy to true
Marxist-Leninism, the end of the class struggle, the—"

He stared hard at Truck.

"Well?"

"Do we have to have this fucking clown in here?"
Truck appealed. But ben Barka, listening to the on-
ion-skins peeling off the Saharan rock in a far-off cold
dawn, only lifted one eyebrow. What did he have to do
with Europe, his eyes were asking, in this or any other
century—?

"You'll address *me*. The colonel isn't responsible for
interrogation. Look here, Captain, we've started out on
the wrong foot here. I'll tell you what we'll do. We'll
cut the philosophy—fair enough, it isn't your line, I
can understand that—and get down to brass tacks.
O.K.?"

Truck shrugged stonily.

"Well then, about this propaganda machine: we
know you can control it. It's in your genes." He
grinned ingratiatingly and repeated, "Your genes." He
narrowed his eyes, as if that might enable him to spot
the actual deformity, there in the bone. "Captain," he
said, "I'm empowered to offer you the rank of Hero of
the UASR." His eyes bulged at the thought of it.
"Also—wait for it!—*immediate* honorary professorship
in Political Philosophy at Cairo University. New Cairo,
that is, of course. What do you think of that?"

It was everything he'd ever wanted, you could see
that.

"I think you're a clown."

"Captain, Captain. You're a spacer. You owe the
Zionists nothing. Plenty of the hinterland people are
committed to a Socialist Galaxy"—it had been fashionable, a couple of years before the New Music—"even

your wife, Captain. She was once a member of the Party—"

"Oh, *shit*." Truck got to his feet, stormed across the room to confront ben Barka. "I'm sick of this little idiot," he said. "Can I go now?"

"Sit down!" yelped the PCO. He danced around in the doorway, fumbling for something in his belt, his nose running horribly.

"No. Look, ben Barka, you don't really have anything in common with this wretched little commissar and his rubbish? You don't really agree with that stuff?"

The colonel blinked once, slowly. Beyond his initial nod, he hadn't once acknowledged the existence of the PCO. Now he brooded on the man's crumpled uniform and great raw ears. He smiled faintly. "Yes, I think I do." After a while, "Yes, I do." In his eyes, the remnants of an old dream, dissolving wadies, camels, and *fellaheen* fading into insubstantiality.

"Then you and Alice Gaw make a fine pair. God help you both."

The PCO had succeeded in hauling out an enormous Chambers gun and was waving it about. "I'm arresting you," he shouted, "in the name of the Peoples of the Galaxy." Sick and hollow, Truck limped out. "You'll co-operate. The exigencies of the class struggle demand it!" In the doorway, fumes from the chancy old reactor catching at his throat, Truck stared back over the greasy, bobbing head of his monkey captor. Ben Barka was sitting on the camp bed. Nothing but an old dream. Sand dunes and an old, sold-out dream.

Outside, filled with disgust, he tried to kick the PCO's face in. But the hashishin, who'd been hanging about in the gloom in anticipation of just such a contingency, grinned and threw him down a flight of steps. They were careful not to hurt him much, and he guessed their orders were to treat him decently unless the other side looked like getting hold of him. It was West Central and Nodes all over again.

They put him in the Cowper stove of the furnace. Someone had long ago ripped out the checkerwork, disconnected the blast pipes, and hacked out a crude door about a foot above ground level. What remained was a domed steel shell, all its ducts but one plugged and welded, and that one too high to reach. From it issued a sluggish trickle of warm air lighted by some peculiar inner quality caused by its passage over the reactor fire, so that his breath took on the palest yellow tinge as he mooched about sucking his split lip. He was too galled to care.

If Grishkin's lunatic violation of his innards in the Cathedral of Intestinal Revelation had robbed him of his sense of proportion—what Pater had called his "fine vulgar iconoclasm"—ben Barka's scruffy little retreat among the rubbish was doing a lot to restore it. He knew a wrecking yard when he saw one, and he remembered the PCO from innumerable hinterland corners: snotty-nosed, one foot in the gutter, leaving small toothmarks on the bone.

It was a pusher's Galaxy all right.

After a bit, he reviewed his situation. His assault on the PCO, however satisfying, had been by nature an exploration; next time, he expected to get the Chambers pistol. He retrieved the knuckleduster from his boot, paced round a few more times—hobbling and cursing—to work the stiffness out of his bruised right arch, then squatted down to wait in a position that would put him behind the door next time it opened.

It stayed shut for nearly three hours.

He worried because he needed darkness, and the dawn must be near. He dozed off, he woke up with a guilty start. His stomach grumbled, his legs developed pins and needles. He recalled the holograms of Howell, and conceived a sudden retrospective lust for sallow Heloise, uncrowned queen of the Aesthetic Asteroid.

Grinning into the luteous gloom, he clenched a fist and rubbed the cold steel knuckles against his cheek . . .

The sides of the Cowper stove boomed faintly as someone outside kicked at the door. He shot to his feet, sweating. He was only partly upright when the door slammed back—grabbed at it for support, found it swinging further toward him as a result, and was shoved painfully into the wall. So much for ambush. Sodding and blinding, he extricated himself and rolled out of the closing gap into the yellow arena—

White light pinned him crouching to the scaly floor like a child caught in the awful act.

"You watch it, spacer," said a soft voice. "What you doing in there?"

He sat on his right hand to hide the knuckleduster, blinked.

"Hey," he whined placatingly, "that hurts. I was having—" Flapped his left hand in front of his eyes. The light went out.

"Fetch him here," ordered the PCO, who'd sensibly sent a couple of commandos through ahead of him. They grinned at one another, pistols dangling negligently from their hard thick fingers. One of them shrugged and advanced.

"You just leave me alone!" pleaded John Truck, cowering away as the brown hand touched his shoulder, so that its owner had to stretch and grab at the last minute. Balance undermined, he swayed. "Right, you sod!" shouted Truck, brought the knuckles round in a dirty gray arc and hit him in the mouth. Something broke, the Arab's fingers went lax, Truck had hold of the gun before it hit the floor.

"Now," he said, trembling with relief and fury. He wound his left hand into the hashishin's belt and held the flaccid body up as a shield. Red unsteady light dispelled the gloom as the PCO and the remaining Arab let go simultaneously with their pistols. Lunchtime smells in the Cowper stove.

"No, no," said the PCO.

"Oh yes," whispered Truck, shuffling inexorably forward behind the smoldering corpse, "oh yes."

All three of them were on fire when he left the chamber, expressions of horror on their rigid features. What else should he have done? He watched them dispassionately for a moment or two, then, weighed down by more guns than he'd ever owned in his life, ran off into the jungle of railway tracks and junkheaps. Rusty gear trains rolled about under his feet as he went, like the fossil bones of preposterous little animals.

Energy fronts resonated silent and dazzling from the cliff-faces of the rolling mills; from the convection currents dancing like translucent veils above the mounds of the city came a wicked, sucking roar; hot-air refraction shifted the positions of the known stars, cold winds howled toward the stricken center of it all across the bleak loading platforms. It looked like a dream of arson. It looked like Hell—

He didn't quite know what to do. Dwarfed and stumbling, a gun in each hand and a spare one stuck down the side of his boot, he took to the lanes of shadow beneath the great corroded walls, drawn toward that essential solipsistic djinn thrashing the confines of its magnetic bottle.

Ianthine light fired the lines and pylons of the high voltage system; it limned the Kaldo converters and the vast corrugated sheds of the borax refinery; it spilled like hot glass over Truck's bald, vulnerable skull as he turned to scan the waste behind him, and discovered twenty cruel black figures leaping through the rubbish—a complete *fellaheen* death-commando, threading the lunatic peep-show flicker in a classic search-and-destroy maneuver.

Ben Barka had decided to cut his losses.

Truck got down on the floor and crawled further into the shadows, shaking. He could see them, but he didn't think they could see him. He rubbed his face into the rust, he bit the inside of his cheek so hard it bled. They'd have found their dead by now, smoking in the Cowper stove. "Oh Jesus," he sobbed. He hadn't got a chance.

He fled down a blind narrow walkway, falling repeatedly into troughs and sumps of lukewarm sticky water—at the end of the alley, fetched up against a blank wall of flaking steel—opened his split lip and dropped one of his guns.

Panicked.

"Oh my Christ, my Christ," staring back, mouth open, bloody-chinned, no way out.

He scrabbled about, discovering rivets.

There was a door.

He wiped his lips with the back of his hand. Spreading his cloak to hide the flare, he fired half a Chambers magazine into the rusty lock; reeled back from the heat with his forehead blistering; stab-kicked the door and dived through it panting and laughing like a madman, reeking of scorch and smoke and death.

He had broken into a gutted pumping station, where a score of small-bore pipelines converged to supply raw organic material to one great conduit fifteen feet in diameter. Most of the transfer valve gear had been ripped out, but a faint odor of partly-processed polymers still haunted the sour air. A shattered inspection window gave access to the conduit; as soon as he had relaxed enough to be able to turn his back on the rapidly cooling door—fairly sure that for a moment the pursuit had gone off in some other direction—he poked his head through it and had a look.

The main stretched away right and left in a slight but perceptible curve, lighted by dim orange bulbs strung from a frayed cable in the ceiling—adopted by the denizens of Junk City as a trunkline for furtive journeys, a rat's highway smeared with cryptic brown graffiti and littered with rubbish. He rested his elbows on the windowsill and wondered if it would get him anywhere. Small drafts fluted through splits in the inner cladding, drying the sweat on his temples.

He was clambering in, and stuff the consequences, when someone came tap-tapping out of the dim Fallopian reaches, footsteps quick and purposeful. He ducked back into the pumping station until the noise got very close, then shoved his pistols through the window and hissed, "Move, and I'll blow you to hell!"

A short, ironical laugh, then a female voice said, "Go on and shoot."

"What?"

"You'd be doing me a favor, Captain."

He peered through the window.

It was Angina Seng, all coppery hair and long body. She stood regarding him with a pinched, censorious expression. Once again, he had the feeling that she was fighting a doomed action to prevent her soul evacuating her skull and boiling off into space. The lines around her mouth were deep and sad.

"I can't seem to get rid of you, can I?" she said. "Are you going to get it over with, or can I go?"

He was amazed to realize that she honestly didn't care. He hauled himself through the window and frowned aggressively. "I've got a bone to pick with you," he told her, remembering that he had.

"I've no time, Captain. You'd better shoot, if that's what you feel, because I'm not waiting around any longer. Whatever you feel necessary."

And she turned on her heel and trudged off, arms folded, head down, breasting some personal hinterland wind.

"Look here—" He watched her receding shoulders for a minute, glanced at his guns. He felt a bit of a fool. He hurried after her like some mad philosopher chasing the Noumenon forever down a gradient of misunderstanding. "Why do you always treat me like a child?" He complained. "If you'd leveled with me just once—"

She stopped, swung on him, her eyes blazing and alive for the first time in his experience of her.

"Because you know nothing! Because you understand nothing! Because people like you are always too puzzled and decent to shoot people like me. Because that's what you *are*, Captain."

She shrugged.

"Oh, what's the use? Truck, you're a baby: there's always someone shielding you and all the other odd little people like you—if you want *me* to apologize for *your* naïveté, then bloody well forget it!"

Off she went again, and this time all he got from her when he caught up was, "Shouldn't you be running away? They've got half the Arabs in Junk City out looking for you."

"I was rather hoping you'd help me," he said diffidently. "You keep getting me into these things. You've conned me twice and I think you owe me for that."

She looked weary and compassionate. "You see?" she said. Then: "Why should I, Captain, why should I owe you anything?" She looked him up and down, shook her head. "I see no reason to help you, Captain, no reason at all."

On the other hand, she did nothing to discourage him; so, despite his armory, he simply followed her. She was familiar, and he couldn't think of anything else to do. Walking at a fair clip, she got about ten yards ahead of him. He could always, he reasoned, shoot her in the back if she turned out to be bait in an ambush. Somehow, he didn't think he'd ever be able to shoot her in the front.

The floor took on a downward slope. Patches of congealed plastic ridged the metal underfoot, trapping little runnels of bitter condensation. Up ahead, there was a ninety-degree bend in the main. He let her go round it, stopped, put his ear to the wall. He was close enough to the reactor to feel its soul in the steel and hear the distant moan of convection currents—but other than that, only moisture dripping from the lighting cable with a sound like tapped porcelain. Angina had stopped moving. She coughed, and shuffled her feet.

Truck checked his pistols, sucked his split lip indecisively. "Oh shit," he murmured, and went around the corner like an armored train. There was nothing up there he feared more than what lay behind.

He was in a shadowy alcove where cold stale air licked his face like a sick animal. The conduit terminated a few feet away in a screen of thick wire mesh, into which was set a wicket-gate of the same material. A vague brightness lay beyond it. In the alcove nothing moved but Angina's sharp black silhouette. She was standing with her face pressed up against the mesh, as if trying to see through it.

Truck crouched there sweating and ready to kill something, then relaxed. "What do we do now, then?" he asked brightly.

"*We* do nothing, Captain," staring through the mesh.

"Sorry I spoke."

He investigated the alcove, rubbing his chin with the end of one of his weapons. "You might be wrong about me not being able to shoot you," he said. "I'm not saying you are—" There didn't seem to be any other way out. "If you'll just stand aside," he said, "I'll open it for you"—sighting up on the wicket-gate— "with no trouble at all."

She gasped, turned away from the grille, an odd complex of fear and yearning in her eyes.

"Don't!"

She stared over his shoulder. Her lips moved, but it wasn't she who whispered eerily into the gloom:

"You don't want to go any further, Captain Truck."

He was there suddenly, but with a look of permanence, as if he'd been waiting just beyond the periphery of Truck's vision ever since the debacle beneath Carter's Snort. As if once acknowledged, he would never go away again. His emaciated and reptilian body was hung with a pale fawn suit cut in that good twentieth-century fashion; his shoes were of the finest alligator; on his head was a straw Panama, bent and grimy at the brim from being pulled down over his eyes. At a glance you could see he belonged to the streets of Egerton's Port, that he'd get you anything you needed: with the end of the longest-running party in the history of the universe, it seemed he'd found his level.

"You aren't a king any more Veronica," said Truck, narrowing his eyes. "Don't try and stop me."

He felt something that might have been sympathy. Chalice Veronica had fallen from grace. He was fading away. What gray cheesy junk flesh he'd once possessed had melted off the bone, which shone through like a lamp behind waxed paper; he was all eyes and resentment, all paranoid jaw and gray stubble; he smelled like an old, old pusher who'd had his hand in the stock cupboard just once too often.

"You're a little fool, Truck," he hissed, "and I wish I'd never seen you. It's still a supplier's Galaxy. The King, even in exile, knows things, sees all—Timelines whip the Moment across the Universe like broken hawsers—Intimations input spinal sensors—H signals flicker like heliographs across the spaces of the dyne—I —see—" He shuddered.

"Ben Barka or General Gaw, what difference can it make to *you* who owns your callow little brain?" He chuckled. "I see one of my little dogs has found you again—"

He swung his blunt, shapeless head and—as if using some other sense than sight, some slow junk radar—located Angina Seng, up there rigid by the wicket-gate. Since his appearance, she had developed little muscle tremors; her face was drawn and white, her eyes were fixed on him.

"I want my stuff, Veronica," she said. "I want it."

Veronica smiled at Truck. "Pardon an old man's sentimentality, Captain. I say 'my' little dogs, but of course I really only feed them. Angina liked what I gave her so much that she came with me when the General withdrew her patronage. It was quite lucky for Angina that we both—left—the General at the same time. The same Moment, eh, Angina?" And he rolled his lizard's eyes to show a thin rim of white veined like hairline cracks in ancient china.

"I want my stuff, Veronica, you bastard," said Angina, and her voice was perfectly empty.

"Oh, my dear, we all want our stuff. But we have to be patient, don't we?"

He took a pace backward into the gloom. Only a ghost, only a thin spirit hanging on, an echo of habits past and a withered kingship under the earth. Truck shot out a hand and grasped the loose wattled skin of his throat. It was like touching a dead, damp leaf. "What are you doing on Avernus, Veronica?" He felt sick. His fingers trembled with the effort of gripping that awful flesh. Only a ghost: but even in eclipse those old junk pores still oozed some stink of mold and darkness. Yellow teeth snapped at him. Veronica's breath rattled, but his head was already dead.

"I'm the paymaster, Captain. Ben Barka needs me as much as the old cow ever did. They all need what I sell, to keep their agents enthusiastic and faithful. Sometimes, ideology isn't enough. The law, the administrators on both sides, why, they're some of my best customers (I'd say 'most regular,' but *all* my customers are that)—"

"What sort of rubbish is this? What's behind that door?" Truck released his grip, flung the eroded bag of bones away from him. It chuckled.

"You're finished, Veronica."

"Don't knock it until you can do it, my boy."

He wasn't even trying to get away. He took out a small pewter pillbox and slipped something into his mouth—the merest delicate flicker of a black, saurian tongue. "The General cut off Angina's supply the day after you refused your services on Sad al Bari, Captain. She's an impatient woman. What could poor Angina do?"

Truck looked at the girl. She had slumped against the mesh, mechanically repeating. "I want my stuff, I want my stuff." She hooked her fingers behind the wire and pulled herself upright. Her facial musculature was cracking up, assembling grotesquely inappropriate expressions—a sentimental smile, a port lady's breezy come-on—but her eyes were calm.

"There, Truck: nobody's protecting you now. I go where the junk leads. Can you say you honestly didn't know? It's a rotten Galaxy, and it doesn't belong to you or I. That bastard"—nodding and grinning and gasping at Veronica—"and the General and ben Barka have it cut up between them. What scraps they leave go to Dr. Grishkin in return for absolution. Politics, religion, and dope: they keep us happy with Hell.

"Veronica, I love you, come in the dark with me and we'll— Oh, *Christ!*"

She dashed forward and, before Truck could move, grabbed one of his Chambers guns. She held it in both hands, whimpered, and blew the wicket-gate to pieces.

There was a writhing motion in the gloom. Chalice Veronica cackled madly. "Down, girl!" He produced something small and black and shot her between the shoulder blades with it. She screamed and fell over, still scrabbling toward the twisted, melting mesh.

Veronica scuttled triumphantly after her. John Truck stepped between them and put a single bolt into Veronica's wet black mouth. The back of the King's head flew off like shell from a rotten egg, but his eyes knew that it's always a pusher's market. Truck stirred the heap of dry reptilian bones with one foot, then knelt beside Angina Seng. There was a hideous, smoking hole, but she was trying to say something.

He turned her over.

She looked up at him, quite lucid, blinked. "I could have gone for you," she said. She touched his hand. "That little guitarist in the Spacer's Rave said you'd eat me. I wonder if you would have?" Blood came out of her mouth. She moaned. Faintly: "Grow up, Captain. It's time someone helped us all. Get rid of the bastards. Stop avoiding the issue. They've no right to do the things they do to us—"

He thought she was dead. He was crying. About a minute later, she said: "If you go in there, don't breathe too hard, and don't get close. It's Paraphythium D-20."

She didn't say anything after that. She'd given him everything she could. It was an act of faith. For some reason, he kept thinking of Ruth Berenici.

He kicked his way calmly through the wreckage of the wicket-gate.

Behind it lay a cylindrical filter tank about thirty feet high. It was chilly and dim. Years of scalding reactor winds had formed the dull *laminae* on its walls.

There, he discovered about half a dozen people squatting in a semicircle around what appeared to be a bundle of old sacks and wool.

Every so often, one of them would stand up unsteadily, go over and take a deep long sniff at it, then sit down again. He leaned on a wall to watch. None of them took any notice of him. He recognized them from streetcorners and the concrete aprons of spaceports on familiar planets—faces you knew without ever having seen them before.

The membranes of his nose itched.

After a while, moving like an automaton (no more capable of feeling, or so it seemed, than one of Pater's holographic images), he went closer to see what they were sniffing. On went the rite: up, shuffle a few paces, sniff, hold the breath, shuffle back; up, shuffle, sniff, as if Truck wasn't there. In a way, he wasn't.

It was a dying sheep.

The fleece had fallen away from its hindquarters in great lumps, like stuffing from an armchair left to rot in the rain; small red blisters connected by thin raised threads of poisoned epidermal nerves covered the exposed hide where the Paraphythium infection had got to it. It shifted about restlessly, trying to find a comfortable position for its scabby legs, nuzzling its sores. It looked sadly up at him, dull brown eyes running and pained, and he stared dispassionately back. He studied the rapt, revelatory faces of the users, searching for some human distinguishing mark, but they all looked like animals, too.

Starting at the nearest end of the semicircle, he went around and shot them, one by one. They never made a sound. It was like being underwater—quiet, removed.

He went back to the sheep.

It tried to get up and run off, but the time was long past for that.

"Hush," he sad absently, "hush."

He tangled his fingers in the fleece at the back of its neck and gazed for some time into its eyes, its sweet, strange breath warming his cheek. When he stood up and put the gun to its head, light from the burning corpses sent his shadow flickering and huge over the sides of the tank. He regarded the carcass, numb and unthinking. Then he turned his face to the invisible stars and roared wordlessly until the tank rang like the inside of a bell—like the inside of his head—with all his horror and rage.

He pulled the third gun from his boot and ran out of that place, blubbering . . .

. . . Paraphythium images of flight and pursuit, fire and steel, ran together like water color in his brain. He'd breathed too deeply of that air, he hardly knew what was happening to him . . .

Warrens and runways led him inevitably too close to
the reactor, pumping and howling and sucking in the
night with a rage as diffuse and frustrated as his own.
He staggered away from it, whimpering and covering
his eyes against the elemental blast . . . With his cloak
on fire, he fluttered through the deep rusting canyons
of the city, like a moth in an unbearable cyanic dream.
He reasoned desperately with himself, "It was only a
sheep," but he knew he was just as culpable as the
Pusher King. (On Morpheus, hadn't he worn the alligator shoes and given the customers their stuff?) He
hoped the death-commando would kill him. Twice,
they ran him down, spilling like maggots from the great
carcasses of the foundries when he was least expecting
them, calling to one another in harsh, mechanical
voices. The first time, he hid in a culvert like a rat up a
drainpipe, promising obscene things to the ghost of
Angina Seng if only they would pass him by . . . The
second time, at bay in a shadowy maze of turbin jigs,
from head to foot in a black cerement (writhing up
like a genie, like smoke from the stacks of the city); it
came to his aid with a strange gun. "Who are you?" he
called, dazzled by the splashback. Its head towered
above him. Had he shrunk? "Leave this city," it advised him, and laughed most sepulchrally. "Leave this
place," and swept its weapon in a withering arc . . .
But he was lost. He came upon the reactor from another angle. "No more!" (Trying to cover eyes and
ears, blind and deaf.) He braced himself in the teeth of
the fifty-knot wind howling into its maw and fired both
his guns at it until they were empty. The magnetic
bottle ran with spectral colors for a moment, the
plasma heaved and raved, but nothing else happened
. . . He decided that if he couldn't kill Junk City, he'd
kill ben Barka; went to find him; stalked three or four
people who resembled him up and down blind alleys
and among swarf heaps; sprang out on each one like a
praying mantis, hands hooked. But, "You're not him!

You're not him!" every time. He killed them anyway
. . . He reeled drunkenly through the city, alone. "Let
me out!" he cried, and shook his fist at the blank
uncaring face it showed him . . .

◻

TWELVE

The Bunkers on Centauri VII

Two hours after dawn in Egerton's Port. At 4 A.M., the bottom had dropped out of the thermometer, and the street details were still pulling the night's crop of defunct and hypothermic losers off the sidewalks. There were plastic syringes frozen into the gutters and skeins of rime on the windows when John Truck stumbled over the threshold of the place he shared with Tiny Skeffern and fell on his face, making instinctive running motions and trying to brandish his guns.

He was covered in blood and soot. The Paraphythium was wearing off—and with it, mercifully, the accurate memory of that horrible night—leaving him with a runny nose and only the slightest notion of where he'd been, where he was, or how he'd managed to make it there. He heaved himself up as far as his knees, explored his raw, flayed face with one hand, and mumbled, "Oh God, Tiny, I have to get out of here." Nobody answered, so he slipped down again onto his belly and went to sleep, the room silent and unrelenting around him.

When he woke up it was getting dark, and still no sign of Tiny. His head ached ferociously. He propped himself up against a door frame and drank a pint of something he'd found in the fridge. Then he fumbled about, cooking eggs and eating them while he tried to read two messages that had come for him. The first one went:

DERE BOSS I COM IN FRUM ERTH ON A FREYTER
WURE THE UDE ENT GUDD WEN I SEEN TH OLD
ELA SPID ON THE APRIN I DISIDED TO COM BAKC
THERS NO HARD FEELINS
FXX.

That, hand printed in Fix the bosun's mephitic script on the back of a crumpled, furry old spare-part invoice from a well-known Dynaflow subsidiary, caused him to grin. His face felt stiff and numb. With Fix's chopper back in its rightful corner of the hold, he could at least fly the old tub without fear of its engines falling out all over the sky. That was what he told himself; really, he just missed the little guy.

As for the other: "The time is ripe, Captain," it said, mad and plummy and familiar. "Come with all haste. God speaks to us from the bunkers, you and I." And it gave a fifteen-figure reference for a planetary touchdown. He didn't think he'd have to check the almanacs to locate the planet in question, either. It was signed "Grishkin." It appeared he'd been activated as the mad priest's agent.

He sat on the floor among the piles of sleazy bedclothes and Opener literature, trying to formulate some sort of policy. Angina Seng had finally convinced him that when the landed gentry cuts up a seedcake for tea it makes no difference to the cake which of them holds the knife: whoever "won" Earth's war, it would be the same old crew who stepped up afterwards to hold out their plates; the squabble over Truck and the Device was nothing more than a polite difference between friends as to who should have the largest slice.

Ben Barka and Gaw would survive; Veronica would be replaced; Grishkin would come waddling on behind. Whole again, the triumvirate of Drugs Actual, Political, and Spiritual would dance and trample its way over the corpses of spacers in hopeless hinterland streets (blinked out like cooling suns, their precious fire gone); caper on the hulls of ships in cometary orbits, each one stuffed ripe and full with dead young men; and tread gleeful measures over the husks of planets circling two hundred suns.

The Ruled never suspect what is being done to them in their own name; how would they dare?

But Truck knew. He'd seen the eyepatch on the face of the ghoul, and the reptile's black quick tongue; he'd seen a burned-out dream of deserts, and shuddered at the entrails of madness. He'd witnessed the death of a sheep in a blasphemous cloister under the ground, and tried to understand the message of its holy breath.

Grishkin had found a way to break the Centauri blockade, confront the Device with the man who could operate it: but wherever Truck went, Gaw and ben Barka could never be very far behind. They were locked onto him and to each other in the excesses of their dance, compelled to lift their legs and laugh and sweat. He wouldn't have a hope if he answered the priest's summons, they'd be after him like dogs; yet he owed Grishkin for his humiliation on Stomach—he owed ben Barka for his scorched face—he owed *some-one* for the deaths of Angina Seng and Sinclair Pater and every single spacer whose flesh had been frozen to the streets of Avernus.

He got up and paced about. It was completely dark, but he didn't dare put the lights on in case the place was being observed.

He shrugged.

He decided to go to Centauri anyway.

Perhaps the Device was calling subtly to its inheritor, perhaps he honestly wanted a confrontation. Certainly, as he slipped out onto the bitter streets of the port, black and ragged in his cloak like a wounded crow, he wanted revenge; by the time he'd passed the high wire fence of the landing field, he had convinced himself that his anger was more than personal; and he believed as he strode between the rocket pits under the white arc lights that the time for passive misery and acceptance was over.

It wasn't.

When he located the *Ella Speed* (he'd somehow forgotten the paint job and the new name), he found her loading ramp extended like the tongue of an immense mechanical mouth.

Fix the bosun was lying huddled up on it.

He was dead.

His lips peeled back from those sawmill teeth, he was curled fetally round a massive abdominal wound, as if his final horrified act had been an attempt to contain the several pints of fluid congealing on the diamond tread of the ramp beneath him. His eyes were narrowed, his fingers were all in a knot; under the port arcs, his features were composed of precise white planes and cold shadows, a brutal, quite alien morphology of emotion, memoir of a hard death.

Truck (down on his knees again, with his hands in the bosun's blood and his mind on the corpse boats of Cor Caroli, where, under the same clinical illumination, there was at least a little peace, an order to the serried rows) heaved and retched. He wiped himself on Fix's yellow jerkin, coughing dismally. ("A pumpkin," he explained, "is what your head is. Don't forget, no vegetable seeds.") Since their government is semifeudal, Chromians acquire early a deep familiarity with death, but: *Oh, you poor sod,* he thought, *you poor little sod.* This was nothing like the loss of Pater, whom he'd hardly known; or of Angina Seng, who hadn't died alone under bleak lights.

Images of Fix: mafficking across the Galaxy in search of freedom and dope and big Denebian whores, his grinning mouth hungry to eat it all down; shivering and blinking on the steps of courthouses in the morning, wondering where to go next after being busted and spending the night telling weird Chromian jokes ("— and were they tits? Not on your life. Intellectual melons!," with nobody among the soreheaded jailed losers knowing quite how to laugh at this hick who found everything new they thought was old); Fix horrible in trashcan alley fights, the morals of a goat, vital, *alive*—dead.

"What can I do?" whispered Truck, cupping the back of the great round head in his hands. He couldn't even bring himself to close the eyelids. He got up. Someone was going to be killed. He gazed speculatively along the length of the boat toward the command bridge, then went inside.

My Ella Speed, a light haulage vehicle of the "Transit" class, registered out of Carter's Snort, Earth, and licensed to transfer up to one thousand tons of freight over distances less than a thousand light years—she mounted three Dynaflow converters (each outputting about fifty gigaton hours per every half ton of fuel consumed) and a "Powerslide" rocket pile for sub-Dyne maneuvers such as planetfall; her cramped little hold had carried everything from neat nitromethane for the curious engines of Anywhere to five thousand live ferrets genetically modified to survive the curious atmosphere of Titus-Bode. Now, except for a few string-tied bundles of "Some Words of Plain Good Sense in a Time of Trouble," it was empty and hollow, amplifying the scrape of John Truck's bootsoles as he rifled Fix the bosun's belongings in search of a gun.

He padded forward through that sweet and dirty ship. In the engine room, where instrumentation flickered and clicked and the display board said *power down* in arrays of colored lights, Fix had left himself a final note: CLENE HTE RUNIN GEER. Truck screwed it up and chucked it on the floor without so much as a smile. He put his shoulder against the command-cabin hatch and shoved. It was locked. Temper gone, he tried to kick it in and was rewarded by Tiny Skeffern's voice from the other side.

"Truck, there's some mad sod in here with a gun." He sounded muffled and distant. Truck said nothing. *Damn him for being in the way.* A scuffling sound. "He says he'll shoot if you don't come in quietly. I think he means it."

"Oh, *Hell!*" Poor old Tiny. "All right then." The electronic lock hummed and chimed, the hatch slid open. Truck dropped Fix's chopper, and the sound clattered back along the subframe of the boat like a laugh. "I'll get you, you bastard," he said, holding out his hands to demonstrate their emptiness.

Tiny had got himself backed up into a corner, his hands well above his head, small beads of sweat on his bald patch. A shallow laceration with bruised edges ran down his left cheek. He looked accusingly at Truck and complained, "I don't think much of your friends." Truck moved a bit further into the cabin, to discover Colonel Gadaffi ben Barka lounging against the approach-radar board with an arid smile on his thin lips.

"Don't think that'll help you when the time comes," Truck told him, nodding at the military issue Chambers gun that had lately blown such a large hole in Fix the bosun's insides. "I owe you for all this, ben Barka. Nobody threatens me on my own boat."

The Arab shrugged elegantly. He had crossed one leg over the other, his whole body unconsciously mimicking the feral repose of his own death commandos. His uniform was as neat as a pin. But he looked tired, and the desert, never very far away, was etching at his brain.

"You shot my bosun," Truck insisted.

Ben Barka's soft brown eyes hooded themselves for a heartbeat. He seemed to be studying his pistol. "You can't think I'm unaware of that, Captain. Neither are *you* aware of how much is at stake. You did plenty of killing last night." Another oasis choked to death in the long, empty night. "He attacked me after fair warning. He was very brave. Do you think I did it lightly? I'm sorry if you do."

John Truck had found Fix the dwarf washed up in the port hinterland of Gloam—disoriented and illiterate among the hustlers and prostitutes, having no real understanding of the twilight subculture that had swallowed him after his escape from the rural manors and squirearchies of Chrome. The two-thousand light-year brawl that had followed was Truck's responsibility; so was its end, down there under the arc lamps of Avernus. Like Annie Truck, Fix was a dependent.

"Are you apologizing to me? I didn't own him. Apologize to him!"

"Come, Captain—"

"I'm going to kick you to death some day, you bastard."

The desert shifted, rustled, extended its perimeters; it had made vast inroads since the meeting in the ganger's shed: from being a means, a sympathetic terrain for imaginary revenges, it had mutated into an end. The olive groves had withered, the aqueducts fallen to rubble. Cairo and Alexandria was bleached shells in the ancient sunlight. High up in mountains ben Barka had never seen, exfoliation was cracking rock enough to make a Galactic sand-sea; sand was already spilling from his skull to submerge everything; in peace, he would slip along the wadies of the mind, stalking Reality's pitiful little punitive expeditions—

He made a small gesture with the pistol. "If you'll take your place at the controls, Captain Truck. Your vessel has been commandeered." His teeth were like bones exposed by the dry winds. "Mr. Skeffern, you'll note, is still alive and well."

"Get your backside off the switchgear if you want the boat to go anywhere, ben Barka."

The command-cabin of a Transit class hauler is laid out with dual controls and duplicated navigational aids; two acceleration chairs provide access to these, and a third can be brought up on runners from the rear of the bridge and locked abreast of the other two. It is a habit of transport pilots to leave this one permanently in place; ben Barka sat himself down in it and indicated that Truck and Tiny should strap-in either side of him. He put his pistol close to Tiny's ear.

"I think you were going my way anyway, Captain. We might as well travel together."

"Oh yes?" Truck powered up his controls. "Where's that?"

Ben Barka sighed and shook his head. "Captain, Captain. The pistol's pointing in the wrong direction for obliquity." He smiled down at Tiny, who hunched his shoulders like a nomad in a sandstorm. "Grishkin, that impatient priest, had it from normally reliable sources that today had been chosen for an Arab attempt on the IWG blockade of Centauri VII (there is in fact an action in progress there; it's significant enough to keep IWG fully occupied, but hardly planned to be an actual military success).

"He realized almost immediately that he could never wish for a better diversion—with the result that you, Captain, received an *en clair* message from him early this morning. (It was couched, I felt, in rather fulsome tones even for a priest.) He expects your landing to go quite unobserved by either myself or the good General Gaw. He may even be down there already, waiting for you—one of our ships reported a boat in Opener livery sneaking a shade ineptly past the perimeters of the engagement some two hours ago.

"It was me who leaked the information to his pathetic intelligence machine; they'd never have got it without help. I don't wonder he didn't bother to code the message. Half his people are working for me or the General anyway. There you have it: we're going to the same place, Captain. We always were."

Truck engaged a bank of rocker switches below the engine-room repeaters and warmed up the Powerslide pile for take-off, wondering just how much allowance ben Barka had made for Grishkin's fanaticism and the General's not inconsiderable cunning.

"Be it on your own head, Colonel."

My Ella Speed rumbled and shook. The cargo ramp pulled itself in slowly, tipping Fix the bosun into the hold like a bale of fresh animal skins. Truck got a go-ahead from the Port Authority, giving his destination as Sad al Bari and his cargo as "mining machinery." Two massive, caterpillar-tracked LTOA vehicles moved in across the dock and stood the boat gently on her tail. He checked that Tiny's controls were shut down, worked the rocket engines through the prelift part of their power-curve a couple of times.

"I can go any time you want, Colonel."

"Do it."

My Ella Speed, well into the spirit of the thing, wiggled along her length like a bitch in heat, and threw herself upward.

While the colossal cruisers of UASR(N) have so-called "autonomic gravity" environments which protect their crews against the devastating G effects of a battle maneuver, third-hand Transit class haulers do not. They are safe from inertia only during dyne-field shifts; and *My Ella Speed,* lustily fighting the attractions of Avernus, made it from relative rest to escape speed in a very short time indeed.

The multi-G blast is a concomitant of the spacer's way of life; Truck and Tiny, who had been lifting like that since birth—and before—took it stoically, with G standing on their faces and stumping all over their ribs.

But ben Barka was used to a more generous kind of travel. Perhaps he simply forgot. Certainly, it was too late when he remembered.

He dropped his Chambers gun when they were about a mile up. He tried comically to move his arms from his sides, sweat breaking out all over his face. His eyes rolled and protruded as Truck poured it relentlessly on. He gasped for breath; his skull snapped back against the head-restraint. When he tried to shift it, Truck—feeling somewhat wilted himself—made a vast effort, steered his hand the full two inches from armrest to controls, and let it fall against the emergency thrust button.

My Ella Speed howled and quaked. Ben Barka made a choked, surprised sort of sound. His eyes opened wide; suddenly, a dark thin trickle of blood issued sluggishly from his left nostril. His tongue poked out from under his mustache like a misshapen fig. He passed out.

Captain John Truck, a haulage man from way back, who, in the dark womb of Annie Truck, had come down the infamous Carling Line in an unguided drone that was little more than a high-G tin can with refrigeration, held it until Tiny Skeffern was unconscious too, just to make sure. Then he settled into a parking orbit, said, "Never mess with a pro on his own ground, Colonel," and began to run checks on *Ella*'s misused hull. He'd been in tougher lifts. Egerton's Port got on to him by radio and wanted to know just what the boy-wonder Rocket Ace in the clapped-out Transit thought he was up to.

He grinned. "Sorry about that," he told them. "Wrong switch." Horse laughs all around.

A few minutes later, Tiny woke up and unstrapped himself. "That was a bit bloody hairy," he complained. He saw ben Barka. "Oh-ho!" he said. "Can I shoot him?" he asked, getting hold of the pistol, which had fallen down the side of his seat, and waving it carefully around.

"No, I'm going to put him out of the rear lock without a suit. It's something I just thought of," said Truck proudly. "He'll look good, going down on the night side. It's quite artistic, really."

Modesty, modesty.

Tiny examined ben Barka's congested face. "You hit me," he said coldly. He reached out and wiped the barrel of the Chambers gun down the Arab's cheek. "Go on, Truck," he said, "let me shoot him, eh?" He grinned ingratiatingly.

Truck took the gun off him, got his hands under the Colonel's armpits, and with difficulty hauled him aft, bruising the limp body in frequent collisions with bulkheads and pieces of machinery. "Sorry, ben Barka." Ben Barka, looking a bit of a mess and still out, said nothing. Truck sniggered. "You're going to enjoy this, ben Barka." And he described to the Colonel just how it might feel out there in the graveyard orbit, down along that firework trajectory. But when he arrived in the cargo bay he forgot all about that for a while; and by the time he had finished composing Fix's poor torn corpse, he'd decided to put ben Barka in a suit after all.

It would give him time to wake up and take an interest in the long drop.

He went forward, sealed the bulkheads, and evacuated the hold with no prayers. Out went Fix and ben Barka, in a white storm of Opener leaflets. Ben Barka's suit began to broadcast immediately and indiscriminately—an all-band distress call. "Damn," said Truck. "Isn't that just typical?"

Egerton's Port came through again. "Are you going to hang around all day, *Intestinal Revelation?*" said the duty officer. "We need that slot." Then, suspiciously: "Is there something wrong up there? I keep getting something that sounds like an SOS."

"It's a fault, actually," said Truck.

"It doesn't sound like a fault to me." There was a pause. "I've got someone here from the Port Authority. They want to know what an Opener vessel is doing hauling ironmongery to Sad al Bari—"

"Oops," said Truck.

"—not to mention going off the field like half a frigate squadron. Can you assist?"

Truck switched the communications gear off.

"Tiny," he said, "start the Dynaflows. We're leaving."

He fired up the navigational systems and set *Ella Speed* hunting like a three-dimensional compass needle until her blunt prow pointed at Alpha Centauri (or a spot where her sluggish internal processes remembered it to be). Tiny got the converters operating and came back up to the bridge. The exterior screens shimmered eerily, already probing out into the mysterious reaches of space.

"Right," said Truck. He cut in the Dynaflows, pushed the throttles about, and the old *Ella* howled down the Galactic freeway toward Centauri, on overdrive. "It's time we started getting some of our own back, Tiny."

There wasn't much hope of getting their own back on anything they found orbiting Centauri VII. Six or seven hundred miles off the wan gray face of that murdered planet, *Ella Speed* pushed her bows into the edge of the immense envelope of debris. Like the remains of huge animals in some valley too deep for dawn to reach, forgotten in a mist of frozen air, dead ships lay in futile ambush for Eternity. It was a dark, still zone, full of dead men drifting in slow curves among fused machinery, rat-trapped with the dull red embers of melted atomic piles, whole engine rooms like lumps of cooling slag, decaying in sullen aureoles of radio-static.

Deeper in, parts of the graveyard were still full of a white, fitful glare, a deceptive and piscine motion, as a few bolt-shaped UASR(N) cruisers slugged it grimly out with IWG. They were outnumbered and unformated, but they seemed to be fully occupying the Fleet—no vacuum commandos were out, communications silence were being observed. Truck tried frequency after frequency, found interference breaking like waves on a beach strewn with smashed and rusting armor at the candle-end of time. He picked up a few desultory syllables of a common Morphian dialect (enough at least to tell him who had done the dying out there), a moan, gunfire scissoring open a hull, distant, decaying, obsessive.

Ella Speed nosed on through a dream of violence. None of the combatants spotted her. Behind her, quite unaware of each other, the cruisers *Solomon* and *Nasser* skulked the graveyard like two pike after the same minnow. Truck never suspected he might be followed; perhaps he was too occupied by the young gunner from Parrot who had attached himself to the boat, tumbling lazily about her bow in some gravitational eddy, beckoning Truck and Tiny on with one stiff arm as if inviting them out there to share his cold peace. His intestines, covered in a hoarfrost of condensation, were spilling infinitely slowly from his ruptured pressure suit, but his insignia were polished and bright.

Truck couldn't tell which side he was on.

Centauri captured them, filled the screens like an accusation.

Only one planet was ever killed—

At the climax, the absolute fervid crux of MIEV bombardment, when defense is a rag of memory in a hot wind and the sky shakes with ionization, much of the surface water is stripped off the crust as "live" or superheated steam. The target vanishes under a cloudbelt several miles deep, there is a corresponding radical increase in its albedo—a last despairing heliograph of pain—

At five o'clock in the afternoon, July 4, 2180 A.M., the shroud covered Centauri and, as a good shroud should, spared the living the ultimate patient indictment of the dead. The General Gaws of the day turned from their bomb-room repeaters, satisfied, shrugging and yawning—perhaps even a little bored—and certainly wondering how they might turn one half of Earth into the same sort of mess without actually damaging the other beyond habitable minimums laid down by their biologists. Ever since that merciful occlusion,

Centauri had been a rubbish heap smelling of wet ashes.

By the time Dr. Grishkin, under the auspices of God and a well-known Galactic encyclopedia, came to sink his first bore in search of the bunkers, a lukewarm rain had been falling evenly over the new landscape for almost two hundred years. He found a planetary fen drained by vast slow rivers: shallow, stagnant meres, inconceivable acreages of mud-flat and salting—and every cubic foot of water filled with corrupt organic matter caught at some point between decay and dissolution, cloudy, brackish with old death. None of the continents resembled anything he found on the pre-Genocide maps; finally, it was beneath the human and animal silts of the estuaries and deltaic fans that he discovered water percolating through the slaughtered regolith in small secret streams, to the abandoned redoubts miles beneath.

There, he dug.

If he was a little mad to begin with, Centauri helped him further along the way. Nothing was alive there, unless you count the echoes of water. Water—and the wind, mumbling thick-lipped between the blasted, mysterious columns of masonry that poked up through the silt like fingers searching the air for the source of their long pain. In continual twilight, corpse-lights shone. The sky was green and gray, luminous with radio-decay products. Wind walking in a rubbish heap; dead lights and water; something was haunting Centauri, but it wasn't the Centaurans—

They were underfoot, even their due corruption suspended for some other time.

John Truck brought his boat home along a line of lavender flame, aiming for Grishkin's fifteen-figure reference. She settled steaming and contracting on a mudbank. Around her stretched the flat, unmarked flood-plain of some vast estuary off to the east. Nothing moved, nothing cried out or ran away. For a moment, the rain had stopped, but there was nothing out here to notice.

After a few minutes, Truck and Tiny emerged from the cargo bay done up in white carbon-fiber helmets, lead-glass goggles, and respirators like squat black snouts. Dark, shiny jumper-suits covered their bodies, which were full of anti-radiation drugs (prescribed) and amphetamine (unprescribed) from *Ella*'s over-stocked medical chest. Truck's Opener cloak flapped drearily in the wind. They stood around in silence, shuffling their feet and gawping at the inhospitable landscape; pointed in different directions and waved their arms at one another; then set off along the indistinct banks of a clogged watercourse.

Despite the amphetamine, Truck became quickly depressed—at first disturbed, then obsessed by the puzzling, fibrous consistency of the mud. When a tangle of thin bones, eroded and luminescent white, caught at his feet, he measured his length in the stuff. Thrashing about with revulsion, he kicked Tiny—who was irritably attempting to help—in the chest. "Do it yourself, then." He wiped himself off. Down there were nests of papery, corroded steel, lumps of stone, objects. He'd come up holding the broken handle of some piece of domestic apparatus, bright blue. He shuddered and threw it away. Tiny wasn't speaking to him.

It was a miserable excursion. Panting and withdrawn, they struggled upstream, looking for a sign—which they eventually found in the shape of Omega Shaft. By then, Truck was convinced by some half-dream that *everything was still going on down there in the silt*. He grew fearful that some initiation lay before him, some induction—inevitable by right of birth—into the strange decomposed half-life of his mother's race, an existence carried on in terms he couldn't quite imagine, in smashed houses among bits and travesties of human paraphernalia accumulated without logic after their drift down the watercourse.

Hidden in a freak fold of land, the Omega Shaft

complex of buildings—from which Dr. Grishkin had
begun the excavation which was to lead to the discov-
ery of the Centauri Device—was a sprawl of massive
precast concrete sheds, dull in color and filmed with an
unpleasant moisture. They served to house the generators, air-exchangers, and lift motors of the shaft, a collection of machinery that in operation caused the
ground to vibrate palpably. It was surrounded by a
chainlink fence into which was set a military checkpoint—a later addition of General Alice Gaw's.

Subsonics from the deeper levels of the bore itself
trembled in Truck's bones as he stood with Tiny just
beyond the reach of the arc-lights that surrounded the
compound, sweating in the heat from the nearest ex-
tractor outlet. A small, stubby ship was parked on its
tail in the gloom a hundred yards from the checkpoint:
hull scorched and deformed by a misjudged high speed
re-entry, venturis sunk fifteen feet into the ooze, it
wouldn't be leaving that place for some time. It was
empty, and a recent, hasty paint job hadn't obscured its
Opener livery. It had the air of something abandoned
by an owner whose mind was occupied elsewhere.

Truck hung about indecisively for a while, human
silt drying and flaking off his coverall. The gates (and
indeed the whole complex) seemed to be deserted. The
Fleet police weren't in evidence, and neither could he
detect any sign of military activity. He turned to the
dim, snouted little figure by his side, and pantomimed
an advance.

"I'm not going down there, mate—"

"Yes, you bloody are."

Tiny dragged his feet. In silence and moving slowly,
like the performers of some decadent choreography re-
hearsing without audience, they made it to the checkpoint. No one greeted them.

Two dead Fleet men lay face up in the mud by the
gates, their respirators torn off. Their goggles had been
shattered by the same explosion that had torn down
the fence, but they were otherwise undamaged. Their

eyes were fixed on Centauri's unforgiving sky, and it was hard to dispel the impression that something had issued from the shifting streams of silt and finished them off without a sound.

THIRTEEN

◼

In the Transit Lanes

Thoughtfully, Truck stole their guns.

The shafthead itself was littered with bodies in IWG uniforms, flung radially away from the center of a second explosion in postures stark and raw and strange. *Has someone been here already*, thought Truck. He stared around at the deserted sheds, doors banging in the wind, all those machines operating away unattended. It was coming on to rain again, thin gray curtains blowing between the buildings like wraiths. Truck attempted to scratch his head through his helmet.

"They've all had it," reported Tiny Skeffern, trotting doggily from corpse to corpse, feeling his amphetamines and elated at not getting into a fight, "I think." His voice, filtering out through the capillaries of the respirator, was flat and ghoulish.

"Come on, Tiny."

Truck left him to it and went to find the elevator mechanisms. The shafthead throbbed around him like a plucked string. Rain smoked at him unexpectedly round blind corners. Smears of rust on the walls. He found the lift cage, wiped absently at a film of moisture on the control panel.

DISENGAGE SECTION 5 AND PRESS FOR DOWN.

Under the earth again, he thought, *under the earth
again.* He felt divorced, disinterested. None of the murder at the shafthead seemed to have affected him; perhaps he was preparing himself for his encounter with
the Device, tying off unproductive sensory channels,
shutting out all irrelevant stimuli.

"Come on, Tiny."

They sealed the pressure doors of the lift cage, removed their respirators, and began their descent into
the crust of Centauri VII.

Truck had no more sense of homecoming. The lift
was slow, there was nothing to look at but Tiny. He
was suspended between realities, he was powered
down. Two miles deep, and he checked his dosimeter
to see if he'd picked up any of the active caesium
floating about on the surface. Two and a half, and he
imagined desultorily the earth groaning and shifting beyond Omega Shaft, swallowing him up. It didn't happen. He breathed on the wall of the cage and wrote his
name in the condensation.

"Oh, wow," said Tiny, snapping his fingers. "Under
the earth, what a blast."

The cage grounded gently. Truck worked the doors.

Shaft Zero: they entered the bunker-chain ("Stay here
and stop anyone who tries to come down," Truck told
Tiny. "Not on your life," said Tiny, shuffling his feet
and looking paranoidally over his shoulder) and almost
immediately became lost in a labyrinth of filter passages, transit lanes, and every conceivable sort of dead
end.

Plate movements during the later stages of the
MIEV bombardment had tilted the whole system, giving the tunnels a general easterly slope of five or six
degrees; some terminated abruptly at fault-lines, others
were waterlogged and impassable. In the rest, power
failure had left natural convection as the sole medium
of ventilation, and the air in them was hot, humid, and

heavy. Curious white clumps of mold, fat and glutinous, clung to the walls, giving the place a musty, evil odor. And while Grishkin's team had introduced fluorescent lighting to the major bunkers and some of the corridors, most were lighted only by the wan phosphorescence of the algae that dripped from the outputs of the ventilation plant like listless hanging gardens.

Despite the faulting, it was still a considerable warren. Truck and Tiny were quickly reduced to choosing their direction at random, wading half a mile at a time through eight inches of filthy water past alcoves full of enigmatic, corroding equipment, broached refrigerator units foul with partly decayed food, and doors that wouldn't open. The water trended east, chuckling around their feet to speed with mysterious echoes into the darkness ahead; they found a stream stronger than the rest and got some idea of following the direction of the current—but it only led deeper in, to pour finally over the lip of a fault into the absolute blackness beneath.

"Christ," whispered Truck, staring at the jagged, tumbled blocks of concrete, the great rock dome the Centaurans had never planned, the long fall. After that, they tried three of the major bunkers—found only rusting consoles and heaps of bones covered in a damp green deposit, each pelvis or femur labeled with a neat white tag ("female," "prepubescent male," "female adolescent") by Grishkin's archaeologists. By pure force of will, they rediscovered the bright fluorescent walkways, but none of them seemed to lead back to the bottom of Omega Shaft.

It was Tiny who first noticed that they weren't alone in the maze.

The transit lanes were full of pathetic alien junk abandoned by the survivors in the aftermath of the war: personal effects, robbed of place and purpose and cultural definition, hard to identify in terms of human equivalence as the belt-buckles, bookends, or athletic trophies they undoubtedly were. Tiny, with the brain of a jackdaw and all the moral sensibility of a maggot in a cemetery, had been pocketing the shinier bits as he went along, exclaiming "Look at that, Truck!" and "Hey, someone's kicking himself for losing *this!*"

When he found the Chambers gun, however, he didn't say a thing: just hurried up and stuck it under Truck's nose. Truck, sodding and blinding with frustration and expecting each new bit of loot to turn out to be a pocket nuclear weapon, tried to ignore him. He waved it urgently about. "Truck? Truck?"

"Look, what the hell are you playing at, Tiny?"—pushing the barrel aside. "If we don't get out of here soon, there'll be murder done—"

"I found it on the floor."

Truck grabbed it, in a spirit of self-defense, and had a look.

"You dropped it."

"Did I hell drop it. Look. Look. You can't tell me that's been down this bloody hole for two hundred years."

It hadn't.

Five yards further on, they stumbled over its owner.

He was stone-cold dead on the ground, a strand-wolf from one of ben Barka's howling personal deserts, clutching a double handful of mud and grinning savagely into the haunted water that flowed past his head.

Silence.

Truck and Tiny looked down at him, appalled.

Then footsteps, quick and muffled, like murder in an alley, skittered down a parallel tunnel: something was keeping pace with them, stalking them out of the phosphorescent dark.

"Christ, Tiny, he's still here!"

A junction loomed ahead.

"Move!"

Truck threw up his pistol, sent a bolt flaring and sizzling down the passage, shadows bickering along behind it. He couldn't see anything, but someone was out there. He dragged Tiny along after him, stumbling and swearing. "If he gets behind us—run, Tiny, run!"

They reached the junction and hauled up gasping—just in time to see the hem of a plum-colored cloak, violently agitated, vanishing into yet a third branch of the maze—

Neither of them felt very much like following it. Suddenly, the labyrinth was full of disturbing echoes. And plum is the color of Openerism.

But Openerism wasn't the end of it.

Fifteen minutes later, they came upon an entire unit of General Gaw's elite police, tumbled about the corridor like burst sacks. A Chambers bolt was still fizzing in the gloom, picking out slaughterhouse expressions on upturned faces, limning an indescribable mess of blood, scorch, and tangled limbs.

"Oh Jesus."

Tiny cocked his head. "Truck—"

Muffled Arabic whispered all around them on the complex acoustical fronts of the maze, a new ambush being set up at their very elbows. Distant but clear came the thump of grenade exchanges conducted through rock and concrete, faint shouts and cries. Ruin was loose beneath Centauri, and the bunkers were full of lost men blundering into invisible, desperate engagements.

Suddenly, and close: "There's a whole nest of the buggers in here! Look alive, lads! Let's have their trousers down! Where's that napalm!"

Truck shuddered. Bitter smoke had begun to drift down the empty corridor, nuzzling the corpses at his feet. He knew that voice, that awful gusto; he stood once more at the fulcrum, with the Galaxy shaking itself to pieces in a mad struggle for balance around him. "Come on, Tiny." He gazed warily round the abattoir. The dead police stared back, their polarized contact lenses grim and gray and unblinking. "I've got to find that bloody thing before they find me."

General Gaw's voice faded in the teeth of an Arab counterattack. Truck and Tiny, hermetic and apart, waded off hopelessly, deeper into the labyrinth, their shoulders hunched, the bunkers vibrant around them with the careless enthusiasm of the Dance—Opener, Arab, Israeli, celebrating the abandoned figures and extravagant rituals of violence.

Tiny Skeffern dawdled once too often, and they missed each other in the dark. Truck ran wildly up and down the transit lanes bawling "Tiny! *Tiny!*" not caring who heard. Only echoes answered him. He stumbled about firing off one of his Chambers guns at shadows until the *click-clack* of the empty mechanism brought him to his senses. Groaning, he leaned on a wall, put his forehead to the cold damp rock. Another dependent astray in the absolute broil of Circumstance.

Thereafter, he wandered with the gradient like a thin jackal, avoiding the larger concentrations of military and trying to surprise smaller ones by leaping out at junctions with bared teeth and oaths. He came to an area of seemingly endless geological disturbance, picking his way through a great choke of rubble and collapsed ceilings to the fault-line lip, where he watched the water spill over and down into the planetary chasm, not quite sure what he was seeing.

By that time, the Device itself was exercising control over the bunker maze; Grishkin, who'd mapped the system for IWG less than a year previously, was roaming it in a mad daze; Arab and Israeli alike were hopelessly confused. Truck was being cut out and guided toward an initiation he'd feared all along. He blundered along the fault-line, not thinking about much.

Twenty minutes walking brought him to the central redoubt, Grishkin's markers and lights, and an anteroom where luminous fungi cloaked the pipes and cables, and the wind hissed up out of Centauri like a voice.

From the anteroom the bunker doors, jammed open for about a quarter of their travel, made a tall rectangle of light, peculiar and leaping, as if some sort of fire was burning inside.

Eyes narrowed, he advanced.

He preferred light to darkness. If that seems trite, then remember that it was a decision made long before he stepped over the threshold of that bunker, and he meant it literally. Though he loved the streets after nightfall—the cold blind littered alleys of the docklands—he found his true environment out among the weird spectral particle displays of the dyne fields, and he had indulged himself under the kaleidomats of a hundred different Spacer's Raves on as many planets until his brain jumped and resonated to the beat of their strobes and their unpredictable shift of wavelength. None of that, however, prepared him for the Centauri Device.

It hit him, the moment he walked in, with a hammer of light and sound designed to crack his head open like a walnut, and the complex antenna of his central nervous system became abruptly a receptor for everything from a 30 c.p.s. epileptic flicker to the ultrasonics of nonspecific anxiety. It was like walking into a brick wall—lights, noise, radiation. Wild bursts of sound set fire to the contents of his skull; white light raped his eyes; pulsed infrared attacked his epidermal nerve endings—

The inhibitory neuron blocks of the CNS depolarized. Synapse points and potassium-sodium exchanges across the axon membranes flared up wildly, went into frantic activity then locked up solid; gate levels disordered, swooped, dropped to zero. Masses of irrelevant information stormed the sensory-motor cortex, smashing up through the thalamus and hypothalamus, howled triumphantly round the reverberatory pathways of the association cortex; nerve ignition reached a frenzy as something bypassed the damping effect of so-

dium ion supply deficiency and total constant excitation
was achieved; all three cortices blew out like candles in
the wind—

Somesthesis became nothing but a memory. Truck
was deaf, dumb, and blind—without feeling, without
volition. His nervous system had been captured and en-
slaved—

In the sub-millisecond period following this on-
slaught, while membrane potentials were bedding back
down into the millivolt range (after measuring in actual
volts and attaining terminal impulse propagation speeds
of more than four hundred miles an hour), the Device
got to work on his biology—

In the limited sense, Captain John Truck was no
longer there, conscious or otherwise: he could sense
nothing; he could not order his limbs, nor was he
aware of any limbs to order or any essential "Truck"
to order them—he existed solely as a metaphysic and a
problem of philosophy. In that, he was lucky. Pain
scorched up every nerve in his body, got in among the
cells and began to unwind the dextro-rotatory helix—
he didn't feel it; fingernails scraped samples from the
marrow of his bones, broached the canal of his back-
bone, and dabbled in his cerebrospinal fluid—he didn't
know; unbelievable methods of genetic exploration
were loose in his skull and gnawing like the larvae of
some parasitic wasp—he couldn't tell.

He couldn't tell. The Device, having research into
his mere chemical credentials well in hand, had turned
to psychometry—of a sort. Off in some debatable
realm where thoughts drag themselves around without
benefit of a single brain cell between them, Truck was
looking at pictures. Pictures—?

Everything he most desired: the secret of a new pro-
pulsion fitted to the *Ella Speed* (which was now somehow longer and slimmer, chased and inlaid, with a
white fire flaring at its stern)—immense brass wheels,
concentric and eccentric, which might enable him to

shoot through into unmapped Galaxies; a girl he had never seen, Ruth Berenici's scar transfiguring her face; the studio of Swinburne Sinclair-Pater, a poem in porcelain; a drug; Fix the bosun alive and well and baring his filed teeth, his stomach all neatly sewed up; finally, and very briefly, a scene at the Spacer's Rave—

Tiny Skeffern, immobile under the lights, a quirky smile on his lips—and a new music to replace the old, boiling from the H-line cabinets in a tidal wave fit to inundate the Galaxy—

Uncouth, clannish, lumbering about the confines of Space and Time with a puzzled expression on his face and a handful of things scavenged on the way from gutters, interglacial littorals, sacked settlements and broken relationships, the Earth-human has no use for thinking except in the service of acquisition. He stands at every gate with one hand held out and the other behind his back, inventing reasons why he should be let in. From that first bunch of bananas, his every sluggish fit or dull fleabite of mental activity has prompted *more, more;* and his time has been spent for thousands of years in the construction and sophistication of systems of ideas that will enable him to excuse, rationalize, and moralize the grasping hand.

His dreams, those priceless comic visions he has of himself as a being with concerns beyond the material, are no more than furtive cannibals stumbling round in an uncomfortable murk of emotion, trying to eat each other. Politics, religion, ideology—desperate, edgy attempts to shift the onus of responsibility for his own actions: abdications. His hands have the largest neural representation in the somesthetic cortex, his head the smallest; but he's always trying to hide the one behind the other.

Standing where John Truck now stood (smashed and overwhelmed by the Device), Dr. Grishkin, Gadaffi ben Barka and, later, General Gaw—all paid-up members of what they liked to call the human race—

had seen what they wanted most, grasped, and in grasping proved beyond doubt their genealogy. They would never see anything else.

While Truck, that mongrel of highly suspect lineage and scruffy demeanor, simply gazed a bit stupidly at what was offered and couldn't make up his mind. When he failed to grab at something with both hands (or even to show any exclusive preference—possibly because of his Centauran heritage, possibly because being a spacer and a loser he desired all and none of it), the Device pulled out its probes and let go. He was a borderline case, but blood will out, and old Annie's genes had done their work.

Truck measured his length on the concrete, twitching and whimpering. After a while, he crawled up to the thing and had a look. It had tested him and passed him, he saw it as its makers had seen it, and he knew he could operate it.

He still didn't know what it did—but then, he had his father's eyes, too.

He fell asleep out of pure physiological relief, and was waked he didn't know how much later by the sound of Chambers fire echoing down the transit lanes outside. He put the Centauri Device under his arm and left the bunker at a run.

He went through the antechamber blind and panicking, careening off the walls and trying to arm his remaining pistol one-handed. The last thing he needed was to be caught with the Device. His mouth tasted filthy, sweat crawled between his plastic suit and his skin. When he got to the outer door he slowed up and listened, stuck his head around hoping no one would blow it off. Pitch black in the transit lane. The fluorescents were dead. Nothing was moving out there.

A low crooning noise started up somewhere off to his left.

He peered into the darkness, seeing only slow violet patterns slipping aimlessly across the surface of his own eye. The noise again, bubbling up out of a wet place in the ground. His dark-adaption was slow in coming after the pounding taken by his CNS in the bunker. He cursed and blinked, cold premonitions burrowing through his head. He shivered, held his breath, released it in a great shout and leaped into the passage, gun first.

He found Tiny Skeffern a few feet down the corridor, lying with his face to the wall.

"Truck, oh Truck—"

Tiny was crying and sniffling with it, his blunt little fingers sidling up to the edge of the pit in his chest then scuttling away again like small terrified animals.

"Truck, it's huge. I want to be sick—" He curled up, rocking himself to and fro. "Where've you *been,* Truck?" He moaned with horror, looking at his wet fingers. "Christ, bloody Christ, bloody—"

Truck carefully turned him over onto his damaged side to give the unpunctured lung a chance—there was nothing else he could do but wait for the breathing to stop.

"It'll be all right, Tiny," he murmured. There were other things to say, but he couldn't say them. "It'll be all right."

"But there's a *hole!*" Tiny shuddered and wept. "Oh, why did I come down here? I'm hurt now—" His blue lips slid back off his teeth; every muscle in his body tensed and quivered. "Cloak!" he screamed suddenly, eyes wide. "Cloak! Cloak!" It was meaningless and eerie. He was silent for a long time. Then he said: "I'm always losing damn guitars," gave a great retching cough and relaxed.

There wouldn't be any more music.

Truck sat down beside the corpse and dropped the Centauri Device. It rolled away from him. He kicked out at it feebly in the dark. He was alone in a desert of entrails and greed, while another Tiny Skeffern chased the Vulpeculan melon down Ruth Berenici's staircase, on Earth a million years before. He put his hands over his face. A noise came from between them.

"Captain?"

A huge, dim apparition with a bulbous, snouted head stepped out of one of the equipment bays that lined the corridor.

Grishkin the mad priest had come to collect, diabolical in his plum-colored cloak and black radiation suit, his whole vast bulk heaving with the aftereffects of some mysterious exertion or compulsion. He stood staring at John Truck, his eyes enigmatic behind the smoky panes of his goggles. His respirator hissed evenly. Had Stomach been only another postponement?

"I kept coming back to the same place," he confided suddenly.

His voice was thick and clotted. "You know, I surveyed this place. I was never lost in it before." He advanced a few paces, still gazing hard at Truck. His arm whipped out, he clutched one of Truck's wrists with the energy of an ambition near-fulfilled. "I knew you wouldn't fail me, my son. The Ark has a special gravity, a—" He put his other arm around Truck's shoulders. "You must help me. There are "—his grip tightened—"others in the bunker."

He saw the Centauri Device.

He rubbed his fingers, clumps of raw white sausage, over his goggles; they left faint beads of perspiration on the blank lenses. Then, quivering and collapsing like a pig in a midden, he knelt before it. One fat hand fumbled at the neck of his coverall, pulled, unzipped it to expose his plastic windows. Things swam there, ferocious and triumphant. Head bowed, he revealed the processes of his soul.

Truck laughed nervously. "You're off your head, Grishkin." Then he remembered something. "Oh my God," he whispered: " 'Cloak!' "

He pivoted on one foot and with every ounce of force he could muster drove the toe of the other into Grishkin's neck.

"You foul old bastard!" he raged. "Why'd you kill him?"

Grishkin keeled over, still in a votive crouch; he swayed about, struggling to get up, but Truck was on him like a snake, full of poison and death, and had one hand fastened in the soft flesh at the nape of his neck. They fought for a moment in the echoing dark. Truck won—lugged him bodily over to Tiny's corpse. He was absurdly heavy. "You disgusting sod! Open your dirty head to *him!* Go on, *look at him!*" And he gave the Opener's right arm a savage twist.

Grishkin squealed and tore himself loose. He knelt over the Device again. "No," he said. "Forgive me," he begged it. "I didn't know what I was doing." He looked furtively over his shoulder at Truck, advancing with steely hooked fingers.

A grotesque ballet ensued, danced out in the depths of a dead planet to the accompaniment of animal grunts and howls: time and again, Truck forced Grishkin to face the dead musician, while on his part the priest, squealing and groaning with fervor, flailed his way back to the Device. He tried to pray. Truck's respirator fell off and he kept kicking Grishkin in the side of the head, shouting, "Pray to *him!*" and "You're not God!" Soon, both of them were covered in blood and filth, panting and incoherent. Neither could get the upper hand, and Tiny Skeffern stared indifferently up at both.

"We made a bargain, Captain! We made a bargain!"

Finally, Grishkin's cloak came off; he lay there, fat and dripping, his radiation suit in tatters. Truck saw only a great white slug, full of something neither human nor animal. He choked disgustedly and gave up.

"I should kill you, Grishkin."

Grishkin chuckled. "Too late for that, Captain." He came up off the ground with a Chambers pistol aimed at Truck's head.

Truck, abruptly calm, almost disinterested (understanding that Stomach *had* been a postponement, that all along there had only been one way to end the dialogue begun on Bread Street, Sad al Bari), shot him in the window of his belly.

"Captain," said Grishkin.

Truck pulled the Device from beneath the body while the sound of the shot was still echoing through the bunkers and wiped the stinking fluids off it with a corner of the Opener's cloak. He stared down at Tiny, shook his head. There was nothing to do then but make his way back to the bottom of Omega Shaft; for him, at least, the confusion or curse had been lifted, and he found it easily. He got into the lift and returned to the surface of Centauri, his mind such a howling waste that even Gadaffi ben Barka might have felt uncomfortable in it.

Halfway up, his dosimeter reported a mild overexposure.

It was a long journey back to *My Ella Speed*. He pushed one foot doggedly before the other through the ooze, rain slashing into his face, the whole desolate landscape a gray-green vagueness shifting and mutating as the water ran off the lenses of his goggles. He stumbled into streams and buried his elbows in stuff he didn't dare look at. He'd been out in it ten minutes before he remembered to put his respirator back on. He coughed miserably.

It was a long journey, and worth nothing in the end. When he got back to his boat, he found the command-cabin blown off it in a tangle of cable and melted girder, the rest leaning and blackened like a dead tree.

Two other ships were squatting on the mudbank, enormous and silent. The UASR(N) *Nasser,* its fifteen million tons half-submerged in the silt, never built to touch the surface of a planet—it was on its side, nose down, all its locks opened up by demolition charges and its cavernous insides gutted; and the IWG *Solomon* like a red and black moon embedded after some inconceivable collision with the planet, her gun ports gaping. She had done the dirty business on the other, it was plain: but she seemed deserted, too. They loomed a hundred feet, two hundred feet, into the dead wet air, heaps of dead commandos scattered in great pools of shadow under their hulls.

Truck stared numbly at it all. It was beyond him. He went over and put his back against the ruin of his *Ella,* slid down into a peasant crouch, and wrapped his ragged cloak around him against the rain. He shivered. He was trapped. Whoever came up out of the furtive slaughter in the bunkers would have him, and the Device. He closed his eyes and waited. *Ella* groaned and leaned a few degrees more, settling into the mud. He had nothing left.

Presently, he heard shooting.

He got up wearily. Off in the direction of Omega Shaft, uncertain in the rainy distance, small ominous figures boiled toward him, spread out across the floodplain and fighting as they came. Nothing was solved, then. He set off to meet them. What else could he do?

"Captain," said a cold, lively voice from behind him, "did Pater pull you out of the Snort for nothing—?"

FOURTEEN

The Third Speed

Down there in the bunker, the Centauri Device had killed him as surely as a Chambers bolt: his reflexes were gone. He spun round desperately, reaching for his gun but knowing he'd never have the time to use it.

No blow fell.

Instead, a long pale hand danced momentarily like a mirage an inch from his face. He stepped back instinctively, blinked. In that fleeting instant of blindness, something was altered; and when he opened his eyes again, the hand belonged to someone he knew, all the menace had drained from the toiling figures on the flood-plain, and even dim Centauri had brightened around him.

Across the palm of that quick hand there lay a single green carnation, long-stemmed and full of grace, beads of moisture clustered in its every fresh, intricate fold.

"We assumed you were dead," was all he could think of to say.

"I may have been," said Himation the anarchist. "Who knows?" And he laughed. The storm collar of his long black cloak was turned up, his wide-brimmed hat was pulled well down: all that could be seen of his face was a glitter of eyes. There was distant amusement in them, and some new thing besides, as if since Pater's death he had pursued in austere and derisive splendor a destiny quite different from any laid down for him. His hands, though, were still full of deft mischief and dishonesty, and discovered a small frog behind Truck's ear.

"Do you always travel with that, Captain? There, you laughed: I saw it distinctly." He looked down at the Centauri Device, sneered, and clasped Truck's free hand between both of his own. "I'm glad to see you."

"It doesn't affect you," said Truck. He wished he could see into the gap between collar and hat. "What do you see me carrying, Himation?"

"Why should I tell you?" He winked. "Other things have 'affected' me since we last met—"

For a moment, it seemed as if he might add something to that; but when he spoke again, it was to say:

"Come on, we have to get you out of here before"—shading his eyes against an imaginary sun and peering at the line of advancing men, who had come close enough for their hoarse metallic cries to be heard flapping over the intervening silt-flats like mechanical birds—"this lot catches hold of you." The line was thinner now, broken in places; a short, stumpy female figure trotted tirelessly at the head of it, strung with bandoleers of vomit-gas grenades and brandishing a pistol in each hand.

Himation grabbed Truck's arm. "Run, Captain!"

"Where to?"

But Truck already knew. They breasted a rise, Himation in the lead, his cloak billowing out behind him. A vast estuary spread itself before them, gray and calm, its far banks lost in a haze of rain. On it, some fifty yards from the shore, there floated a great golden ship. She was fully a quarter of a mile long; her raked and curved fins shone like sails in some exotic Byzantine wind; enamel work writhed deliciously over her lean hull, words in a lost language of rose stems.

" 'The wolf that follows, the fawn that flies,' " whispered John Truck.

"Look"— black shrouded arm, long white finger, an extravagant swirl of cloak—"they've sent a boat out for us!"

Himation flung up his arms. Playing cards showered from the mirthless air of Centauri, colored ribbons burst like fireworks from his fingertips; when he bowed right and left, small animals could be seen scuttling round the crown of his hat, while unruly red hair escaped its brim. Awed by his own genius, he shouted with laughter—in a kind of possessive joy, a laugh that went on and on.

When General Gaw struggled over the rise, she found only the echo of that laughter to comfort her, as *Atalanta in Calydon,* the last raider, shook off the water of the bay like a gilded hound and raced up into the sky on a blaze of white light.

"Where are we going?"

Centauri displayed its scars like Ruth Berenici in a Carter's Snort dawn. *Atalanta in Calydon* hung a thousand miles above that wan face, a cobalt blue light washing her exquisite alien metalwork, dead men bobbing round her hull in thankless, eccentric orbits. Himation drew himself up and turned from a long contemplation of the wretched embers of the battle. What he saw out there was anybody's guess, but it made him tense and withdrawn.

"A hundred thousand men died out there," he said, ignoring Truck's question. He fidgeted with a pack of cards. "I hate this place." He sighed with a kind of fierce, impatient compassion. "Why do they do it?" Then, in a low voice:

"You're going to Earth, Captain. I've only got one thing to do before—" He hesitated, then shrugged. "I'll drop you off there first."

"But—"

Truck guttered into silence. He'd expected more: if not a conjuring trick—a spiriting away—then at least some lessening of his responsibility. The anarchist's appearance had lifted his spirits; now they fell again, and he felt betrayed. He shrugged helplessly. "You aren't even coming with me? What can I do with it on my own?"

The Device was wrapped in the remains of his old Opener cloak in case it affected Himation's crew; it was heavy, and lately it had become slightly warm to the touch; a faint resonance, a distant thready pulse of vibration, crawled beneath its skin. Did it arm automatically on the identification of Centauran genes? He was alone with it again, and without hope.

"We should dump it, Himation. Right over the edge, where nobody'll ever find it again."

"It must end on Earth, where everything ends up. Otherwise there'll be more of this—" He nodded at the orbital graveyard outside, the corpses floating like wet cardboard on dark water.

"I can think of a time when you'd have laughed at a few killings. It was you who licked the knife at Carter's Snort, not me. You might at least come to Earth to help me, if Earth is so bloody important. Tell me why you won't."

Alarm bells filled the ship.

Himation whirled to the screens, snapping his fingers at the quarterdeck crew. "Captain, I—later." He glanced over his shoulder at Truck for a moment, shrugged eloquently. He conferred with his fire-control room.

"We have a strong trace in the one-fifty mile band, Himation. She's lifted from Centauri. Do we fight?"

"We leave."

Atalanta in Calydon throbbed and moaned with the power buildup. Waxy blue light drowned the bridge. On the screens, the image of the graveyard quivered and broke up, those wretched hulks taking on for a precious instant the gaudy colors of the orchid, the forms of imaginary beasts. With this transfiguration, panic jumped out of a dark hole and shook him like a dog with a dead rat.

"Tell me *why!*" he shouted across the bridge. "You owe me that!"

Heads turned toward him. *Atalanta* toppled over the thin edge of space and into the dyne fields.

Himation relaxed. He crossed the bridge and said, "All right, Captain. It's hard—I don't belong here any more—you can't imagine—" He shook his head, made a dismissive gesture with one hand. "All this—" Finally, it tumbled out:

"Captain, I've been outside the Galaxy since we last met!"

"Listen, Captain," he continued: "you know how it was at the end of Pater's last fight—

"*Atalanta* was lost under the Arab guns, running like a fawn. I heard Pater cry 'Dyne out!' I could see him flaring along in my wake, trying to draw their fire. But my bridge was exploding with mad light, and long reaction guns had breached our hull. He came in time and again, sowing torpedoes, spouting fire 'Dyne out!'—but his forward batteries were shot away, the *Green Carnation* was ripped open down her length like a golden pike. He stormed past one last time, then I saw him flicker—'Dyne out!'—and fade. Twice, three times, he wrestled with the dyne fields. He was superb: no other man could have forced that wreck into the Impossible Medium. Rolling like a bitch, still shooting, she vanished.

"I tried to follow. *Atalanta* clawed with dreadful energy at the fabric of space, desperate to push herself clear. Her bridge trembled with ionization—metal ran with a fire that consumed nothing! I knew we were wedged like those pathetic hulks we had seen earlier in the battle, mere specters caught on the edge between two hypothetical eternities. Then I had her through—flip!—like a grape pip flicked across a darkened sickroom. I sweated. Captain, I swear I prayed with my relief. But when I noticed my bridge circuitry, I knew I was no longer in control: it had melted to slag! My crew were helpless—

"*Atalanta* had taken over.

"None of our own equipment was operating; instead, the alien machinery shivered with an intense white light. The hull seemed to melt and withdraw—we swam in senselessness—all solid forms vanished in amazing twists and contortions; and when we looked at one another, aghast, we were no longer men! *Space* had somehow entered the ship, and was crawling through us in slow, luminous waves. We were steeped in it: we were birds of paradise, we wore the masks of gilded deep-sea fishes in some tideless ocean, we were glass effigies with infinitely thin, attenuated limbs—

"I knew we would die, if we were not already dead (and trapped forever in some unimaginable posture of unreality). But even as the thought formed, space coughed us up—

"And out into darkness!

"Nothing moved beyond the hull. I rushed to the screens—they were dark; we restored our circuitry, but they remained dark. We pushed out sensors and probes—they recorded a terrifying distant trace; we regained power, we spun her like a compass needle to face it—

"There before us lay the Galaxy, faint as an afterimage crawling across a dead man's eye!

"We've seen it, Captain, from the outside. Aboard *Atalanta,* we've seen them all: Andromeda, M32, NGC205 for our first, hesitant, skeptical journey—and later to others so unbelievably far out that they have no names. There is a third level of Space, Captain; a Third Speed. I've spoken with its denizens, and learned the glory of the moth in the lamp-bowl—can you un-

derstand why I hate this rubbish heap, with its putty
brains and feet of lead? I've been beyond!

"Since that day, *Atalanta in Calydon* has flown herself: we simply navigate. We brought her in triumph
back to Howell after that first wild flight—only to find
Pater still and cold in his peacock room, yourself gone,
no one knew where. That fastidious prince! His life
was the purest fabrication of Art, the most gilded of
lies—but I loved him. We outfitted the *Driftwood of
Decadence* as his bier; we filled her with prints and
porcelain and fans of the utmost sophistry; all Howell
gathered to watch her final firework leap into the un-
known. She went off on a sigh, on a whisper, like a
dream of unaccustomed beauty.

"She's traveling still, Captain, at the Third Speed;
Pater may have reached the edge of the Universe itself
by now. He deserved nothing less.

"After that, all I could do was come in search of
you—

"I found a trace of you on Stomach, a memory in
the eyes of an androgyne whore. But the trail was cold.
I spent a week stalking the city of Intestinal Revelation, dressed in a stolen Opener cloak. From there, I
tracked you to Avernus. Avernus—the worst place in
the universe! But I ceased to fear for you when I heard
that some lunatic Opener novice with a gun had wiped
out Chalice Veronica and his whole Paraphythium operation in a single night. And I was up there in the
parking orbit—not alone—to watch you blow your
hatches on not one body but two.

"You would seem to have become something of a
nemesis—"

"One of them was Fix," said Truck. He felt bitterly angry: for Pater, for himself, for what they had so nearly
achieved on that last ride into death, with the *Green
Carnation*, her heart burst, falling to bits around them;
and for what he had in exchange—dead friends, and
the Device like a yoke across his back.

"They've killed Fix and Tiny now. I haven't anybody left." Himation had rescued something from the night, but Truck's boots were full of lead. He felt like crying, but, "I still owe them for that," he said, with as much defiance as he could muster. "And if I did for ben Barka, I'm glad. I meant to."

"But you didn't, Captain. That parking orbit was somewhat crowded, I'm afraid; and everyone in it there to watch you: *Nasser, Solomon, Atalanta*—oh, we made a fine procession later, following you to Centauri. Ben Barka was plucked out of the murder trajectory by his own flagship. He was in the fight that destroyed *Nasser* and the *Ella Speed;* he was in the bunkers. Like the General, he is a survivor."

Truck was aching in every bone, whether from weariness or misery or his untreated overdose he neither knew nor cared. He sat down on the deck. He put the Device down beside him, stretched out his legs, and examined his hands. What could he do? All along, his gestures of defiance had been crude and fruitless. He stared desperately up at the anarchist.

"They'll hound me till I'm dead, Himation."

No reply.

"What do you imagine I can achieve on Earth? I don't even know what this thing does."

Himation shifted uncomfortably, looking at the hull above Truck's head. "None of this means much to me since I went out there. Space is a habit." His eyes clouded, probing out past the hull. "Pater saw something in you, some strength that neither he nor I possessed. He wanted you to take the Device and do with it as *you* chose. He thought that that action in itself, whatever the purpose of the thing, might be enough. You understand? Your importance has always lain in your skepticism.

"And he intended you to take it to Earth. That's the only reason I came back at all. I hate this place after what I've seen outside."

"What *have* you seen?" said Truck angrily. "Tell me

that." But he wouldn't explain, and for a while each man was absorbed in himself—Truck rubbing his hands nervously, full of self-pity, while the anarchist gazed at the flying streamers of illusion on *Atalanta*'s screens, at his crew—at anything but Truck's face.

Finally, Truck said: "You don't know that Pater was right. You don't even know what he meant. Neither of us do. I'm not even sure he did."

Himation shrugged. "No," he admitted.

Truck shivered. He couldn't control his hands: Independent, they moved gently over the Device, taking its thready, secret pulse. "Himation, I want to go with you," he whispered almost inaudibly. He jumped to his feet. "Please. You owe me that. You're using me, Pater was using me, just like the rest of them—!"

But Himation had turned away, and pretended not to hear—whether out of consideration or embarrassment, Truck couldn't decide.

Midnight on the German Strip. All real life had fled this place with the Rat Bomb wars. Hard frost and a lunar desperation lay on the land from Lübeck south to Plauen. Coburg and Marburg, Dresden and Magdeburg—white ruins under a cold sky; Hanover and Hamburg, names on acres of rust and concrete, old weapon pads, interconnecting pits and craters. Somewhere through it ran an old, lost frontier.

Beneath a bright acidic moon, John Truck stood with Himation the anarchist on the lower slopes of the Brocken. In the shadow of the mountain—confirmation of an old despair—lay *Atalanta in Calydon*. The northeast wind, full of ice particles and the smell of the cold gray Baltic brine, whipped Himation's cloak out like a flag.

"This is as close as I can get you to Göttingen." The wind boomed over the bare rock above, stole his voice, and howled off with it to the frozen nightmare of Thüringen.

"What the hell am I supposed to do there?"

"There are people, at least. You couldn't have expected me to put her down at Albion."

Truck blew on his cupped hands. "No." He set his back to the wind—he would let it blow him along: when had he ever done anything else?—and hunched his shoulders, looking along the valley. "I'd better go before I freeze to death." Nothing moved down there in the wind. Boulders or buildings, everything was covered with *verglas* and frozen snow.

"Look," said Himation, holding out his hand, "I'm sorry if this seems hard—"

Truck laughed bitterly. "It's hard," he said. "And it's no good me saying that I don't blame you, because I do. But"—he grinned—"I'd do the same myself." He touched the anarchist's hand briefly and walked quickly away, before he was tempted to say anything more. He'd gone about ten paces when Himation called "Wait!"

He went back.

Himation had taken off his cloak and hat. He was thin and hollow-chested, younger than Truck had imagined, perhaps nineteen or twenty. His great shock of red hair and dead white face made an astonishing contact with his bright blue eyes. Shivering and jogging from one foot to the other, he bundled the clothes up and held them out.

"It's bloody bitter out here—and I shan't need them any more."

He looked suddenly diffident and boyish.

Truck took them from him. "You don't look much like your father," he said.

Himation smiled uncertainly. "My father? Oh, *Pater*." He laughed. "Did he tell you he was my father?"

Truck shrugged.

"It doesn't matter." He held up the bundle. "Will these do tricks for me?"

"Who knows?"

Himation smiled shyly. He reached out and plucked

a green carnation from behind Truck's ear. "I'd better have this back. Good-by, Captain."

He made off toward his ship—stooped, lean, full of energy, as if he'd been newly released from some prison. A flurry of snow whirled round him, like the prop to an illusion.

"Tell them to look for me in Andromeda," he called.

He raised his hand. A flower fell from it and was snatched away by the wind.

Truck slung the cloak around him, buttoned its collar, and pulled down his hat. He retrieved the Centauri Device from a small puddle it had melted for itself in the snow, and went into the darkness of the valley, alone. Behind him, he heard *Atalanta in Calydon* lift into the air.

" 'The wolf that follows, the fawn that flies.' "

He didn't dare look back.

Perhaps four hours later, exhausted and covered with snow, he blundered into an IWG early warning post somewhere in the derelict suburbs of Göttingen. "I've come to give myself up," he said, and peered bemusedly into the twilight of the operations room, the skin of his face smarting in the sudden warmth.

Thin, unnatural faces squinted back at him through a haze of tobacco smoke, underlighted by the backwash of green light from plotboard and ultrasonic map: red-eyed, eerie and frightened, like underground animals blinking up from burrows—

After a month in one of those places, waiting for the war to start an operator begins to see things up on the empty slopes of the Vogelsburg, where nothing has stirred for over three centuries; he imagines massive troop movements among the drowned stormcellars of Braunshweig and Salgitzer; he discovers an intruder in every silent fall of powdered mortar in a vacant city. He wears five keys chained to his neck—used in a proper sequence, they will kill the world.

After two months, he can hardly remember in which order to avoid using them—

Halfway through the graveyard shift, tired and sick among a litter of disposable plastic cups, all they saw was a faceless, threatening figure in a dark cloak, snow swirling behind it; and under its left arm an indistinct, shifty object that somehow chafed at their irritated eyes. All they heard it declare, in a muffled, deadly voice, was: "I've come—"

A Chambers gun spluttered in the gloom.

Shadows hurled themselves over the walls, jerky and panic-stricken.

"You bastards!" screamed John Truck, and clutched at himself in astonishment. He snatched his own gun from his boot and dived behind a radar module.

It was a short exchange. At twenty-five or less, photophobic and with the ulcers of a sour responsibility eating at their insides, they were already old men. He killed them all, lay for a minute behind the console, whimpering. When he came out, he saw that some of them were clutching their keys, while others simply stared relieved at the low ceiling, blood on their rolled-up shirtsleeves—each one thankful, perhaps, that it was only his own death and not the world's.

Truck moaned. He was seeing in halftones. "You should have given me a chance," he murmured, supporting himself against the doorjamb.

Outside, the wind was gusting up to Force Eight. There was a small VTOL pad behind the building. Halfway to it, he collapsed, lay there surprised under the sickening slow sweep of the ultrasound antennae and examined his wound. The bolt had eaten its way into his ribs, low down on the right side. The fire had gone out, but something was leaking from a fist-sized hole.

"Oh God," he prayed. "Oh, Christ."

He leaned on one elbow in the frozen slush and retched with fear. He couldn't feel anything down there, no pain, nothing. He wiped his mouth, looked up. A single aircraft was on the pad. He hauled himself laboriously toward it, hissing and gasping every time his right side touched the ground, out of horror that he'd get something in the wound.

He hadn't once let go of the thing under his arm. It was warm enough now to give him comfort in the wild night.

FIFTEEN

◙

The Last Anarchist

It was 6 A.M. Christmas morning in Carter's Snort when John Truck brought the stolen VTOL into the abandoned rocket-mail field at Renfield Street. Snow was on the ground, Sauchihall was full of crepe paper streaming in the wind; in warm entrances and fuggy hallways, the port ladies were singing carols to their customers.

He came in hard, failing to kill all the vehicle's forward momentum. It slewed drunkenly over the concrete, falling apart, to fetch up finally with a surprised grunt against the base of an old launching gantry. For a minute or two it pushed itself in a grinding, obsessive circle round the obstacle, like a blind and dying crab on an empty beach. Then the engine gave up, and there was only a thin hiss of low-pressure air escaping from a fractured puff-pipe in the wing.

Off in the dark, undercarriage wheels rolled toward the edge of the field, bouncing and spinning like tossed coins.

Truck let his forehead rest against the landing-computer display. He was delirious, full of morphine and amphetamines from the VTOL's survival kit; his lower chest was an awkward, pulpy bag of pain; visions came and went like minutes of wakefulness in a week of sleep. "We made it, Pater," he muttered.

After a while, he raised his head, feeling a pressure, a radiation on the back of his neck. He couldn't see Cor Caroli, but he knew it was up there somewhere, one bad eye winking sardonically down on all murder and death. Cor Caroli, dog into wolf. He pondered his own transmigration, accomplished somewhere between Sad al Bari and Centauri VII. Where had his old body gone? He was sick now, but he was all wolf.

The Device whispered urgently to him. He ignored it as much as he could, occasionally waving one preoccupied, impatient hand in front of his face as if to dispel the persistent fevers that hovered round his skull. It showed him movies of Omega Shaft. He was gray-faced, he was burning up. It cost a century of effort to drag himself out of the cockpit. Civilizations rose and fell while he blundered up and down Renfield Street, trying to remember who he was.

"I'm coming," he said petulantly. "Don't rush me."

The Snort hid coyly from him in a maze of side streets, then jumped out with no warning at all. Truck closed his doors to it——neon, mercury vapor, a piddle of sleet coming from somewhere up above the buildings to light up in the glow from the barfront windows—but it got to him somehow, warm and alive in the teeth of the compass wind, and guided him through the murk along thoroughfares that led only to places he didn't want to go. He staggered on, blue-lipped and anoxic; and at every corner, at every landmark, he picked up passengers to ride the lower decks of his skull—

The Boot Palace on Sauchihall: echoing and sour, haunted by a feeble echo of music. Its walls glimmered at him. Tiny Skeffern stood in the shadows there, kicking an amplifier in ghostly pique, shrugged, climbed aboard—as if Truck were some biological *Ella Speed* to lift him out and away from that place. Fix the bosun

stumped after him. "We'll need big protection, boss."
And settled down inside to keep watch through Truck's
runny eyes—

West Central Detention: damp and dirty and down
by the river. Out on the street among the rubble—
maybe even hoping to be arrested and taken in to
where he felt comfortable. Singing and weaving: "You
look like I feel, Cap'n." He turned away in that classic
6 A.M. pose, one hand flat against the wall to steady
himself, head down crucified to vomit emptily. "Give us
a lift, bosun, eh?" And he climbed on, too, winking
and nodding. Behind him came Picking Nick and Angel and Og—caught holding for a friend, vagrant and
eccentric—judged, sentenced, and condemned to become graffiti on a wall—

Bayley the Wrecker's: wind moved among the broken spines, chains clanked, but the specters there were
tender enough to hurt him in regions beneath his delir-
ium. Angina Seng smiled and winced—"I could have
gone for you." Out among the giant metal, Annie
Truck, port lady from way back, waddled toward him
with dignity, massively up the stick with his own self,
materializing from the scattered ribs of a refrigerator
ship. Wherever he looked, sheep's eyes full of regret
met his own—

They came to him whether he'd known them or not,
until he thought his skin would burst from the pressure
of their essence: every loser, every spacer who had
ever lifted from a planet; every tired mute refugee who
ever came down the Carling Line; the confused, the
accused, the misused—the spiritual, moral, and metaphysical basket cases of fully two hundred years. They
crowded—their odors of loss, all their heart-luggage,
all their badges of despair—into the space behind his
eyes, to stare out passive and inarticulate at the hinterland of all hinterlands: the displaced, the disgraced, the
arrested, the outcast and unarmed, all his longtime
dependents coming home to that inevitable junction

after who knew what long uncomprehending trudge across the years and light years—

The new Centaurans.

Down by the prison he leaned over the parapet of a bridge. The river disappeared beneath him, oily and magical, constantly renewed. He owed them nothing, he owed them everything, and they were still pouring in. He knew he'd been drained, turned into an empty and purified vessel to receive precisely this draught, this visitation—"What do you want?" But they simply stared on. What could he give them? How long could he hold together? He could only drag himself away from the bridge and take to the streets again, going— where?

Four hours later, Ruth Berenici Truck, rising late after a lonely night—turning the other, unscarred cheek to face the world as she opened the door—found him on her doorstep. Where else should he be, now? He was curled up tight round his wound or the Centauri Device, and snow was in the hollows beneath his cheekbones.

He looked up at her with a pain so intense as to wake every echo of her own and said distinctly, "No more. I'm full up. I'm hurt, Ruth. Can we come in?"

"All you have to do is be born," he said later, trying to explain himself. And when she showed no sign of understanding (because you have to be crazy to live in the general rather than the particular). "I can feel them in me. All us losers are Centaurans."

Ruth Berenici sighed. She took away the chlorhexidene aerosol, the sulfanilamide powder, and the fouled dressings. "What do I have to do to get in there?" she called from the kitchen. Reappearing in the connecting doorway, slightly stooped, arms folded across her stomach: "Die?" She went and frowned over the Centauri Device, continued almost absently, "Is there a place for the living in your cosy little colony?"

"Ruth."

"I'm sorry. Truck, what is this thing?"

"Whatever you see." He laughed, coughed. "It's an operator of entropy."

Outside, it was afternoon: gray. Clouds raced through the sky. He was propped up on his side on the bed, where he'd been since she manhandled him in (floppy and apologetic, nothing new).

The cough went on and on, like a paper-shredder working in his chest cavity. She had plugged the hole, but the bolt was still in there; deflected downward by a rib, it had passed through the bottom of one lung and lodged in the upper part of his abdomen, where it could be seen pressing up against the scarred plastic of his Opener window (looking at which for the first time, Ruth had merely compressed her lips and shaken her head—just another funny hat). As the last of the morphine wore off, the pain was becoming unbearable. He wondered idly if the ghosts in his head could feel it, too.

"They're late," he said presently, watching the twilight creep out of the high corners of the room.

He waited the afternoon away, immobile, his sunken eyes following Ruth Berenici as she moved restlessly round the room. He was trying to find ways of apologizing to her for being himself—even now, when they both so desperately needed him to be something else.

He slept a little. When he raved, she held him down; when he woke moaning, "You could go to a hospital," she begged.

"They're all using me!" he screamed. Use and owe: was it the only language? "Don't cry, Ruth." He rolled onto his back, stared fearfully at the ceiling; dropped off again, to relive Pater's fatal flight, the Cowper furnace, the Central Bunker—to enumerate all the coffins he had already occupied.

"John!"

Pigs squealed in some dream, wriggling in comical flabby fear from under the knife, like mad Grishkin in a bunker; but the squeal he woke to was of brakes, and

in the street outside. Half a dozen armored vehicles
had arrived beneath Ruth Berenici's window—doors
slammed, turbines raced up and down their power
curves then died abruptly.

"John!"

Both ends of the street were sealed off. From down
in the hallway came a curious muffled thud as a small
explosive charge knocked the outside door off its
hinges. The stairwell rang with falling debris, then footsteps. A two-hundred-watt amplifier truck began to
broadcast garbled Martian commands into the night.

"John!"

At first, he didn't realize what was happening. He
struggled up out of the abattoir with his mouth hot and
gummy, worked his tongue round it, blinking at the
ceiling, where streetlight made an asymmetric screen.
Ruth's dark figure bent over him, caught at his shoulders. *"John!"* He shook his head. It wouldn't clear.
Then, on the second flight of stairs, someone manufac-
tured an illusion of resistance from the shadows—fired
off his Chambers gun.

"IWG!" yelled Truck. "Christ!"

He clawed at Ruth's hands and flung her away from
him. He threw himself off the bed and rolled across the
floor, scooping the Centauri Device up as he went.
Ruth was sobbing softly somewhere off by the window,
and all around him the hinterland seemed to be full of
sirens—faint, distant, of impersonal intent, rising and
falling on the compass wind like an anxiety on the edge
of reflection.

With sweat pouring into his eyes and his teeth chat-
tering, he dragged himself to where he could set his
back against a wall and face the door. Ruth looked
desperately down into the street. "Truck?" she
pleaded.

He was on the edge of a dark hole. "Ruth, I—"
They were on the landing outside, kicking lumps out of
the wall while they waited for an order. "Ruth—" It
was too late for any of that.

He bit his lips.

The door caved in.

"I promised we'd meet again, sonny," said Alice Gaw complacently.

She stood in the doorway, squat and brutal, dust and fumes from the explosion downstairs drifting up the stairwell to settle on the landing behind her. She seemed preoccupied. "God, what a leprotic hole this place is." She was back in the black short skirt of her WA uniform, stomach sagging over the leather belt that held her holster up.

She studied the room amusedly for a moment, then sauntered in and stepped aside. Fleet policemen hurried past her and began to go methodically through it, breaking up the furniture with careful efficiency. Truck coughed dismally, the paper-shredder at work in his lung again. Now it had happened, he felt curiously remote. The General looked him over, chuckled.

"I see they made a bit of a mess of you in Göttingen." She shook her head. "Was it worth it—? You might have started a *real* war this time. If it hurts, I'll get a quack in as soon as we've got this little business over with."

"Don't bother, General. I'll survive."

She ignored him, absently watching the Fleet men as they tore up some loose boards. "Look sharp, you lot," she chided them, "or I'll do it myself. You haven't got all day." Her features went lax. Still looking away from him: "I'm not sure you will, Truck. And I don't have all that much time here myself." Her one eye focused on him suddenly. "Frankly, you've made it a shade difficult for me with the people I answer to. They're sending me over to the Strip to sort out the cock-up you caused there—"

She ran a hand through her hair. Her attention wandered. "Truck, my love, why haven't you introduced us?"

And she smiled over at Ruth Berenici—

—who, emerging from whatever personal nightmare found its expression in the street below only to find herself in a more public one, cried, "Who are *you?* How can you just burst in here like this— Animal!"

Alice Gaw cocked her head to one side like a small deformed bird. "My my," she said. She planted herself, feet apart, in front of Ruth and stared up at her with an expression of chilly intimacy. "Look, lovie," she began evenly, "I like you. I liked you on sight. If I hadn't, I might have resented that."

She reached out lazily and captured Ruth's lower jaw in one hard hand. She tutted sympathetically.

"That's a nasty scar. No, don't be shy. Let's have a look at it."

And, with the muscles of her forearm trembling slightly, she forced Ruth's marred profile into the light.

"You know, that really is nasty," she mused. "Look duckie," she murmured confidentially, "I'll tell you what: I'm fifty-six years old, and I've been on my feet all bloody night long. Just you keep on the right side of me, and I'll keep on the right side of you. Hm?"

"Leave her alone, General," said Truck quietly.

Since his trip across the long floor, it cost him pain to breathe, to speak—even to concentrate. A warm brown fog had crept up while he was unaware and filled the room: events filtered through it to him only after a peculiar delay. There was a salty taste in his mouth.

"You can leave her alone, now."

The General relaxed her grip. Ruth Berenici twisted out of it and fled whimpering toward the door, her long body ungainly with fear. One of the Fleet men caught hold of her. "Just see she doesn't do herself any harm, lad," said Alice Gaw. Tiredly, gazing out of the window: "All right then Truck—where is it?"

Keeping his eyes open had become difficult—some kind of grit had worked up under the lids. He got the Centauri Device out from under his cloak, painstakingly stripped the charred and blood-stained rags of that other garment off it, and set it on his lap. It didn't look much.

"What do you see, General?" he asked. He shrugged painfully. "I don't think I really want to know. No— I'd stay put if I were you. You're talking to a Centauran."

And she was.

His eyes closed. In twos and threes, driven across airless spaces by a wind no one can name, coming the long way round from the gutter-edge outposts of the Galaxy, they were still drifting into his head, pressing up against the shuttered windows to await a glimpse of that crucial room—a direct, inevitable link between the Centauri Genocide and the deaths of all his friends.

All us losers are Centaurans—and that conceit established his ancestry more effectively than any biochemistry. Eyes open again he discovered General Gaw squinting across the room at him.

"You'll regret that, sonny," she promised. And: "It doesn't look like the thing I saw in the bunker."

"I think it armed itself when I picked it up. You only saw its dormant phase."

Something caught at his throat; he swallowed, coughed, tasted blood again—and this time the contraction of his diaphragm muscles triggered off a quick, uncontainable spasm of his lower intestine—he'd dislodged the spent Chambers bolt and it had fetched up somewhere in the mess behind his window. "Oh," he whispered. "Oh, shit."

Then, hearing a sharp intake of breath, a scrape of feet, "I can set it off at any time, General!" He raised his head slowly from where it had slumped on his chest. She had moved in a couple of yards and stood before him in a relaxed professional crouch. "What made you think you'd be any closer to owning it when you found your Centauran?"

She showed her teeth.

"Come off it, Truck. I'm your only chance. From

the stink in here, I'd say somebody stuck one right in your guts. What's to stop me waiting? You're going to die, Truck."

"I promise you I'll fire it off if that looks like happening, General. I've got nothing much left to lose."

Confounded, she withdrew; and through the thickening fog he watched her confer with one of her policemen, who presently nodded and left the room.

"Ruth?" said Truck, but she didn't hear him. He wiped his hand across his mouth, and it came away wet and shocking. Successive storms of fear and pain and vertigo swept through him, each crisis leaving him weaker—while the Centauri Device, a high, electrical voice, vibrated in every cell of his brain.

There wasn't much left of him up there—a thread of memory, the odd little bit of personal stuff. It came down to streets and faces in the end, scraps that still defined him, a fading signal from the hinterland. He was a proxy, he was a junction box—

"I'll tell you what *I* think, Truckie."

He had almost fallen asleep. He peered about the room. He was deadly tired.

"I think you're waiting for your gyppo friends to pull you out of this. If you are, forget it. Bring him through, lads!"

When "he" came through, under the watchful eye of the Fleet, he was much changed. Occupying the same space as he occupied, coextensive yet divorced, breathing—if it could be said to breathe—the same air as he breathed, came his long-time specter.

The flat and watchful planes of his face were simple implications of the bleached and jawless skull beneath, pouring fine sand from the sockets of its eyes, generator and epicenter of all deserts; resident in the marrow of his spine were other vertebrae—scattered beneath a dead tree, polished, mourning; as he moved, he shed brittle echoes of past deserts and intimations of the Desert to Come. And, far off in his liquid brown eyes—broken white columns, like reflections in a failing cistern—

Ben Barka. The ghost encompassed him. It wore his uniform without pity.

"General—" The promptings of a parched wing. "I am a prisoner of war. This is a charade. I object to taking part in it."

"Cut it out, Gadaffi," advised General Gaw. "I know you." And she gave him a breezy grin. He shrugged infinitesimally and seemed to forget her. "What I *don't* know, Truck," she went on, "is what deal you two scabs cooked up in the Avernus parking orbit—"

Ben Barka chuckled sourly. "General—"

"Speak when you're spoken to, ben Barka. Truck, you aren't denying that you shipped him up to a rendezvous with *Nasser* in that sardine can of yours?"

"There was no deal, General; there was no rendezvous. He killed a friend of mine." Truck couldn't understand what she was getting at. "You must be mad."

But it was hardly worth it. Her voice rose and fell, endless, accusing, endlessly beside the point; ben Barka's deserted husk replied with the dry song of the locust; above them both, electrical, crystalline, angelic—the voice of the Centauri Device reminded how certain things might be done, ushered him, a particle of human silt down the long slow watercourses of Centauri VII.

Where at last he might be initiated into that queer half-life beneath the ooze, the purgatorial suspension of his mother's race—

He woke up abruptly, in a panic because he thought the Fleet men were ushering ben Barka from the room.

"Wait!" he cried. "General, make me a bid!"

She had crept closer while he dozed, hands tense and outstretched. Now she looked wonderingly down at him. "It's you who's out of his mind, duckie. We've got you now, unless you do something quickly—" She sounded almost sympathetic. "I wonder if you'll have the guts to work that ruddy thing?"

Truck groaned impatiently.

"General," he whispered, "now's the time! You want the Device, and me to operate it for you. Nothing's changed. Tell me why. Tell me how it— Look, just tell me *who* will benefit!"

This time, he knew for whom he was asking: they waited—as they've always waited, at rocketports, *pneumatique* stations, in delousing sheds and hand-out queues; in the greasy front offices of courts and refugee camps and detention bureaus—tired and grimy and stoned. He was asking for a dwarf, a musician, and a dead Centauran whore, for everyone who had nowhere to sleep at night, the new incumbents of his brain—

She opened her mouth.

Three quick explosions shook the street outside.

The whole room was flooded briefly with an intense, ominous red glow. Ruth Berenici moaned and flung herself toward Truck; one of her guards reached out and carefully hooked the feet from under her. The building shook and shuddered, plaster drifted down from the ceiling. A Fleet noncom, his face bloody and convulsed, appeared in the doorway.

"On the roof!" he shouted, eyes wild. "General! Two detachments, and another in the street!"

"Christ, ben Barka, you're going to regret this," said Alice Gaw calmly. She rounded on the noncom. "Hold them. I need five minutes here. Get some support in. How the fucking hell were they allowed to get this far in the first place?"

"They're jamming everything, General; we can't raise Fleet—"

Alice Gaw whipped her Chambers gun out of its holster and rammed its barrel up into the soft place under ben Barka's chin. "Hold them!" she screamed at the noncom. "Chummie, I'm going to blow your head off the moment any of that filth gets down here—" She pulled his head back with her free hand.

He overbalanced, plucked at her arm, eyes wide and

empty; and for some seconds they tottered about in a circle, locked in the excesses of the Dance. Harsh, mechanical grunts and sobs, an eerie, obsessive shuffle of feet.

She pushed him away and raised the pistol, breathing in great noisy gasps. Her eyepatch had come adrift, and raw pulpy horror stared out of the hole in her head.

"I think I'll do it now—"

The window exploded inwards, and a stray shot from the street buried itself in the opposite wall, fizzing and spitting like an angry cat. A spatter of glass, a sudden stillness. Into which John Truck said:

"It's now or never, General. Quick! Make us a bid!"

The pit in her face gaped above him. Her chin was wet.

"Growth," she croaked, and he hardly recognized her voice. She swallowed. "A free market economy. Law and progress. Peace with honor. You know all that." She thrust her face up very close to his. Cosmetics were caked in her pores. He wondered how old she really was. "Truck? We must stop them! They're a threat to every worth-while human value!" she said.

"Freedom and dignity, Truck, how much are they worth?" she demanded, her single eye blazing. "You've had them all your life *because we kept watch!*"

From the windy concrete plains of Anywhere, the bleak industrial complexes of Parrot and the radio-deserts of Weber II, from the filthy vapor-lighted alleys of the Snort, the new Centaurans—disenfranchised by poverty, barred from action by law, a pusher's market—crowded into that junction box between past and present atrocities that was John Truck's skull.

They were silent.

"Well, Truck?" She bent over him anxiously, as if sensing a little of what he represented at that moment. He knew she didn't.

"Let ben Barka make his bid," was all he said.

She threw up her hands in disgust.

"Laddie, I was hoping for a minute there you weren't completely out of your head—

Fighting had broken out on the stairs as ben Barka's death-commando pushed its way off the roof. Dust and smoke billowed into the room; a dispute over the third turning of the fourth flight became an action, a battle, a siege; screams, burning meat, and bellows from the amplifier truck outside. Somebody in the street had brought up a small rocket launcher and was busily pounding the top floors of the building to rubble with it.

Truck could see nothing now unless it was within a couple of feet of his eyes. He felt his substance boiling off into the void with the effort of holding himself together against the twin pressures of the Device and its inheritors.

"Let him speak!" he hissed.

In the event, ben Barka came up of his own accord. The General's police vanished to back up a holding action on the stairs, but he made no move to escape. He studied Truck's white and sunken face impassively. He brushed at something that might have been fine sand, lodged in a crease of his uniform.

"What precisely are you offering me, Captain?" he inquired. He raised his hand. "No, General Gaw. Consider: what have either of us to lose? Our footing"—a thin smile—"would now seem to be equal." The muzzle of the pistol wavered, dropped. "Captain?"

"A chance to speak, ben Barka."

"Very well, then." He looked to Alice Gaw for confirmation. She nodded, shrugged, pursed her lips. "It'll get you nowhere, duckie. Mark my words."

Ben Barka clasped his hands behind his back.

"Captain: IWG rapes and plunders, exploits criminally the labor force of the Galaxy. Used in the service of a genuinely Socialist revolution, the Device will bring about redress, stability, peace—and a just share in the profit and the adventure by the labor force."

He glanced toward the door, speculating on the state

of the conflict. "Social forces work like natural ones, Captain—blindly, forcibly, erosively. I know what you want. If we are to be a viable alternative to the corruption of IWG, we must be a hot, corroding wind—stripping off the topsoil where we must, reshaping—"

Truck closed his eyes.

"You haven't any conception of what I want. Either of you. The odd thing is that you both actually seem to believe all this stuff. We've heard enough."

A quick, frightened movement in the fog: Ruth Berenici, bruised and dirty, unable to understand. She pushed between Alice Gaw and the Colonel and, kneeling, touched one of Truck's hands.

"John, this is mad! You're *dying!* What does it matter which of them you give it to, when either of them could get you a doctor?"

He regarded her in silence. There simply wasn't enough of him left now to tell her anything.

"Don't I get a chance to bid?" she pleaded. "What use are you to either of us dead?"

"I'm sorry, Ruth."

"Sorry? John, it's *me* in here!" Then, quietly: "Damn you. Damn you for a loser."

They were leaving him the way they had come, through some back door of his brain—evaporating into fields and fluxes more subtle than any Dynaflow can create. Dogma means nothing to them. Personal relationships they take where they can, and always lose them somewhere between the Right and the Left, somewhere in the scorched field, in the urinal smell of the transit camp or the subway station.

It comes down to scars and empty bellies in the end. It comes to numb brains and the long trudge.

When they had gone—refugees from life and death, shuffling back down the light years and the centuries, hunched up against that eternal bitter Compass Wind—he smiled over his bitter disappointment. He saw quite clearly again. He saw what the hat and the cloak meant. How much better Himation or Pater would have been able to say it.

"It isn't enough," he decided. "So I am left with this thing after all.

"Listen, General. The Centauri genes have been scattering themselves over the Galaxy for two hundred years. There's a survivor of the Genocide in every drifter who ever lifted from a planet.

"But more: all of us down here are survivors of some personal atrocity, even if it's only birth.

"We breathe the dust of tragedy, and you offer us politics.

"Colonel—both of you—we're sick of ideology. It doesn't seem to work for us, only for you. You watch us crawl round the world—because there's nothing else for us to do—and see in us the reflection of a dream that was never worth the words you use to describe it; everywhere, you discover the symbols of your own obsession, codified but unreal—just as you discovered them in the bunker on Centauri."

He touched the thing on his lap. It seemed to swell beneath his hand.

"This is the only thing that has ever belonged to us. When we hurt, you sell us something to ease the pain. This is the power to say, we aren't buying any more, *and to mean that we're not buying it from either of you.*

"Let's see what it does, shall we?"

Outside, the street erupts in silent flame. The Snort is burning. What does it matter, now? It was never worth anything, anyway.

Earth's old diplomatic grin splits wide open, to reveal a scaffolding of bone.

The room spins like a top and whirls away. Ruth Berenici, unattainable warm declivity, wounded, fading, falls away. Behind her Arab and Israeli, plucked away insensate, topple from the bloody stair.

"Christ, Gadaffi, stop him!" screams the General.

They might hurl themselves forward forever, open-handed, gripped by eternal preternatural fear—

To hang, a dying-insect-hum on the moving air, while John Truck transliterated, last of the Old Centaurans and first of the New, allows that other voice, electric, to flood his inner ear.

His hands move: precise, elegant.

The thing on his lap like an animal stirs to meet them . . .

Nothing is lost . . .

something twists the world away . . .

Epilogue

So little comes down to us.

While the above is not solely fiction—being, as the reader will have realized, a dramatized account of some of the events leading to the Sol-Centauri Hypernova of 2367, and the formation of what is still known in hinterland argot as "Truck's Gap"—sources are few and scattered: a handful of secret files relating to the mysterious Centauri Device recovered from IWG and UASR embassies on Sad al Bari IV, Avernus, and—oddly enough, considering its backwater position—Gloam; records of coded tachyon transmissions by the cruisers *Solomon* and *Nasser* prior to the battle of Centauri VII, and of Earth-Fleet communications right up to the moment of occlusion; and, perhaps less bare but no less tantalizing, evidence gathered over some years—and in difficult conditions—from spacers who had known or talked with Captain John Truck.

We have no record of the mode of operation of the Centauri Device—here we follow (somewhat inaccurately, we fear, to the end of a more satisfying drama) the most popular of the current "psychic" theories. And nothing, not even the unstrictured imagination, can explain that curious spatial discontinuity which engulfed everything within a radius of ten light years from Earth in the winter of that, Earth's most urgent year: Sol was destroyed, along with Centauri, to produce the power for this vast sleight of hand; the chains of Terran politics were broken; no more can be said. Further, we have no clue whatever to the appearance of the Device in its armed phase—the sole descriptions extant refer to what was seen in the Omega Shaft bunker by Dr. Grishkin's archaeological team, General Gaw and two of her police force, and the UASR agent Colonel ben Barka. It was never our intention to produce original research, or shed new light on these matters, but to concern ourselves with what is more relevant in human terms.

Of the golden ship *Atalanta in Calydon,* there has been no sign since. She called at Pater's secret base shortly before the engulfment of Earth, and evacuated those of its complement who wished to leave. Many of these anarchists chose to remain in the Galaxy. About eighty of them were put off on the night side of Avernus some hours before the hypernova took place, and it is from them that we have our accounts of the "Third Speed," of the asteroid Howell and its fastidious prince, and of Himation's last words to Captain Truck. Whether *Atalanta in Calydon*'s stopover on Avernus was in any way connected with the reactor accident which finally destroyed the warren known as "Junk City" will never be proved. The events, however, were undeniably coincident.

But our greatest concern must undoubtedly be with the greatest mystery: The character of Captain Truck himself.

Say what you like of him: that his friendships were shallow and callous; that his morals were those of a cretin or a small animal; that his interests were tawdry. Say that he had sold drugs on nine planets and abused them on ninety more; that he had fought in dishonor and squalor in every back alley of the Galaxy, display-

ing only the courage of desperation. Say that he was
young and unformed and uneducated, and of a depth
of naïveté matched only by his premature bitterness—

But admit also that while he found life unpleasant,
he found death worse. He loathed killing and conscious
hurt, hypocrisy and cant, and the glib lip-service solu-
tion of human misery provided by ideology—but could
find no means to articulate that loathing. This most
honest of dishonesties could only find its expression in
surliness, in bravado, in a constant search for impermanent oblivion. He had in fact, despite it all, innocence. Only that innocence or Grace made his gesture
possible: only innocence can ever make such gestures
possible, or acceptable.

Did he see his action as a belated revenge for the
Centauri atrocity? Was he simply disgusted by the ir-
relevance to reality of the politics of his time? He has
been cast in both these roles in previous accounts, and
both are forceful human activators. Again, though: a
more simple, direct revenge for the killings he had seen
or taken part in during the last few weeks of his life
may have motivated him—or he may simply have triggered the Device accidentally, while delirious from the
injuries he received in the Göttingen early-warning station.

There are even grounds for that peculiar and poetic
myth of the spaceport subculture—the belief that John
Truck destroyed Earth as a proxy of the "new Centaurans," those fabulous underground denizens of the
dockland slums and the dyne fields, who will someday
emerge as the true inheritors of the Galaxy. The reader
must judge for himself.

OUT OF THIS WORLD!

That's the only way to describe Bantam's great series of science fiction classics. These space-age thrillers are filled with terror, fancy and adventure and written by America's most renowned writers of science fiction. Welcome to outer space and have a good trip!

THE EXCITING REALM OF STAR TREK

FANTASY AND SCIENCE FICTION FAVORITES

antam brings you the recognized classics as well as
e current favorites in fantasy and science fiction.
ere you will find the beloved Conan books along
ith recent titles by the most respected authors in
e genre.

] 01166	URSHURAK	
	Bros. Hildebrandt & Nichols	$8.95
] 13610	NOVA Samuel R. Delany	$2.25
] 13534	TRITON Samuel R. Delany	$2.50
] 13612	DHALGREN Samuel R. Delany	$2.95
] 11662	SONG OF THE PEARL Ruth Nichols	$1.75
] 12018	CONAN THE SWORDSMAN #1	
	DeCamp & Carter	$1.95
] 12706	CONAN THE LIBERATOR #2	
	DeCamp & Carter	$1.95
] 12970	THE SWORD OF SKELOS #3	
	Andrew Offutt	$1.95
] 14321	THE ROAD OF KINGS #4	$2.25
	Karl E. Wagner	
] 11276	THE GOLDEN SWORD Janet Morris	$1.95
] 14127	DRAGONSINGER Anne McCaffrey	$2.50
] 14204	DRAGONSONG Anne McCaffrey	$2.50
] 12019	KULL Robert E. Howard	$1.95
] 10779	MAN PLUS Frederik Pohl	$1.95
] 13680	TIME STORM Gordon R. Dickson	$2.50
] 13400	SPACE ON MY HANDS Frederic Brown	$1.95

Bantam Book Catalog

Here's your up-to-the-minute listing of over 1,400 titles by your favorite authors.

This illustrated, large format catalog gives a description of each title. For your convenience, it is divided into categories in fiction and non-fiction—gothics, science fiction, westerns, mysteries, cookbooks, mysticism and occult, biographies, history, family living, health, psychology, art.

So don't delay—take advantage of this special opportunity to increase your reading pleasure.

Just send us your name and address and 50¢ (to help defray postage and handling costs).